11/05

Books by Clare B. Dunkle

THE HOLLOW KINGDOM TRILOGY:

The Hollow Kingdom ★ BOOK I

Close Kin ★ BOOK II

In the Coils of the Snake ★ BOOK III

By These Ten Bones

In the Coils of the Snake

CLARE B. DUNKLE

In the Coils of the Snake

Henry Holt and Company
New York

Special thanks to my editor, Reka Simonsen, for her wise, well-crafted suggestions and thoughtful assistance; she was my Merlin on the magical quest that became this trilogy.

Henry Holt and Company, LLC
Publishers since 1866
175 Fifth Avenue
New York, New York 10010
www.henryholtchildrensbooks.com

Henry Holt® is a registered trademark of Henry Holt and Company, LLC.
Copyright © 2005 by Clare B. Dunkle
All rights reserved.
Distributed in Canada by H. B. Fenn and Company Ltd.

Library of Congress Cataloging-in-Publication Data
Dunkle, Clare B.
In the coils of the snake / Clare B. Dunkle.—1st ed.
p.   cm. (The hollow kingdom trilogy; bk. 3)
Summary: After learning that the new goblin king, her promised groom,
plans to marry an elf instead, the human Miranda flees the goblin kingdom
and is rescued from despair by a mysterious elf lord.
ISBN-13: 978-0-8050-7747-6
ISBN-10: 0-8050-7747-2
[1. Goblins—Fiction.   2. Elves—Fiction.   3. Magic—Fiction.
4. Marriage—Fiction.]   I. Title.
PZ7.D92115In 2005   [Fic]—dc22   2004060748

First Edition—2005
Book designed by Amy Manzo Toth
Printed in the United States of America on acid-free paper. ∞

1   3   5   7   9   10   8   6   4   2

For Joe,
who told me to write it down

In the Coils of the Snake

Prologue

"But why do you have to die tomorrow?"

The great round throne room was empty. No crowds thronged its floor, and the paving tiles of rose, cream, and serpentine marble displayed their dizzying patterns. The polished walls of red and green porphyry gleamed vermilion and olive in the light from the chandeliers, and the eighteen colossal black granite columns that held up the golden dome glittered with countless flecks of silver mica.

Only two people occupied this room that could hold hundreds, this vast chamber designed to contain the business of a realm. An old goblin sat on the throne that stood upon the dais, and a human girl of seventeen knelt before him, their voices damped into whispers by the expanse of space and the velvet and brocade curtains that hung before alcoves and doors. He was ugly and bony, with dull straight hair that fell to his shoulders, and his unmatched eyes gleamed like coals, one green and one black. She was statuesque and beautiful, with brown eyes and auburn hair, and her delicate pink skin contrasted with his gray fingers as she clasped his hands tightly in hers.

"Why tomorrow? Why so soon?" she asked. "Couldn't you die next week?"

Marak just smiled at her.

"Catspaw has waited his whole life to be King," he said. "I've ruled for more than half a century now, and it's time I passed the power on. There will be new advisers, new projects, the bustle of retirements and appointments, new fashions, too, I wouldn't doubt. There will be energy in this room again, with a young, dynamic King—mistakes, quarrels, absurd plans—I can hardly wait to die and set it all in motion." He didn't mention his inability to eat and sleep now, his failing magic, his labored breathing. These things, he thought, were entirely beside the point.

"Miranda." The young woman looked up at him, her eyes full of pain and grief. By the Sword, she was magnificent, he thought proudly. He had trained her from the cradle to take her place in his underground kingdom, and she would not disappoint him.

"Miranda, three months from tomorrow will be the ceremony that makes you a King's Wife. I've thought it best to keep you and Catspaw at a distance, but you'll find him to be a gifted ruler and a good man. He doesn't have my temper. He's more like Kate. And he's completely devoted to those he loves."

The young woman listened gravely. "I like Catspaw," she whispered.

Marak nodded his approval. "Ruling a kingdom is hard, especially at first," he continued. "The new King will need your encouragement. And your people will watch everything you do. They'll look to you for help, for comfort, for a thousand different things. You've grown up knowing this, and I'm sure you'll meet your obligations."

"I will," she promised softly. A tear sparkled on her eyelashes before slipping down her cheek. Marak watched it with idle interest. He thought it made a very pretty effect.

"Can I stay with you?" she asked, but the old goblin shook his head.

"No, the time I have left belongs to Kate. You need to leave now, but I want you to come to the crypt in the morning so that I can say good-bye."

Quiet, unmoving, in an agony of suffering, Miranda stared at the gray hands holding hers. Her guardian had always been there to guide her. Now, in less than a day, he would be gone. All that learning, all that brilliance lost, like galaxies disbanding. Like a universe collapsing into dust.

"I want to come with you," she said miserably.

The goblin King's eyebrows went up, and he chuckled at this absurdity. "But, Miranda, I don't know where I'm going!"

"I don't care," she said quickly. "I want to be with you. All my life, I wanted to come home with you, and you always made me wait, but you promised that I could one day. And then, when I finally did, it was for such a short time, and now——" She stopped herself with an effort.

Unperturbed, Marak gave her hands a little shake. "Catspaw will be all that to you," he said. "I certainly didn't raise you to escort me to the grave. You're going to be a King's Wife in a thousand, Miranda! What a pity I won't be here to see you."

The lovely girl mastered herself again. She even managed to smile. Then she turned and left him, crossing that empty desert of colored marble under the great golden dome.

Chapter One

The goblin King had not planned to raise a human bride for his son, but when the opportunity presented itself, he grasped its possibilities at once. Grasping possibilities was Marak's special genius.

Jack, the human boy whom Lore-Master Ruby had raised in the goblin kingdom, knew that he would have to leave when he grew up because no woman in the kingdom could marry him. But Marak's foster daughter, Til, always wanted what she couldn't have, and she spent years daydreaming about this forbidden man. She was in love with Jack before she ever even saw him.

Marak was not particularly impressed by her tears and protests of undying devotion. The stormy Til was always distraught over something, and he decided that she would soon forget her sweetheart. But the more he thought about the matter, the more he liked the idea. Why not let Til marry Jack? The young human was shaping up to be a fine businessman, and he could arrange the selling of their dwarf-made goods without the need for goblin trading journeys. The neglected estate of Hallow Hill had recently gone up for auction. Kate's distant relatives had fought over it in court, bankrupting her inheritance, and it had changed hands several times since then. If Jack purchased the land with Marak's wealth, the goblin King could build safeguards into the legal documents, protecting the goblins' borderlands from human misuse.

But there was a reason for allowing Til and Jack to wed that was far more compelling than these simple practical concerns. The clever goblin savored the chance to launch one last great scheme. His son would not end up bound to a madwoman, as he had been for fifteen years in his first marriage. Instead, he would permit Til to marry Jack and demand a daughter from them in exchange. He would leave her with her parents to develop her human nature fully, but the child would be his from birth. No other goblin would visit her; he would raise her himself, and she would have the benefit of all his wisdom and magic. The child would be extraordinary, his greatest and best achievement, a King's Wife down to her bones. If Til loved Jack before they ever met, Marak loved their daughter Miranda long before she existed, from the moment he first planned out her life.

Little Miranda adored her strange guardian, who sincerely cherished her and praised her for all her childish accomplishments. The goblin King was a huge secret in her life: he visited Hallow Hill only after the sun went down and everyone else was asleep. No one but Miranda and her parents ever saw him, and they were magically forbidden to mention goblins to anyone.

It was Miranda's love of Marak that led to her greatest misfortune, many years before she was old enough to understand it. Til never forgave Marak for choosing one of her children to marry the prince. Her hatred of Catspaw ran very deep. She could do nothing to harm her nemesis; Catspaw was out of her reach. But the young Miranda was sensitive, and Til took out all her harsh anger on the child. The entire household, to one extent or another, followed the mistress's lead. It was far better to stand with Til than against her.

The goblin King didn't force Til to be fair. Instead, he taught his ward to be brave. He was not at all displeased that his little girl had such a bitter opponent in her life. Humans measured themselves by adversity, he reminded himself. Miranda would be the stronger for her misfortune. And her attachment to goblins would be all the greater for her unhappiness in the human world.

But the cruelest thing young Miranda had to deal with was one of her own beloved Marak's ideas. He decided to teach the child goblin. This difficult language required years of study and practice, and because she could never explain to anyone how she learned about it, even the kindliest members of the community decided that Miranda was unwell. Goblin divided her from everyone else and kept her from having friends. The more the others taunted her for her efforts, the more fiercely proud and aloof she became in the face of all their ridicule.

And so Miranda grew up with only one source of comfort: Marak became everything to the lonely child. Between the formidable per-sonalities of her mother and her guardian, the young girl was molded and shaped, like hot iron between the hammer and the anvil.

The one great wish of Miranda's wretched heart was that her childhood would come to an end. When she grew up, she could go with Marak to his realm and escape her unhappy existence at last. Then she would always be with someone who loved and appreciated her. She would live the life of a queen, surrounded by admiring crowds, and no one would ever treat her disrespectfully again.

But Miranda had come into the goblin caves only weeks before, and now her beloved guardian was leaving. She stood in the hallway outside the throne room, trying to comprehend what this meant. The few people Marak had allowed her to meet in the kingdom couldn't begin to replace him. He had been her whole world from her earliest years, and tomorrow she would have to watch him die.

If a goblin King lived long enough, his magic told him when his strength was almost gone. Then he had to make a choice. Either he could lie in bed with his face to the wall, hoarding that strength for several days, or he could arrange a few final meetings, bid farewell to his court, pass once more through his solemn people as they lined the path to the Kings' crypt, walk on his own two feet to his tomb, and lie down within it. That was what Marak chose to do. He led the way, moving more rapidly than he had for months. Why shouldn't he? He would be resting soon enough.

The crypt was a long cavern deep underground, completely silent and bitterly cold. No monuments lined it, and no elaborate carvings marked its walls. Only the goblin King's family came there, along with the dwarves who had charge of the place. They guided the sober group down the narrow path between smooth rock formations that seemed to drip and flow. The torches the dwarves were holding flickered, as if the light couldn't settle on anything. Darkness waited outside their feeble circle, steady and final.

Miranda walked at the back of the little procession, just in front of the last dwarf, her thoughts chaotic and trivial. The goblin King's sister-in-law, Emily, walked before her with her handsome husband at her side. Ahead of Emily walked the goblin King's Wife, Kate, small and slender, her long golden hair gleaming in the torchlight. Taller than the others, the prince walked with his mother, blocking Miranda's view of the goblin King.

The quiet group assembled by Marak's tomb, a shallow coffin chipped into the rock. Its lid rested on the cave floor beyond them, waiting to be fitted on. Once Miranda had seen it, she could make out the other lids nestled into the rocks, their outlines betrayed by the narrowest of cracks. Goblin Kings lay entombed all around her.

Marak went from person to person, saying a few words to each. Miranda couldn't hear what he said to the others, his voice was so low. Now he was in front of her, saying good-bye to her, a parting that would never end. She hugged him tightly and wouldn't let go, keeping him alive as long as she could.

"I want to come with you," she told him, just as she had at the end of every visit.

"Be brave for your King," he whispered. Then he pulled away.

When Marak came to his wife, he didn't say a word. Instead, he gazed at Kate with that look he had just for her, as if it were a comfort and a joy to see her. Kate's blue eyes were bright, and her expression was untroubled. She refused to ruin his last moments by crying. The petite woman was descended from the greatest of elvish warriors, and she called upon their courage to sustain her. It worked. She saw his relief that she was taking it so well. He had no idea what the effort cost her.

"Marak," she said in a low voice, "no wife ever had such a King." And the smile that he gave her in return was worth all her pain.

He kissed her and looked at her for a few seconds, stroking that beautiful hair. Then he turned away. As he did so, he worked the Protection Spell on her, the most cherished of all the things he had to leave. Kate didn't even know what he had done. She had no idea that she was the reason he stumbled and almost fell into the tomb. Marak had planned and weighed his strength down to the last. He had used it all.

Once a goblin King lay in his tomb, he lost the power of breath. His son was there to help his death be peaceful. Catspaw laid his paw on the King's striped hair. Marak's unmatched eyes closed in sleep. The golden snake around Kate's neck awoke and flowed smoothly down to the floor at her feet. Then it stretched out and shuddered and became a sword once more.

There was no ceremony. Catspaw knelt for a few minutes, watching over his dead father, thinking about the reign that was ending, the reign that was beginning. When he stood up, the dwarves were ready with the coffin lid. They lowered it with a click, and Marak was gone.

Miranda stared at the plain rock surface that hid her guardian from view, conscious of nothing but a feeling of numb stupidity. Beside her, Emily burst into tears, and she fought down an answering whimper. Violent emotion alarmed Miranda. She had spent too many years hiding her feelings.

The new goblin King came to put his arms around his mother, and Kate looked up at him with a reassuring smile. That was how a King's Wife acted, thought Miranda, watching her. They shouldn't indulge in tears. Catspaw glanced toward her, perhaps to put an arm around her, too, but Miranda quickly turned away. She didn't know him. He was a stranger to her—now, more than ever before.

Instead, she edged closer to Seylin. He and Emily had looked after her for the last few weeks, so she could have accepted sympathy from him. But Seylin had his arms around the sobbing Emily, his face buried in her hair. Miranda realized with a shock that the man was crying. She stared at the ground as they started up the path again. The world had become a place in which she was alone.

Inside the safety of her own rooms, she could cry at last. She sat in the small apartment, desolate, filled with sadness and dread. The stylish furnishings fit strangely in the stone rooms, and the place was dim and gloomy. The whole underground world was full of shadows, she thought, a twilight on the verge of eternal night.

She hadn't minded as long as Marak was there.

A member of the Guard summoned Miranda to the new King. She followed the grotesque creature into a formal reception room. Around the low dais hung green brocade curtains, looped back in elaborate scallops. The goblin King sat upon it in an elegant armchair of gilded wood.

Marak Catspaw's two lieutenants stood beside him. He had appointed Seylin, his former tutor, to be his chief adviser, and the streetwise Richard to be his military commander. They made an eerie trio. The elvish Seylin's black hair and eyes and stately bearing made him look nothing like a goblin. He was dressed in English fashion, and his trousers, waistcoat, and frockcoat of gray matched

his dignity and reserve. Richard was wearing the King's Guard uniform of black shirt, breeches, and boots. As goblins went, he wasn't
hideous. His long hair was white, and his eyes were an arresting pale
green, but his face and build were reasonably normal. One of his
fangs had been knocked out during a boyhood fight, so the dwarves
had made him a false fang of gold.

Catspaw was a big man, larger-boned than his father. He
reminded Miranda of a Viking. His face was striking, not handsome: the jawbone was too pronounced, giving him a stubborn
appearance. But he wasn't particularly ugly, either. His short hair,
marbled with streaks and blotches of dark blond and pale tan, was
not entirely unattractive, and his eyes, one blue and the other green,
were rather interesting. He could almost have passed as a very
unusual human with grayish skin if it were not for the big lion's fore-
arm and paw that served as his right hand. Having grown up with
Kate's expectation that he be a gentleman as well as a goblin, he
favored impeccable jackets and trousers of dark green or blue cloth,
white linen shirts, and a well-knotted cravat. He stood politely for
Miranda's entrance, and she appreciated the gesture. A King, she
knew, had no need to stand up.

Catspaw had already found his fiancée to be a self-possessed
young woman. Although her eyes were red, she wasn't crying, he
noticed with relief; he had grown up with Miranda's mother, Til,
and his foster sister's constant dramatics had given him a distaste for
emotional displays. Miranda was wearing a midnight-blue gown
that formed a pleasant contrast with her auburn hair and rosy com-
plexion, and the new King thought her quite lovely.

"I concurred with my father's plans to bring you into the
kingdom as my bride," he began. "I have known of your work
together, and I could not imagine finding a better King's Wife."

Miranda blushed a little and inclined her head courteously to
acknowledge the compliment. At least this stranger shared Marak's

high opinion of her. After enduring years of ridicule from her family, she didn't take such things for granted.

"The King's Wife will be the most important person in my realm, just as she was in my father's day," he said. "I would like you to begin accompanying me to the banquet hall and taking your place by my side in the King's Gallery. Starting today, I will have a member of the Guard posted outside your apartment. You may use this guard to send me messages, and you may ask to see me at any time, for any reason."

Again, Miranda gave a gracious nod at this recognition of her value. She felt steadied by it. Life was falling into its proper pattern.

"Allow me to make you a small gift," Catspaw continued, "on this official inauguration of our engagement." Seylin opened a small box for him, and the King withdrew a golden bracelet. Then he stepped forward and placed it around her wrist. Miranda watched curiously, wondering how he would manage to clasp it since the big tawny paw was so clumsy, but he did it with his normal hand and magic.

Miranda studied the bracelet, and Catspaw stood by to watch her. In honor of the King, it was a chain of lion heads, their unmatched eyes tiny emeralds and sapphires. "Thank you," she told him. "I like it very much." But actually she felt dismayed. She was in mourning for Marak, and women in mourning shouldn't wear ostentatious jewelry.

"Is there anything you would like to ask of me?" he inquired. "Nothing is unimportant."

Miranda hesitated. "I don't have any black dresses," she began.

"Ah! The English custom of remembering one's dead," said Catspaw, returning to his place on the dais. "I've already had this discussion with my mother. You may certainly instruct the tailors to make you a black dress. Because of its resemblance to the King's

Guard uniform, it will be seen as a patriotic gesture. But if you decide to wear black every day, you will cause confusion and concern. My father's reign was happy, and his death was peaceful. A public display of somber feeling would be out of place."

"I see," said Miranda slowly. "But the three months' delay of marriages—isn't that a period of mourning?"

"The delay of our own marriage, you mean," clarified the goblin. "Other marriages are still taking place. No, the delay is purely practical. It goes back to former times. Before the elves disappeared, new Kings were often injured in the quest to capture a bride. The three-month delay allows the new King time to appoint his court and bring the kingdom into good order before embarking on such a risky ordeal. I grant that this ceremony is unlikely to pose a threat to my health, but a law is a law, even for kings."

While Miranda considered this surprising information, Catspaw gave her appeal further thought. "I understand your desire to demonstrate your love for my father," he concluded. "Why don't you choose something that he gave you and keep it with you as a remembrance? Then you can do your mourning in a way that won't seem so extreme."

Later, in her dressing room, Miranda considered this suggestion. It was true that Marak had given her many things when she was a child, but she hadn't brought much with her when she had left home. As she rummaged through her jewelry box, looking for items that linked her to him, she drew out a small bracelet decorated with a blue enameled butterfly.

The little girl awoke and sat up in excitement. He was here! She pelted down the dark hallway, calling out his name.

"Marak, Marak!" she yelled, dashing through the parlor door. Her father looked up with a smile from the chair where he was reading a newspaper. Her mother stood with her back to them, looking out the window into the darkness.

The black-cloaked man caught her and swung her up onto his lap. "How's my Miranda?" he asked.

"What did you bring me?" she demanded breathlessly as she hugged him.

"You'll have to find it," he replied. She drew from one of the pockets of his cloak a gold bracelet with a butterfly on it, and Marak helped her put it around her wrist.

"What does it do?" she asked, her brown eyes owlish with anticipation.

Marak threw back his head and laughed. "Must my gifts always do something?" he asked.

"They always do," she said.

"Maybe this one is just supposed to look pretty," he suggested.

Miranda studied the bracelet for a second, a little disappointed. Then she smiled at him. "It's pretty," she said, and he bent down so that she could give him a thank-you kiss.

"That's my Miranda," he said, pleased. "Now, how have you been?"

The little girl promptly tugged up the hem of her nightgown to reveal a scab. "I fell out of the wagon and skinned my knee," she announced. "I didn't cry."

"Good girl," he said approvingly. "I'm not raising a crybaby." He smeared salve on the knee, and the scab bubbled back into skin. Miranda sighed with satisfaction.

Her mother turned away from the window to glare at them both. "She's torn that scab off three times so she would have a wound to show you," she said.

"That's good," said Marak, smiling at his Miranda. "I'm not raising a coward. She's not afraid of a little pain."

"You said you wanted a normal human girl!" said Til sharply. "How can you call that thing normal when you come around here every few days working new spells on her?"

"Work a spell on me! Work a spell on me!" begged Miranda happily.

Marak grinned at the frustrated Til before bending over his little girl again. "What spell do you want me to work?" he asked her.

She stopped to think. "Nurse told us a story, and it had a girl, and she was spelled to be the beautifulest in all the land," she told him.

"I can't work that spell on you," he responded sincerely. "You're already the most beautiful girl in this land." And that little face lit up with a beautiful smile.

"Work another spell on me!"

"Just anything?" he chuckled. "How about this?"

He cupped his hand over her butterfly bracelet. When he pulled it back, a real butterfly sat there, deep blue, trembling and fanning its wings. It fluttered crazily up before her wide eyes and clung to the front of her nightgown. Miranda was beside herself with joy.

"I knew it did something!" she exclaimed triumphantly, and the goblin King laughed.

Miranda sat at her dressing table and watched the blue butterfly loop about on its whimsical travels of the room. "You shouldn't act so cheerful," she whispered as it landed on her wrist. "He won't be coming to see us anymore."

Chapter Two

In the short time that Miranda had been in the goblin caves, Marak had kept his ward very much to himself, determined that Catspaw would hold for her the thrill of the unknown. Miranda had lived quietly in an apartment on the elves' floor of the great palace, content with her ongoing studies and Marak's daily visits. If she had seen almost nothing of Catspaw, she had seen very little else of goblin life, either.

Now the girl found herself propelled to the very center of goblin society. The new King kept her by his side at every social occasion, and the fascinated monsters thronged around her. Miranda played her part to perfection, exhibiting the fine manners and graciousness that Marak had drilled into her. She hid her true feelings from everyone—including, at first, from herself.

Because the fact of the matter was that many goblins were hideous. They didn't just look funny, as Marak had always said. There were deformities among them that sent a chill down Miranda's spine, a shock such as she might have felt at the sight of a corpse. She could barely swallow food in their company.

There was the goblin, for instance, with the huge flat head, burly arms, and tiny body. His doll's legs dangled uselessly a foot above the ground as he swung himself from place to place on his hands. There was the genial little goblin with the common abnormality, eyes of two different colors. One of his eyes was dark brown, twinkling with good humor. But the other eye was huge and bright red. And there was an entire family of goblins who were the color of dark gray earth, with the look of things too long underground. Their hairless heads were round and bulbous, like soft rubber balls. Their pale eyes bulged alarmingly, as if they were being strangled.

Seen in the light of an honest day, these forms would have been frightful enough, but far worse was their appearance in the thick shadows of the kingdom. At any moment, Miranda might turn a corner in the dim hallways of the palace and find herself face-to-face with a horror she had never even imagined. And when she met it, she had to remember to smile.

It didn't occur to the girl that Marak's death had left her over-wrought and that her repugnance was compounded by her grief. All Miranda knew was that she was pretending to be happy when she had thought at last her hiding and pretending would be over. She had looked forward all her life to coming to Marak's kingdom and being a King's Wife. She had never once considered that it might be difficult.

The long years of protecting herself from her brutal mother guided her conduct now. Miranda smiled her way through to the end of each day, and no one knew she was pretending. The callous goblins never hid their feelings, so they didn't doubt her perfor-mance. Seylin or Kate might have seen through the act, but they were too busy, and they had their own sorrow.

Little by little, Miranda felt herself sinking beneath the weight of her own perfect manners. Her smile seemed frozen on her face, like a lead mask that she couldn't remove. She was performing on a stage that she couldn't leave. She could never step out into the sunlight. And where her appreciative audience should have been, cheering her on, there was only the silence of death.

What a pity, he had said to her. *What a pity I won't be here to see you.*

"I want to see Marak's grave," she announced one morning to the dwarf in charge of the Kings' crypt. The little creature stroked his long white beard. Then he led her through the hallways to the thick, leaden door that closed off the end of the crypt.

"He doesn't have anything graved," he pointed out. "There's not a thing graved anywhere amongst the lot of them. It's not allowed, you see—no names or nothing. Shame, really. Your stone, though, it's graven real nice. I got to help on that one."

Miranda pushed from her mind the thought of her own marble headstone, placed in the Hallow Hill graveyard when Marak had taken her away from home. He had worked a spell on the whole community to make them dream her funeral. It was uncomfortable to remember that her own family thought that she was dead.

She followed the diminutive man down the twisting path of the narrow, chilly cavern, watching nervously as his torch pushed away the inky blackness of the never-ending night. He kept up a cheerful patter, pointing at the all-but-invisible tombs. "That one, he was eight feet tall from the tips of his horns to his cloven hooves." Miranda tried her best not to listen.

They came to the turn of the cavern where the last tomb was, and Miranda's grief hit her like a blow. Right here, he had stood and said good-bye. Then, he had turned and walked away from her.

"This will be for the new King," the dwarf noted, gesturing at a rocky outcrop with his torch. The shadows dipped and swayed with the torchlight, rushing around the cave walls, and Miranda's nerves stretched taut.

"If you don't mind," she said, "I'd like to be alone with him."

"With who?" The dwarf peered past her in surprise.

"With him." She pointed at the tomb, and the dwarf's expression cleared.

"Oh, him! Now, that's what I call being alone. I'll be right outside then, making sure the door don't shut. I'd hate to think of you locked up in here. I'd get in no end of trouble."

He started off, and the shadows leaned to embrace her. Miranda gasped in alarm.

"Your torch!" she called, and remembered just in time to give

him a smile as he turned around. "I'm afraid I need to borrow it."
She took the smooth pole from him and was rather surprised at its
weight; it was stone, not wood, and top-heavy as well. Its flame, she
realized, came from something like a match head, coated with a
chemical that burned.

The little man took his pickax from his belt, and the blade lit
with a clear white light. Miranda watched it bob away up the winding path. She sat down next to Marak's tomb and laid her head on
the sloping lid, resting the bottom tip of the torch on the ground.
The rocks within the circle of torchlight were dull and sandy-pale,
devoid of interest or appeal. "Marak," she whispered, but no answer
came. She wouldn't find comfort there.

"I never knew you were going to leave," she continued. "I
thought you'd always be with me." The echoes of her whisper hissed
up and down the cave, turning corners and coming back again.

"You wanted to go," she accused the empty darkness. "You were
happy about dying. First you made me a stranger to my family, and
then you brought me to all these strangers, and then you couldn't
wait to leave."

Her reserve was breaking down. The smile had cracked off her
face. The manners that had carried her through began to desert her.

"I told you I didn't want to stay here without you," she insisted.
"I told you I wanted to be with you. It's so hard here, and I'm tired,
so tired of it all! Please come back and take me with you."

There was no reply, only the echoes, like a thousand snakes, crawling around the edges of the cave. Nothing changed in the bright,
blank circle of torchlight, and nothing changed in the darkness
beyond. Miranda felt her despair and isolation rise up to choke her.

"Marak!" she cried, beating on the tomb with her fist. "Come
back and take me with you!"

The tomb lid reverberated like a drum with deep, sonorous
booms that swelled into a rumbling roar. They seemed to shake the

cave walls, to come from the earth under her feet. Miranda stopped, startled, but the noise only increased, its echoes resounding like thunder. Too late, she remembered that every goblin King was named Marak. When she had called him, she had called them all.

She started to her feet, but the top-heavy torch slipped from her grasp, shattering in an explosion of sparks. Flaming pieces rolled away and fizzled out, and the shadows leapt upon her. Marak's tomb vanished in the darkness.

Miranda seized the largest piece of torch that still burned and held it up in trembling fingers. She could still see just the hint of a path in the wavering rays of light. Would the dwarf hear her if she called to him, or would the echoes just come shrieking back? At any moment, the last flames might go out and leave her trapped in the dark.

She started up the path, staggering a little, her feet clumsy and heavy, as if she were a puppet trying to work her own strings. Desperately, she clutched the piece of splintered stone, trying to navigate the cavern by its flickering light. She kept herself to a walk, reasoning with her terror. Another stumble, and the light would be gone for good.

Past the King with the bat wings who had choked to death on mutton. Past the King whose fingers had ended in hooks. The waning gleam barely suggested a path, and the rock formations beside her seemed like tall, twisted shapes. She tried not to see them as centuries-old bodies, lining the way to watch her pass. She tried not to hear the echoes in the cavern as the shuffling of long-unused feet. You don't want to die yet, her pounding heart told her. You don't want to be with him after all. But Miranda kept her eyes on the path before her and spoke no more words to the dead.

She stumbled through the doorway and into the tunnel beyond it, lit with the warm glow of hanging lamps. Only then did she feel a painful throb and look down to find blood on her hand. She had split her knuckles open hammering on Marak's tomb.

"What happened to you?" asked the dwarf, peering at her interestedly.

Miranda was far too upset to smile at him this time. "Do you hear anyone following me?" she gasped.

He chuckled. "No. That's just your fancy. Those Kings—they're dead. They don't go following people about anymore."

Of course. How absurd. Miranda felt her face grow hot as she blushed. But the shaken girl had no time to nurse her injured feelings or her hand. Marak Catspaw was giving her a tour of the Kings' trophy rooms that morning, and her visit to the crypt threatened to make her late. She felt a little frantic at the idea of keeping a King waiting. Twisting her handkerchief around the bloody hand, she hurried off.

Catspaw was already there when she arrived, studying the various display cases in the first of the long, low rooms, but the courteous goblin didn't seem annoyed with her. Miranda apologized prettily, aware that the King would interpret her shaking hands and flushed cheeks as anxiety over causing offense. While he led her from case to case, explaining obscure points of history, Miranda began to calm down. The frightening episode receded from her mind as she concentrated on the task of making witty conversation in order to charm her royal fiancé.

They spent several hours in the quiet trophy rooms. To her escort, the place clearly represented both a legacy and a challenge. These galleries had become, over the centuries, the kingdom's national museum, and each King selected one or two exhibits to add from his own reign. Marak had added a display about the sorcerer and a case holding the rags that Irina had worn on the night she arrived. They were a sad testament, he had thought, to the end of the elves.

"I wonder what exhibits will date from my time," mused Catspaw as they examined a display of elvish weaponry. "I wonder what stories they'll tell. 'In the reign of Marak Catspaw . . .' Stories used to begin with both goblin and elf King names, but no longer, of course. That made for a better beginning, and they certainly made the most thrilling tales. There's almost nothing for a goblin King to do these days, with the elves gone. Humans don't make particularly threatening adversaries. The times are dreadfully peaceful."

"Isn't peace best?" asked Miranda. Her suitor responded with a noncommittal shrug.

She was enjoying Catspaw's company. He made her feel important, and his conversation was worldly and knowledgeable. She knit her brows, preparing to turn his offhand comments into a debate, something that both of them relished. But the goblin King interrupted her thoughts.

"What are you doing to your fingers?" he wanted to know, seizing her bandaged hand. Fresh blood stained the wrap. Miranda had been rubbing the skinned knuckles with her thumb, breaking through the dried blood and newly forming scabs.

It was an old habit. She had hoarded her injuries even when she was very small for the pleasure of watching Marak heal them. If he didn't come for several days, she tore open the wounds to make sure they couldn't heal on their own. Later, she had sneaked the nursemaid's scissors to administer her own cuts. It made her proud to bear pain without a murmur: she felt that she had mastered herself. Some days, when the household was particularly harsh to her, it seemed the only thing she could control.

Miranda's mother had soon guessed what she was doing and had triumphantly denounced the girl to Marak. He didn't seem particularly concerned, but the girl had learned caution. Afterward, she only indulged in the habit when she was really desperate, when her mother was more than usually severe and she hadn't seen Marak for days. She couldn't talk to anyone about him, so she couldn't share her private worries over whether he was ever coming back. Then it was a relief to give herself a small cut to fret over. It wasn't as if she was misbehaving: no one knew what she'd done. And the pain was like a friend, sharing her silent vigil until he returned to heal it.

Now Miranda watched the new goblin King examine her damaged hand. The skinned knuckles were an outlet for her wounded feelings, a focus for her internal pain. If Marak wasn't coming back to mend them, she didn't want them mended at all.

"I think some wounds shouldn't be healed," she proposed.

Catspaw had a high opinion of her intelligence and was ready to be interested in the idea. "Why shouldn't we use magic when it's convenient?" he inquired.

"I'm not magical," said Miranda. "Is it good for a nonmagical body to undergo magic for no reason? These will heal on their own."

"They might scar," observed the goblin King calmly.

She studied the smashed, skinless knuckles. It was true that they weren't a pretty sight. But she felt again that sense of mastery over pain, and the exhilaration of it carried her along. Certainly the straightforward Catspaw had no insight into her complicated feelings on the subject.

"Humans are proud of their scars," she debated. "Scars can be a badge of honor."

At that moment, Seylin walked up beside them, on business with the King. The handsome man caught sight of Miranda's injured knuckles and grimaced in concern. "Miranda, what did you do?" he cried out, genuinely distressed. His reaction was like a splash of cold water. Miranda felt guilty and embarrassed.

"Here's a thought, Seylin," remarked the King with cheerful unconcern. "Should some wounds be left unhealed?"

"No," answered his chief adviser sharply, and Miranda didn't protest when he mended her hand.

Catspaw excused himself and went off with his adviser, leaving Miranda alone. After her traumatic visit to the crypt and Seylin's unpleasant reaction to her wounds, she felt nervous and unstrung. She edged cautiously up the stairs, hoping not to meet anything too revolting, but even the picturesque goblins startled her today. She was relieved to reach her own floor and glad to find that the guard posted there was one of the least distasteful goblins in the kingdom.

Tattoo, Sable's youngest son, had only recently become a member of the King's Guard. His black uniform made him inconspicuous against the dark green marble of the hallway. Big and handsome like his father, Tinsel, Tattoo got his name from an unusual feature: many faint black lines crisscrossed his silver face, as if someone had marked it with ink and he hadn't washed it all off. His straight black hair flopped untidily into his blue eyes and about his shoulders.

Miranda liked Tattoo, who had his father's easygoing, friendly manner, and she seized upon his presence as an opportunity. Now, instead of just hiding in her rooms, she could go somewhere more interesting. Facing the deformities in the hallways wasn't nearly so disturbing if she had company along.

Where did she want to go? Miranda loitered in the hallway, considering her choices. There were many fascinating and exotic places in the underground realm, she reminded herself, trying to ignore the nagging whisper that she really wanted to go outside. To leave the goblin caves, to stand in the sunlight again . . . Miranda forced the thought away and held her breath. Sometimes the gloomy shadows here seemed almost to choke her, like layers of dark cobwebs winding themselves around her face and throat.

She couldn't leave the caves, so she would do the next best thing. The kingdom contained two places that Miranda thought of as "outdoors." When she had first come through the goblins' front door, she had emerged in what seemed to be a narrow valley, it was so vast a cave. This lamplit, subterranean cavern was called the palace gardens because of its ornamental beds full of jeweled replicas of living plants. Near the goblins' great iron door, a grove of brass and silver trees caught in clever artistry the changing of the seasons. The enormous palace, with its great square windows, overlooked these dark gardens, and a shallow river foamed over rocks at the valley floor.

Did she want to visit the palace gardens? Miranda hesitated. Of all the wonders in the goblin realm, they were the most eerily exquisite, but for all their beauty, she didn't really like them. They were so silent, the colored lamps so faint and ghostly in that black place. They seemed to be frozen in an eternal midnight.

No, she would go look at the other place in the goblin kingdom where one felt that one was out of doors. There, at least, she would find light. "Tattoo, come with me," she ordered, but the big guard looked uneasy.

"I'm not supposed to, King's Bride," he said. "I got in trouble last time. I have to stay at the door. That's my orders."

Miranda frowned at him and folded her arms in imitation of her imperious mother. "Which would you rather do?" she demanded. "Upset me or risk a little trouble?"

"Upset you," answered Tattoo fervently. "Mother found out that I was written up for leaving my post. I think she'll kill me if it happens again."

This Miranda could understand. The two elf women, Sable and Irina, were her neighbors, and they formed the nucleus of a small clan of oddly attractive elvish-looking goblins. Sable was a stern matriarch with very high expectations. She didn't put up with much nonsense from her children and could be very blunt about telling them so.

"All right, you don't have to come with me," Miranda generously decided. "But you still have to deliver messages to Catspaw for me, don't you?" Tattoo nodded. "Then deliver a message to him in the royal rooms, and I'll come with you. I'll tell you what it is on the way."

Tattoo pondered this for a minute and then walked resignedly to the stairs. Miranda followed him, feeling smug. She wasn't concerned that a lowly guard might think her behavior strange. Delivering eccentric orders to the servants was a cherished privilege of the upper class, and Miranda had seen a great deal of it during her childhood.

"What's the message?" asked Tattoo as they climbed the stairs.

"Let's see," reflected the girl. "Tell the King that I hope his day is going well."

"I have to tell Marak that?" Tattoo looked glum.

"The goblin King will be very pleased," Miranda stated with breezy self-assurance, and she was quite sure that he would be. Catspaw was making no secret of his fondness for her: his attention was becoming real fascination. There were many things in her new life about which Miranda felt dubious, but the new King's regard was not one of them.

Keeping pace with the goblin guard, she climbed steps until she was short of breath. The royal rooms were on one of the highest levels of the palace. That palace fooled the girl into thinking it was a normal building because of its rooms, halls, and stairways, but Miranda already understood that it was much more than it appeared to be when viewed from its ornamental gardens. Many of those hallways burrowed deep into the rock. Its contours could never have been built aboveground; they had had to be mined away.

The pair arrived at the elaborately decorated royal floor of the palace, and Miranda studied the stately hallway with pleasure. On one side, square windows without glass stretched from ceiling to floor, and across from them stood two uniformed guards watching the set of golden doors that led to the royal rooms. The brilliant mosaics and gemstone-encrusted furnishings shamed the Taj Mahal. Not a single human monarch in the entire world lived in such splendor, and Miranda enjoyed thinking of her imminent residency there. The life of a goblin King's Wife, she decided, did have certain tangible rewards.

Tattoo conferred with the door guards and then passed her on his way back to the stairs. "Marak isn't here," he said bitterly. "He's in the palace town, inspecting some hybrid grain." He didn't add that this meant an hour's walk to deliver her inconsequential message, but Miranda was fully aware of it.

"What a lucky thing for you not to be stuck so long in that boring hallway," she noted. "I'll see you later then." The young goblin's unhappy expression as he walked off indicated that he viewed this last statement as a threat.

Miranda's goal was the balcony overlooking the lake valley on the other side of those stately windows. This valley came closest to the world that Miranda had left behind. Hollow Lake, in which she had splashed and played as a little girl, was a large oval body of water several miles across. Beneath it lived the goblins, in simple villages and farms, raising the crops and animals that fed them and the dwarves. The shores of the lake were like mountains hemming them in, the impassable boundaries of their deep round valley. The waters of the lake were the only sky that most of them ever saw, a trembling firmament of shifting cobalt twilight by day, and a bland and featureless velvet blackness by night.

Miranda stood with her hand on the cold stone of the window frame, taking in the view across the round valley. Here, birds flew, although they took care not to fly too high, or they would find themselves swimming instead. Here, plants grew, although no trees could survive. And here, if nowhere else in the kingdom, the sun shone— after a fashion.

This valley was a dim and murky place, the sunlight reaching it through the filter of deep water. Only when the sun stood straight overhead did the water become more translucent. For just a little while, the aquamarine gloom lightened. The difference wasn't dramatic, but she had already come to treasure it. More than anything else that she had lost, Miranda missed the sun.

But today, she found to her dismay that the balcony was occupied. Marak's widow, Kate, was already there. Miranda felt shy and reserved in the presence of the dignified woman. She knew that Catspaw thought the world of his mother.

"Hello, Miranda," said Kate. "I'm glad to see you." Miranda greeted her politely in return and sat down a little distance away. Now, here was a perfect King's Wife, she thought, a bit overawed. Kate worked constantly for her people, and everyone adored her. She was graceful and formal without seeming in the least snobbish. Miranda reflected unhappily that Catspaw's mother probably never gave selfish orders to her door guards.

"I love to come here," Kate volunteered. "It's the only place in the whole kingdom where one can see a real horizon. I hope you won't mind sharing it with me sometimes. My new balcony faces the gardens."

Of course, remembered Miranda: Marak's widow had just moved out of the royal rooms. She instantly felt worried and guilty about her own impending possession of them. Perhaps this important woman resented that. Miranda murmured something civil, and silence descended once again, but now she felt obliged to break it.

"I come here to see the sunlight," she confessed. "I like to see the valley brighten up at this time of day, but it looks as if today must be cloudy." The remarks were harmless enough, but her longing showed on her face, and now Kate looked as if she were the one feeling guilty.

"I'm so sorry," she answered. "I hate it that you can't go outside. Catspaw says that it's too dangerous to allow every King's Wife to go outside the way I do, but maybe he will make an exception now and then. I'll ask him to let you go outside with us on the next full-moon night."

After her ghastly experience in the blackness of the Kings' crypt, Miranda could think of few things worse. "Please don't!" she exclaimed in horror. "I appreciate your thoughtfulness," she amended, blushing deeply, "but I wouldn't like to be outside at night. I'm afraid of the dark."

"Oh." The lovely woman stared at her, quite surprised. "Please excuse me for a moment," she said and left the balcony.

Miranda reflected in consternation on how rude she must have sounded. Up until then, she had hidden her phobia quite well. Now her future mother-in-law might use this information to torment her, just as her own mother had. She could hear Til's voice in her mind, elegant and scornful: *Really, darling, what a stupid thing to say.*

Then Kate was back, sitting down close beside her and clasping a bracelet around Miranda's wrist. "A dwarf made this for me," she explained. "It lights up if you're ever in the dark. I remember how dark it seemed when I first came here and how glad I was to have it with me. I'd like you to have it now."

Miranda studied the triple rope of diamonds, completely won over by the unexpected kindness. "Thank you," she said. "And I'm sorry," she added sincerely, "that you had to move out of your rooms."

"Oh, I don't mind," said Kate lightly. "All that gaudy decoration! That sort of display has never been to my taste." She gazed placidly over the valley while Miranda studied her out of the corner of her eye. Did she feel as betrayed as Miranda did about Marak's abandonment of them? He hadn't even spoken a word to her before climbing into his tomb.

"Doesn't it make you angry sometimes that he just walked away?" she ventured.

The beautiful woman turned toward her. Deep in those blue eyes, there was a preoccupied look, as if she weren't really paying attention. She seemed to be listening for certain footsteps, or the sound of a familiar voice. In a flash, Miranda understood why Marak's widow was handling her loss so well. Kate undoubtedly knew that her husband was dead—but part of her was still waiting for him.

"That who walked away, dear?" asked Kate mildly. Miranda didn't have the heart to answer.

A few days later, the girl sat with Catspaw in his library. While the busy goblin King recorded the day's decisions, writing left-handed because of his awkward paw, she ran her eyes over the closely packed shelves, scanning the long sets of matched volumes. She was bored with her inactivity and annoyed at her own boredom, and she wasn't feeling particularly gracious. But that didn't matter; she would have the right smile ready for her royal fiancé when he looked up at her.

With a slight frown, the goblin King took her hand and examined the jewelry she wore. Among his own gifts, he spied Kate's bracelet and touched it with a finger.

"Mother tells me you're afraid of the dark," he said. "I hadn't known."

Miranda was taken aback by the revelation and felt anxious about what it might mean.

"Did something here cause it?" he asked.

"No, it started when I was young," she answered reluctantly. Then she realized he had noticed her hesitation.

"How?" he demanded, and she decided that she had better tell him the truth.

"One day Mother was scolding me, and I told her I was glad that I was going away when I grew up. There were lots of things we couldn't say because of the magic, but there were still things that we could say.

"Mother always hated to hear that sort of thing—I don't know why; as much as she disliked me, you'd think she would have been glad, too. This time, she glared at me and said, 'You'll go away, all right. You'll be locked up forever in the dark. Let's try it out and see how you like it.'

"She dragged me downstairs to the cellar and shut me into a room. Not one ray of light came in. Then she stood outside and talked to me while I screamed and pounded on the door. 'There are things in the dark that can't come out in the day,' she told me. 'You're cursed. You'll never escape.'"

"She could say that because it was a lie," growled Catspaw. "The magic only blocked her from speaking the truth about the kingdom. It's unfortunate that Til is part of my family; I can't take goblin revenge. All the same, I don't see why her life should be going so well. I'll have to give the matter some thought."

"I'm sure she didn't keep me there very long," Miranda told him, oddly uncomfortable over the calm threat. "Papa let me out. He was yelling at Mother, just as upset as I was. He was probably afraid of what Marak would do. But Mother was very cool about it. I remember she laughed at him. She said, 'Maybe now she'll want to stay with me.'

"She was right, too. I was afraid to see the sun go down, terrified all night, and the nurse wouldn't let me keep a candle. I crept out of bed and huddled in a patch of moonlight, thinking about how Marak always visited after dark. The next time he came, I didn't run to greet him, and I cried when he walked into the room. It sounds silly, but it was the first time I noticed how different he was from everyone else."

"What did he do?" asked Catspaw with interest. "Did he work any spells?"

"I don't think so," she answered. "He was just himself. He held me on his lap, and he talked to me—" Her voice wavered because of the lump that had formed in her throat. She stopped abruptly and studied the diamond bracelet. Sometimes it still hurt terribly to think of him.

Catspaw leaned toward her as she glanced up and held her gaze with his own. "My spells keep the lamps lit, Miranda," he said quietly. "I won't ever leave you in the dark."

Miranda was touched by his consideration. She hadn't imagined the goblin King like this. She saw her royal suitor as someone to charm and impress, but she hadn't realized that she would have to trust him. Maybe he wouldn't always seem like such a stranger, she thought with relief. She remembered Marak's last talk with her: *Catspaw will be all that to you.*

"That night when I was frightened, Marak told me about my future," she recalled. "It was the first time that he said I would be a King's Wife."

"Then I remember that night as well," said Marak Catspaw. "It's one of the only times I saw Father worried. I was up late, studying political economy or some such thing, when he came into my room. 'You've got to marry that girl,' he said, shaking his head. 'I just promised her that you would.'"

Miranda felt startled. "I thought he knew my future," she protested. "He sounded so sure of it. I thought he could see it in my face."

Catspaw smiled. "He was just being a King," he said. "Kings are never supposed to seem uncertain. I don't see anything about your future in your face. I only see the character from the Door Spell."

"You can see that?" wondered Miranda, rubbing her forehead. "I didn't know it left a mark."

"It's gold, and it shines a little," said the goblin, tracing over the script character with his fingertip. "I think it looks attractive."

Miranda pondered that, unsure how she felt about displaying a symbol that she herself couldn't see. She wondered how many other goblins could read it, and whether it really was attractive. Catspaw continued to study her, hesitating over something. If Kings weren't supposed to seem uncertain, he was breaking his own rule.

Then he leaned down and kissed her.

It was a nice kiss, Miranda decided. It made her feel appreciated, and she felt affectionate in return. For once, the smile that she gave her fiancé wasn't a charming mask but an expression of honest feeling instead.

The goblin seemed to have enjoyed the kiss, too. He looked excited and resolute. "Only two more months until our wedding," he remarked. "Then I'll erase this"—he touched the Door symbol—"and write the King's Wife character there."

"Will I notice any difference?" she asked.

"Yes and no," admitted Marak Catspaw. "The doors still won't let you go outside, but they'll treat you with more respect."

A little uncertain, Miranda thought about being his wife, living in luxury, locked in by those iron doors. There certainly wasn't much left to worry about, was there? What a tidy future. She just wished she would stop feeling so edgy about it.

It was Sable who finally pieced together the clues and saw through Miranda's pretense. The elf woman listened to her son Tattoo's descriptions of the erratic behavior of the King's Bride and felt wholeheartedly sorry for the girl. It was clear to her that Miranda was struggling to find her place in the kingdom, and this was something Sable could understand. She herself had not had an easy time finding her place in life.

The black-haired woman combined in one person the sensitivity of an elf and the frankness of a goblin. Polite and distrustful, Miranda never mentioned her problems, so Sable did it for her. "Goblins take getting used to," she told Miranda matter-of-factly, and the girl felt as if a weight had dropped from her shoulders. Miranda was too reserved to come by for a visit, so the elf woman kept inviting her over until the visits became routine.

"You're losing weight," Sable remarked one morning as she opened her door for the girl. "I have bread and cheese for you in the basket on the table. Tattoo," she added crisply, leaning out into the hallway to speak to the young man posted at Miranda's door, "I've mended your Guard cloak—again. Come by for it once you're off duty, and be more careful next time."

Miranda walked into Sable's forest room and looked around with pleasure. The large space was full of dwarf-made trees, hung with tangled cloth greenery, and small fish swam in an ornamental pool by the door. The illusion of a stretch of shadowy woodland worked particularly well for Miranda because she couldn't distinguish much in the dim light. She sat down on a cushion at the strange low table that was only a few inches from the ground.

"One week left until your wedding," noted the elf woman. "It's a shame that it won't be held at the full moon. Weddings and full moons belong together."

Miranda gave a grimace and rubbed her palms where the knives would cut them. "I'll be glad when it's over. Catspaw says he will be, too."

"He's Marak now," Sable observed. "You should call him that." Miranda just frowned by way of an answer. She hadn't yet promoted him into that exalted position, as the elf woman knew perfectly well.

A small silence fell over the room as Miranda pulled food from the basket and Sable began working on one of her math problems. She sketched it out rapidly in three dimensions a few inches above the table, silvery lines and circles appearing as she drew. Then she set it all into motion.

Miranda watched the silver figure spin in the air, wobbling slightly as it turned. "Sable, did you always like it here?" she asked.

"I was frantic when I first came," the woman answered absently, jotting down numbers. She paused and gazed off into space. "I remember how hard it was to get used to the bright light. My eyes would start stinging after a few hours."

"Bright!" murmured Miranda. She could barely distinguish colors in the gloom. "Did you ever try to escape?"

"No," answered Sable. "I couldn't go back. My people would have hunted me down. You don't know what elf men are like, Miranda. They're horrible brutes. I don't think they're born with a heart in their bodies."

Miranda pondered this interesting disclosure. "Isn't Seylin an elf man?" she asked. "He's not a brute. Marak never said that elf men were horrible, just that they were pretty and silly."

"Of course Seylin isn't an elf," replied Sable. "He's a goblin; he just looks like an elf. And Marak never had to live with them like I did."

All in all, it was a strange coincidence that Miranda learned what elf men were like that day. That very night, an elf man returned to his ancestral home, and Miranda's tidy future began to crumble.

Chapter Three

Marak Catspaw and his two lieutenants stood outside the cliff face that concealed the entrance to the goblins' underground kingdom, studying the early night sky. The northern constellation that the elves called the King's Throne was glowing very brightly. The W of stars appeared to flicker and flash.

Seylin was beside himself with excitement. "It's the traditional summons to a truce meeting!" he exclaimed. "A meeting between goblins and elves. But how?"

"And not just any summons, but the highest level," reflected Marak Catspaw. "Adviser, what do you advise me to do?"

"Go, of course," replied Seylin. "The goblin King always went personally to a King's Throne summons. And I certainly advise you to bring us along. I wouldn't miss this for the world."

The three of them walked through the whispering forest not far from the Hallow Hill mansion, where Til was holding a supper party, and up the hill toward the old truce circle, wondering what it might contain. Its double ring of ancient oak trees guarded that secret well, the massive trunks blocking completely any view of what lay within. Marak Catspaw was pleased and intrigued. Some elves still existed, then, and they still remembered their manners, unlike Sable and Irina's savage band. Perhaps his reign would prove important. Richard was remembering the last time he had faced elves, and they had tried to turn him into a rabbit. They wouldn't find that so easy to do this time. Seylin was attempting to recall useful lore from his studies, but the thought of elves blotted out all else. His powerful elf blood gave him a powerful interest in the subject. The goblin Scholars believed that he himself had found the very last elves thirty years before. It had been the disappointment of his life that they were so primitive.

The men passed through the rings of gnarled, hoary trees that enclosed the crown of the hill and walked to the center of the large, open circle of turf within. The half moon lit them with its pale light. A single elf stepped out of the shadows and walked over to join them.

When Seylin had hunted for elves in his youth, he had hunted for an elf like this. The man was noble and stately, and he was dressed as his people had always dressed. He wore a sleeveless, belted tunic and loose breeches of dark green cloth cross-gartered up to the knee, leather straps wrapping around the lower legs in X patterns to hold the breeches close to the calves. His short boots were of soft deer hide. Over tunic and breeches, he wore a dark green cloak, the hood pushed back, and at his belt was a proper elf knife sheathed in leather. The belt lacked the sophistication of a buckle. It simply crossed through a loop in one end and knotted over itself, the free end hanging. No metal, noted Seylin: the cloak tied with leather thongs. True elves, he knew, hated metal.

The man who wore this true elf clothing was a true elf in every sense. The smooth skin of his pale face glimmered with a silvery sheen in the moonlight, and his eyes were large and black. His black locks clustered around the pale, high forehead and fringed the edge of his face, just brushing the cheekbones. In the back, thick, loosely curling hair just reached the lowered hood. Seylin shared with this stranger the impatient eyebrows that slanted up where a human's eyebrows slanted down and the well-formed, pointed ears that showed through the black hair. But even to Seylin, who saw an elf every day in the mirror, this stranger's appearance was remarkable. Strong and strikingly handsome, he possessed a cold authority that demanded respect. The chronicles told tales of great warrior lords who had slaughtered goblins like sheep. This man could be such a warrior, concluded Seylin.

The goblin King merely noted a properly dressed elf man who had the black eyes of an aristocrat. Good, he thought: a rival with manners and distinction. His reign might turn out to be quite interesting.

For a moment, none of them spoke. Seylin was too excited. Richard knew his place. Marak Catspaw didn't intend to speak first. What the stranger felt, knew, or intended was impossible to guess. His expression was very guarded. His eyes betrayed only the slightest gleam at the sight of the goblins, the faintest hint of fascinated distaste.

"I have to speak to Marak, the goblin King," he informed them in English.

"I am Marak, the goblin King," replied Catspaw. "These are Richard and Seylin, my lieutenants."

The elf turned toward Seylin, his manner relaxing somewhat. "I know of you," he said. "You are the goblin who showed himself to be a friend to my people. Even though you raided for brides, you didn't murder the men. You left them in safety and provided them with supplies."

"We did that on the orders of the old goblin King," answered Seylin.

The elf paused, and his expression once again became guarded. "The old goblin King," he murmured, looking at Catspaw. "You are a new goblin King. And unmarried."

His tone was hostile. Seylin considered the matter from his point of view. The most dangerous thing in the elf world was an unmarried goblin King. The Kings had always tried to capture brides from the very highest noble families.

"A good guess," replied Catspaw calmly. "And who are you?"

"My people call me Nir," said the elf. This revealed nothing. *Nir* was only a polite term of address, the elvish word for "lord."

"What sort of lord are you?" demanded Seylin. "Did your ancestors lead a camp? What is your proper name?" But the elf just glanced at him and then turned back to the goblin King. He plainly intended to stay with business.

"I am here to propose a treaty," he announced. "My people were widely scattered after the death of our King, and we have been hunted down to a handful. Over the last twenty years, I have gathered all of the remaining elves."

"All of the elves you could find," corrected Marak Catspaw.

"All of the remaining elves," declared the lord in a firm voice. "In order for my people to survive, we have to come back to our own land and live in our own forest. I need the goblin King to swear that he will do what is best for the elves. He must swear not to hunt us or allow brides to be taken during his reign. We must be able to live freely on our land, with no goblins spying on us."

"How many elves are left?" asked Marak Catspaw.

The lord hesitated as if he were ashamed. "Sixty-seven," he replied bitterly.

"Such a treaty is reasonable," mused the goblin King. "We couldn't raid such a small number for brides and expect the elves to survive it."

"But that isn't all," continued the stranger. "You goblins took the magic books from my people so that we couldn't defend ourselves. We lack many spells that we need to survive, spells for healing and for making our way of life. I must have those books back."

"That you can't have," answered the goblin King. "We use those books ourselves."

The elf lord's expression hardened. "The books belong to us, and you have your own magic," he said heatedly. "What do you need with ours?"

41

"We can work elf magic, too," said Marak Catspaw, "and the spells are essential to the care of the elves who live with us."

At this mention of captives, the distaste in the stranger's eyes became definite. He glanced away from them, looking over their heads at the stars.

The goblin King gave the matter further thought. "I well under-stand your need for the spells," he concluded. "I would be willing to give you copies."

The elf lord looked at him again. "An elf should copy what elves have written," he replied. "I would rather copy the books myself. They will be safe in my care and promptly returned. But I must have writing materials and the materials for books. My people don't yet have these things."

Marak Catspaw was well aware of the importance of the elves to the goblins. The discovery of sixty-seven elves still alive was an event of tremendous significance. Catspaw didn't mind meeting the lord's demands, either, and even augmenting them with his own con-cerned vigilance. But the new King was growing tired of this pretty stranger's arrogant attitude.

"The elves are asking a great deal of the goblins," he remarked blandly. "What do they intend to do in return?" Nothing, he was sure, and he wanted to make this elf admit that and swallow a nice dose of humility.

But the elf lord didn't look in the least humiliated. He glared at Marak Catspaw. "We will give this unmarried goblin King a bride," he retorted.

"A what?" gasped Seylin. Catspaw just stared. The elves never sanctioned the marriages of their women with goblins. Goblins stole elves. They didn't accept them.

"I will give you a bride," repeated the elf lord emphatically, his handsome face set in a look of bitterness and contempt. "My people are too poor and too few to wage battle. We won't survive without our own land and magic, but we aren't strong enough to take them. I will give you one bride in exchange for these things. I have no other choice."

He dropped his gaze and stared at the ground, plainly overcome with despair at the thought. Good, thought Marak Catspaw. He's taking that dose of humility after all.

"Sixty-seven elves," mused the King. "But how many of those could be brides?"

"I've been forbidding the marriages," replied the elf lord. "Four women are unmarried, and one is old enough for marriage at the full moon."

"Five women," considered Catspaw. "Is any from the high families?"

The elf studied him with loathing. "I don't know their ancestry," he replied.

"What color are their eyes?" put in Seylin. Now those black eyes glared at him.

"Blue. Gray. Green. Blue. Green," he enunciated carefully.

"It doesn't sound as if they are from the nobility," said the goblin King. "I reserve the right to take any female child, even a baby."

"To keep like a penned sheep," retorted the elf lord angrily. "Then I demand a right as well. I want to see the elves you already have penned up. I need to see for myself that these women are not mistreated before I let another one fall into your hands." He glanced down at the goblin King's hands as he spoke, saw the great paw, and looked away with a grimace.

"Very well," replied Marak Catspaw. "When will we meet?"

"I can return with my band in six nights," replied the elf. "We will be here on the night of the new moon."

"Then I wish you a safe journey," concluded the goblin King. He turned and left the truce circle. As he and his lieutenants reached the outer ring of trees, he glanced down at his chief adviser. *Follow him,* he told Seylin in his thoughts.

Seylin gave the barest of nods and dropped behind as they walked into the forest, assuming his cat shape and cloaking himself in shadow. He waited a prudent amount of time and then crept through the forest to the other side of the circle. The elf was already gone. Seylin hissed the Tracking Spell. Now he could see the elf lord's footprints, bright against the dark grass, only a few minutes old. Seylin didn't follow them directly; this elf might be watching for him. Instead, he slunk on his belly within sight of those prints, keeping to the thickest shade under the trees.

In the morning, he woke up and stretched luxuriously from head to toe. He was very stiff. Stiff and cold. He had fallen asleep out in the woods. Seylin glanced down, a little confused. He had fallen asleep as a cat!

He jumped and sputtered as memory broke in on him. The elf lord! The tracks! What had gone wrong? Fluffy tail drooping, he looked around. The great trees of the truce circle towered behind him. The elf had stopped him before he had gone thirty feet.

As Miranda came into the royal rooms to accompany Catspaw to breakfast, she could hear Seylin speaking loudly and a little frantically. ". . . Not just any lord, either," he was protesting. "I'm telling you, goblin King, he's one of the great elf lords, a descendent of the elf King's own lieutenants!"

"Maybe," Catspaw answered, unruffled and a little amused. "But you should tear yourself away from your books, adviser, and practice your spells a little more. Great elf lord or not, you gave yourself away."

Miranda put her head in at the door, and the two men looked up, startled. The Guard, knowing that she would be the King's Wife in a week, didn't bother to announce her anymore.

"Who is a great elf lord?" she asked. There was a slight pause.

"An elf has turned up," replied the goblin King. "But don't mention it to anyone, Miranda. It shouldn't be known."

"Of course not," she said with a smile. "Are you ready for breakfast?" There was another slight pause.

"No, I don't have time," answered Catspaw. "Go without me."

So Miranda went on her way. She was feeling cheerful this morn- ing. A great elf lord, she thought idly. She liked the sound of that.

The men watched the door shut. Then they stared at it for a few seconds.

"For pity's sake, Seylin!" exclaimed the goblin King. "What do I do about Miranda? I don't want to marry some wailing elf girl. I want to marry her!"

"I'm fond of her, too," agreed Seylin bleakly. "But the King has to think of his people, and you know what an elf bride means for the magic of the Heir."

"I'll tell you this, I refuse to give her up for some commonplace elf," threatened Catspaw. "Not for anything less than a lord's daugh- ter." He sighed. "But I suppose we have to plan for that possibility."

"She will still be a strong human bride," noted Seylin. "Miranda's settling in well, and she'll get over her disappointment. She'd make an excellent bride for one of the strong elf crosses, to extend the elvish bloodlines. Tattoo would be a good choice. He has his father's pleasant nature, and she knows him well. She and Sable are always together."

"Tattoo and my Miranda," growled the goblin King. "I don't like it at all! That infuriating elf! Why couldn't he have shown up next week? Why did he feel he had to offer a bride? I would have signed his treaty."

"In the meantime," said Seylin, "may I suggest that you embark on that triumphal tour of the dwarf mines that new goblin Kings always take? There's no sense making Miranda suspicious if this all comes to nothing. You can be gone the whole six days."

"Ah, yes," sighed Catspaw. "Days of being dragged through endless miles of four-foot-high corridors on a little stone sledge. But it's best to get it out of the way before these elves come back. I don't want you and Richard to speak of this business with anyone but each other, and have the elves and elf-human crosses assembled near the main door on the evening of the new moon."

Meanwhile, Miranda sat with Kate at the table overlooking the banquet hall. She was becoming more used to seeing monsters at mealtime, but it still affected her appetite. Instead, she studied Kate's golden hair and perfect porcelain skin. Marak's beautiful widow showed not the least tendency to age. Perhaps that was a benefit of being elvish.

"Tell me something about the elves tonight," said the sleepy girl as she snuggled down under the warmth of the covers. It was cold in her room, and she could see her breath when she talked.

Her ugly guardian smiled at her from his chair and shook his striped hair out of his face. "What do you want to know about the silly elves? All right. Here's your story. Once a very ugly human man met a very pretty elf man. The human was poor and miserable, gathering firewood in the winter twilight. His face had been disfigured by a ghastly burn. The elf was magnificent, tall and noble, and he was disgusted at the sight of the poor man. He reached out his hand to work magic, and the human knew that his last hour had come.

"'Spare me!' he cried, dropping his sticks and falling at the feet of the elf. 'I know I look awful, but I'm a very intelligent man.'

"'You, intelligent?' scoffed the elf. 'Then I'll let you go if you can answer a question. How many stars are in the sky above us?'

"'A hundred thousands,' replied the human without a second's hesitation.

"'That's not right,' declared the elf triumphantly. 'It's not even close.'

"'Of course it's not right,' agreed the human. 'How would I know some-thing like that? But you just said I had to give an answer. You never said it had to be right.'

"Then the elf laughed heartily because elves love jokes and pranks. 'You may go,' he told the human. 'But not looking like that.' And he healed the human's face."

"What happened when the human got home?" she asked. "Did his family know who he was? Were they glad?"

"I can't tell you that," Marak admitted. "The human didn't write that story, the elf did. That was Aganir Dalhamun, the elf King named Dust Cloud."

⊙—

Miranda smiled at the memory. It didn't hurt so much to think about him now. She looked at the hideous shapes filling the huge room and felt a surge of affection. They were Marak's goblins, after all. She loved them for that. And he had been right, just as he always was. She belonged here, even without him.

Chapter Four

Marak Catspaw came back from his tour of the mines late on the evening of the new moon and met the elves and elf-human crosses who had been summoned to the grove of jeweled trees near the goblins' front door. The crowd was larger than he had expected. Sable's and Irina's families had been spending the evening together, and they all had come to the meeting.

"An elf lord is bringing elves back to our forests," he told them. "I'm signing a treaty with him tonight. He wants to see you elves to make sure that you're well treated, and for reasons that I won't reveal yet, we need to do as he asks." A stunned silence followed this announcement.

"I . . . I don't want to see an elf," faltered Irina, holding her daughter-in-law Fay's hand. "I don't want to meet elves at all, not without Thaydar." Her husband had died the year before, and she had taken the loss very hard.

"I don't need any elf man checking up on me," declared Sable scornfully. "As if he really cared whether I lived or died."

"This is important to the kingdom," replied the goblin King. "I have to bring you tonight. But you're welcome to take along any of your family, if that would make you feel better."

"I'll be there, Irina," promised Tinsel, putting his arm around the unhappy woman. "I won't let anyone bother you." She smiled gratefully at the big silver goblin.

"Why don't you want to see an elf, Grands?" asked Fay's little daughter. Trina was only five. She hugged Sable, looking up at her in excitement. "Grand Sable, I want to see an elf," she announced.

"Do you?" said the woman, giving her granddaughter a reluctant smile. "Elves aren't everything you think they are. Of course I'll come, Marak, since you need me, but I won't smile and dance for him. And, Trina, you can come with me since you want to see an elf."

"He hasn't asked to see the elf-human crosses, but he doesn't know we have any," continued Catspaw. "Mother? Em? Do you mind coming?"

"Not at all," answered Kate. "I'd like to see an elf, too." Emily nodded her agreement.

As they walked through the forest, the goblin King had Seylin explain to the small group about the proposed treaty and the offer of a bride. Kate was staggered and upset at the thought of what this would mean to Miranda and even more distressed at the thought of bringing home some poor elf girl. It would be worse than when Sable and Irina had come, even worse than her own awful wedding. But there was no sense worrying about what hadn't happened yet. She couldn't help feeling that what was about to happen was going to be thrilling.

When they came through the double ring of oaks, Kate saw that the elves were already there. The elf lord had brought his entire band with him, even the children. Perhaps, she considered, it was something of an education for them: their first chance to see a real goblin.

The elf lord wore a green tunic and cross-gartered breeches. He lacked any sort of emblem that might symbolize his status, and all the other elf men were dressed as simply as their chief.

The elf women wore plain, sleeveless dresses that fitted them closely to the waist and then flared into a full skirt that ended a little below the knee. Their soft hide shoes looked like slippers, and they had no stockings. The women wore their hair long, some with it pulled back and partly braided, but there was not so much as a hair-pin among them. They wore no jewelry, no ribbons, and no lace. But they were all so lovely. Why should they care about fashion? They looked even more beautiful because of the simplicity of their clothing.

Marak Catspaw and the elf lord met at the center of the circle to read the treaty that Seylin had prepared. Then they walked back toward the small group from the goblin kingdom. Catspaw wore the black shirt and breeches that belonged to the King's Wife Cere-mony, and over it the short black cape painted with golden let-ters that stood for his kingship. No matter how this meeting ended, he clearly planned to marry tonight.

Richard had assembled the elves and elf crosses in a short line for inspection. Seylin carried the book in which elf brides were regis-tered and introduced them one by one.

"This is Em, my wife of thirty-one years, a weak elf-human cross from one of the high elvish families," Seylin said. "She volunteered to come to the goblin kingdom in order to accompany her sister."

"That was brave," commented the lord quietly.

Emily stepped forward, smiling at the tall elf. "Oh, not really," she assured him cheerfully. "I've enjoyed every minute of it. Well, most of them, anyway. And I'm not really elf at all. Marak—the old Marak," she added, glancing at Marak Catspaw, "always used to say that I was a model human."

"But the registry indicates that she is part elf," corrected Seylin. "When the test was done, it showed up."

Nir listened courteously but didn't look at the book. "I have my own test," he said. "May I?" And he placed his hand on her hair. After a few seconds, the right side of Emily's face began to shine with a very faint glimmer, but the left side remained unaffected. Seylin watched, fascinated. The elf lord dropped his hand.

"Barely elf," he told Emily, "but no goblin blood." This last had the sound of a mild compliment, like a consolation prize.

"Really?" asked Emily. "Mightn't there be a little goblin in me? How can you be so sure?"

Nir paused and then turned to Seylin. "May I test you just to show her?" he asked politely, and he put his hand on Seylin's head. Instantly the right half of Seylin's body glowed brightly, but the left half turned as black as ink. Seylin looked down at his arms with a sigh. The elf lord turned back to the surprised Emily.

"You see," he said, "your husband is a goblin. Powerfully elvish, but goblin nonetheless. He looks like an elf, and some of my people didn't recognize him, but he knows what he is."

"Yes, I do now," admitted Seylin, "but when I went out to find your people, I honestly thought I was an elf."

"Your King knew what you were," remarked the elf lord. "He must have known." And he glanced at Marak Catspaw with a troubled frown. When he turned back, he was facing Kate, and the frown vanished.

"Here's an elf," he said, smiling, and Kate felt rather overwhelmed. Although she had long ago gotten used to being called an elf, the term had never had a real meaning for her. It was just an attribute, like being slender or being blond. Now she finally understood. It wasn't that she was an elf, it was that she was one of the elves, a whole separate people with their own blood and ways. She was just a part of it, a part that had never known before that it was part of anything.

"This is Kate," announced Seylin, "the old King's Wife and the mother of the new goblin King."

Kate saw the elf wince at these words, and he reached out and took one of her hands in his. He turned it over to reveal the scar from the King's Wife Ceremony, the long, straight slash glimmering across her small palm. He didn't study it as a goblin would, he just stood looking down at it, an expression of pained aversion on his face. Kate saw it as he did: a cruel deformity of a beautiful thing, a barbaric savagery. It was the emblem of a slavery to an evil cause. A wasted life, his face said, and another goblin at the end of it.

He laid his hand on her head to test her, looking into her eyes. As he did so, Kate saw a vision. She was in another world, a forest more beautiful than she had ever seen. The sky glowed with a deep blue twilight, and stars hung overhead, as brilliant as colorful jewels. Sweet, haunting music floated on the air. But even as she saw this world, she knew that it was beyond her reach. It was a place that she could never find again. When he removed his hand, the vision faded, and she was in the truce circle once more.

Everything that Kate had ever lost burst like a bubble in her mind: Til, her mother, her father, her great-aunts, Hallow Hill, Charm, her dog. And then there was Marak, eyes closed, face stern, lying in the goblin Kings' crypt. Maybe he still walked in some world beyond hers, but she didn't know how to reach him. Lost. Hopelessly lost. He was gone from her, too. She could see his dead face before her eyes as the lovely melody drifted away.

The elf lord turned to Seylin. "An elf cross, but more powerful than most of the members of my camp," he commented, and then stopped short as she burst into tears.

"Kate!" cried Emily, coming to hug her, and she put her head on Emily's shoulder and wailed with grief. Seylin stared at her, astonished, and the goblin King looked stunned.

"What did you do?" demanded Catspaw angrily. "What kind of magic was that?"

"I don't know," said the elf, at a loss. "I tested her. I don't know why it would make her cry."

"A test!" exclaimed the goblin in a fury. "Do you expect me to believe that? I'd like to see what you would do if I did that to one of your people!"

"I'm sure you'll have your chance," murmured Nir bitterly.

"It may be an aspect of elf healing," suggested Seylin, "something only an elf could do for her. She needs to cry. She hasn't cried over your father at all."

"Why would she cry over the goblin King?" asked Nir.

"Because he's dead," snapped Marak Catspaw in an icy rage.

"Because she loved him," answered Seylin a little more helpfully.

Nir's frown deepened. He was genuinely distressed. He hadn't meant to make the poor woman cry. Stars above, her life must have been abominable enough without that. He wondered what had happened. So often he didn't understand his own magic. He turned back to Seylin, ignoring the outraged goblin King.

"I won't touch the others," he promised, and he and Seylin walked on, leaving Kate sobbing in her sister's arms.

The two elf women stood together, and Tinsel had his arms around them both. Irina gazed at the ground, plucking nervously at her bracelets. Sable was glaring across the truce circle at the band of elves, and Nir turned to see what had attracted her attention. Willow stood there with his arm around his own wife. The elf lord turned back to look at Sable again, his gaze thoughtful.

"These two are Irina and Sable, both brought to the kingdom thirty-one years ago," Seylin announced.

"I know their history," he responded quietly. That they were elves he knew without needing to test them; he could feel it about them. And yet they weren't his people. They didn't even look like elves in their shiny, fussy dresses. Nir looked at the big gray goblin who was holding them, at his bright silver hair and blue eyes. Here was elf blood, too, he could tell, warped into grotesque ugliness.

"Sable is from the high families," said Seylin. Nir stared at her angry, fixed expression and the faint scars on her cheeks. "They both showed up as pure elf when their blood was tested."

The elf lord turned to Seylin, struggling to control his agitation.

"Their blood?" he echoed, a gleam in his dark eyes. "How could blood go through a test?"

"The goblin King mixed a number of ingredients with the blood," Seylin answered. "I could show you the spell."

"You mean he bled them," said the elf angrily, walking away from the enslaved women. "Tell me, does all goblin magic involve slicing open elves?" And he eyed the King with cold distaste.

"Does all elf magic involve reducing women to wrecks?" countered Marak Catspaw with a steady glare. Nir glanced at the goblin King's mother. She wasn't crying anymore, but she still huddled in her sister's arms. He felt himself growing even more angry at the inexplicable wrongness of it all. Something bumped into his leg, and he looked down into the face of Sable's little granddaughter. Trina beamed up at him, her arms around his knees.

"The pages laugh at me and say I'm an elf," she said, "so I'm coming to live with you now because you're an elf."

Nir knelt down, eye to eye with the little girl. He didn't test her because he didn't need to. She had a lovely elvish face and long blond hair, but when he lifted her hands to look at them, they were a goblin's hands. The slender elf fingers were unnaturally long and bony, and the fingernails twisted into claws. He stared at the little goblin paws, his anger ebbing away into sadness.

"You're very pretty," he told her gently, "but you're not an elf. If you came to live with me, all my children would start having nightmares. You can tell your pages that you were the most frightening thing the elf lord saw tonight. You're more terrible than the fiercest monster because you're a goblin who looks like an elf." Trina giggled, pleased to be distinctive in some way even if she didn't understand how, and Nir climbed slowly to his feet again, inexpressibly sad.

"Well, elf lord, are you content?" asked Marak Catspaw, gesturing at the line of captured elves.

"Content? No," sighed Nir, still looking down at the bright little face. "But I can see that the women are treated humanely," he added with an effort, glancing up. "At least they seem well fed."

"You'll honor the terms of the treaty, then?" Catspaw continued, and the elf lord nodded.

He walked over to his band of elves, the goblin King beside him. Nir brought the five unmarried women forward with a gesture, but they wouldn't have been hard to pick out anyway. All five were sobbing in terror.

"They speak only elvish," he noted. "Shall I translate?"

"I speak elvish," responded the goblin King, annoyed.

Catspaw surveyed their frightened faces. They were pretty enough, he thought moodily; for pity's sake, all elf women were pretty. There was a sameness about these five that prevented any one from attracting attention. He thought of Miranda's auburn hair and warm smile. It would take an amazing elf, he decided wrathfully, to make him give her up.

But Marak Catspaw was a King who had trained his whole life for kingship, and he gave no sign of his feelings toward them. With great courtesy, he coaxed a name out of each sobbing girl. They wailed and turned away from the touch of that horrible paw, but he managed to test them for magic without provoking too much of an outburst. Nothing but a few sparks rewarded his patient efforts. They weren't a very distinguished group. Not one was from the high families, and not one was worth his Miranda, he decided in relief.

But the goblin King couldn't give up so easily. He owed his people an elf bride if possible. Frowning, he walked down the line of elves, watching as they stepped back, shuddering, or closed their eyes in horror. Nir walked with him, his heart sinking. He knew what would happen next.

The goblin King reached the children. Horrified, they were also

55

fascinated, as curious children of any race are likely to be. Among them were two young girls with black eyes, he noted; perhaps one of them would do. Then he stopped in surprise. Standing with the older children was a young woman with the black eyes he had been seeking. He turned to the elf lord, angry and suspicious.

"Why wasn't she with the other unmarried women?" he demanded.

"She isn't old enough to be married," the elf replied evenly. "She doesn't reach her marriage moon until almost a year from now."

"Then she's seventeen," concluded the goblin. "That's old enough to be married."

"That is *not* old enough," answered the elf lord with some heat. "She won't be a woman until the third spring moon. She's still a child."

"That's just custom," scoffed Marak Catspaw. "Many goblin women marry at seventeen, and humans, too. My grandmother married at sixteen," he added coolly.

"Monster!" snarled the elf lord in revulsion, and he turned his back on the goblin, glaring out at the stars. No elf man, no matter how immoral or depraved, could even imagine marrying a girl before the full moon of the month she reached eighteen. To elf men, she didn't seem like a woman at all before that date. Nir was aware that humans and goblins didn't honor this law, and he found it almost unbearable to consider.

Marak Catspaw turned back to the elf girl, perfectly serene. Coming from this nauseating elf lord, he felt that *monster* had the ring of a compliment. He studied the girl admiringly. By the Sword, she was a pretty little thing, he thought, forgetting that he had just concluded in annoyance that all elf women were pretty. Masses of silky black hair fell in soft waves down her back, and her small oval face was almost heartbreakingly lovely. She was standing perfectly still, staring through his chest at some point far away. She wasn't sniffling like the others, and he warmed to her for that.

"What's your name, little elf?" he asked her.

"Arianna," she answered in a whisper so faint that the furious Nir couldn't even hear it. But standing so close, Catspaw could make it out.

"Arianna, is it?" he replied. "Arianna, hold out your hand."

The young woman extended her shaking hand, but when the goblin King reached out to lay his lion's paw over it, she jerked back with a little cry of disgust. Nir flinched at the sound and set his teeth. He had known what would happen for months now, but that didn't make it easier to accept.

Marak Catspaw sighed in exasperation. It was just a big paw; it didn't drip slime or glow green, and now she was going to burst out crying. But Arianna didn't cry. She stood exactly as before, eyes wide and solemn. Oh, well, considered Catspaw, warming to her again, the poor, deprived girl wasn't accustomed to meeting goblins. He reached out his normal hand and took her by the wrist. This time he held her hand in place as he laid the heavy paw over it.

The truce circle filled with a soft light as golden sparks formed all over the small hand. They glittered like stars as they grew in size, shaping themselves into delicate golden lilies, and dripped off the hand in a gentle shower, replaced by new sparks. The silent rain of radiant blossoms continued for an entire minute as the elves and gob-lins murmured in wonder. Only two people in the truce circle didn't watch the charming spectacle. Arianna still stared straight ahead, petrified by the unwelcome attention, and Nir still stood glaring at the stars. He didn't need to watch. He had tested her years ago and knew perfectly well how magical she was.

Marak Catspaw looked at her for some time after the sparks faded away. He knew what he had to do now, but he hesitated, studying that solemn face. He frowned as he thought of Miranda's smile. This girl probably wouldn't smile at him for months—maybe not ever. He did wish that she would at least look at him, though. Putting his hand under her chin, he tilted her face, and Arianna lifted her large dark eyes to his.

She had been watching the goblin King curiously before he had come close, so she did have some idea what to expect, but she stared in horrified bewilderment at the face looking down into hers. Everything about elf beauty was harmonious, but everything about this creature was discordant. His eyes, blue and green, made no sense to her. They weren't a pair of eyes; they didn't belong together. His short hair didn't belong together, either, the golden and pale locks swirling in violent disarray as if they were fighting a battle. Used to the faces of sensitive elves, she found nothing in his expression for her to read beyond a kind of complacent cruelty. Arianna was rendered incapable of thought by that strange face. She simply stared at him without moving a muscle, her eyes huge.

Elf beauty had its degrees, and black eyes were the limit of that beauty. They appeared only in the nobility and in the elf Kings. Gazing into Arianna's eyes, Catspaw felt their powerful allure. He still preferred Miranda's brown eyes, he thought loyally. Then he wondered if this were really true.

"Arianna," he asked in a low voice, "would you like to be a King's Wife?"

Even on the brink of disaster, Arianna didn't cry. She stared up at those eyes that didn't belong together, and felt in confusion that two people were looking at her instead of one. She looked from one eye to the other, baffled and repelled. Blue to green and back to blue again. "I'm promised to Nir," she whispered faintly.

"Oh, are you?" remarked Catspaw, and that settled something in his mind with a neat finality. He dropped his hand and stepped back. "Elf lord," he said in a loud voice, "I'll sign the treaty for this one."

Released from the terrifying force of those eyes, Arianna finally understood what was happening. A wave of icy dread poured over her. She turned her head and looked in mute appeal toward her fiancé, but he still had his back to her. She tried to call out to him, but no sound came. "Agreed," she heard Nir say, and Arianna's world shattered. When she opened her eyes again, that thing had her around the waist.

The elf woman who had been crying before was crying again, coming to take her in her arms. The goblin said, "Mother, stand back. You know how dangerous desperate magic can be." But Arianna used none of her quiet, prodigious magic. She couldn't. She didn't have the right. She wasn't a stolen bride who could fight her way back to her people. Nir had said she had to go, and so she had no choice. On the verge of unconsciousness, Arianna gasped in a breath. She wondered how many more breaths she would have to take before she could finally die. There would be so many, she thought in despair. Millions and millions. She closed her eyes and began drearily to count them.

Seylin spread the treaty out on a stand, and Marak Catspaw came to sign it, his human arm around his drooping bride. He dipped his paw into the bowl of golden ink and put his print on the treaty, holding out the paw for Seylin to wipe clean. The elf lord came up then, eyes averted from the horrible sight as the goblin King guided the faltering Arianna away. Dipping his fingertips quickly in the ink, he signed in a sideways W. Then he jerked the towel away from Seylin and rubbed the ink from his fingers, turning to the stars again. He wouldn't watch the goblins leave the truce circle.

"Elf lord," asked Seylin with interest, "why did you sign like that?"

Motionless, face still, Nir glared at the stars. "Why?" he murmured absently. "Because it makes it binding." He thought about what it had bound him to do and felt a rising sickness.

"But why didn't you sign your name?" persisted Seylin.

Nir continued to gaze at the stars, ignoring the goblin completely. He was bound by the treaty. No, *he* wasn't bound. Arianna was the one bound now, bound, shackled, and enslaved. He had known her fate months ago as soon as he had known what he had to do. He had warned his elves that the goblins might take any unmarried girl, even a small child. He had given them the chance to leave, but he had known that they couldn't leave him, and he had known, too, that Arianna hadn't paid any attention. She had been his responsibility since she was thirteen, and she couldn't imagine that he wouldn't protect her.

For all those months, he had eaten with her and slept by her side, and he had never once told her of her danger. He might as well have wrapped that horrible snake around her himself. He had betrayed her into hell. His magic had told him to do it, and his magic was always right. It was the best thing for his people, he had always known that. But he had destroyed a sweet elvish life because it was the best thing for his people. He only wished that he could have destroyed himself.

"Seylin," he heard the little goblin girl say as they walked off, "I don't want to go back. I want to be an elf."

"I know just how you feel" was Seylin's reply. And then they were gone.

Chapter Five

"Goblin King," said Seylin, catching up to Catspaw, "let me tell Miranda." He glanced down at the silent elf bride. She had her eyes tightly shut, and she kept stumbling. After a minute, Catspaw picked her up and continued walking. Her head dropped onto his shoulder as if she were asleep.

"No," replied Marak Catspaw in a low voice. "Seylin, I'll tell her myself. It's only fair," he added bleakly.

"Nothing's ever fair about the goblin King's Bride," commented Seylin, "not even when we think it's going to be. But you did the right thing. Such a King she'll give us!" He remembered Kate's dreadful homesickness when he was a boy. "She'll settle in," he said encouragingly.

"Poor little elf," growled the goblin King. "Completely aban-doned! I can't understand how he could simply hand her over like that. I would never do that to one of my people," he added, pleased to have another reason to despise the elf lord.

"You wouldn't have much need to do it," observed Seylin. "I don't think the elves are interested in a goblin bride. You're sure about talking to Miranda? There's nothing to be gained by it, and there are some things to lose. She's bound to be distraught, but she'll calm down after a few days. And you'll be facing enough hysteria tonight."

They came to the cliff face and walked through into the

underground kingdom. Seylin glanced curiously at the quiet elf. She had missed her last look at the stars.

"I know I will," sighed Marak Catspaw as they walked down the polished black corridor. "I'm going to leave Arianna in the King's Bride chamber with Mother while I talk to Miranda. She won't be afraid of her, they're both elves. The door will be locked, and Mother can join the women in the inner room if Arianna panics and tries spells. She could certainly do it, with such impressive magic," he added admiringly.

"I'm not so sure she could," Seylin mused as they walked past the great iron door. When it clanged shut behind her, Arianna shivered in Catspaw's arms, but she still didn't open her eyes. "This girl's not reacting like any bride I've ever read of. She's not fighting at all. I don't know why not," Seylin concluded with a puzzled frown.

"I think she's being brave," said the goblin King complacently as they passed the lovely grove of slender metal saplings. Sometimes Seylin still sounded like the tutor he had been. "Adviser, I want you to go wake up Miranda and bring her to the blue throne-room antechamber. But don't tell her anything about tonight, and that's an order."

"All right," said Seylin. "Goblin King, please don't make any promises to Miranda. And that's a request," he murmured gloomily.

⌒

Miranda paced the small room nervously, waiting for Catspaw to arrive. The King must have come home early from the dwarf mines and decided to hold the marriage right away. She felt a little anxious at the thought of the bloody ceremony, but a King's Wife needed to be strong, so she gave Catspaw a bright, unworried smile when he finally came into the room.

The goblin King stopped at the sight of that smile and just

looked at her for a minute. He realized how deeply attached to her he had become. She was so lively and interesting, so proud and sophis-ticated. They would have been very happy.

Miranda's smile faded as he stood and stared at her. "What's the matter?" she asked, nervous again. "Has something happened? Is the ceremony tonight?"

"Yes," replied Marak Catspaw. "Yes to both questions. The cer-emony is tonight, and something has happened." He paused, but there was no point in pausing, so he went on again. "Miranda, I can't marry you," he said. "I have to marry someone else."

Miranda stood there, completely stunned, her face turning white. Catspaw tried to think of something to say that would make her understand. He had done the right thing, of course. Everyone knew that. Everyone except her, and she was the one who mattered.

"I have to do it," he explained. "The elf lord gave us a bride. I wouldn't have given you up for a regular elf, but she's an elf from the highest noble families. She's very magical, and that's important for the Heir."

Miranda fought back tears. Marak hadn't raised her to snivel. He had raised her to be a King's Wife, but she wouldn't be one now.

"An elf bride," she said evenly. "She's very beautiful, isn't she? Of course she is," she said, tossing her head back. "All elves are beautiful."

"That has nothing to do with this," said Catspaw. "That's not why I'm marrying her."

"But she is, isn't she?" persisted Miranda, fixing him with a deadly look.

"Yes," said the goblin King. "So are you." He watched as she turned away and glared at the wall. "Miranda," he tried again, "I'd rather marry you. If I had my choice, I would marry you. But I have to do the best thing for my people."

"And I'm not it," she concluded. "After all those promises. I'm not the best thing, am I? And your people deserve the best."

He didn't answer her. There was no point. After all, it was true.

"And how convenient that I'm not one of your people," she added. Her tone was still even, but her voice was beginning to shake. "You'll do the best thing for them, won't you, but it doesn't matter what happens to me."

"Of course it matters," he said. "You know you matter to me. I'll do anything I can for you, anything."

"Except marry me," she said bitterly. She dropped her head and began to cry. She didn't care anymore that Marak hadn't raised her to be a crybaby. He hadn't raised her to be anything, as it turned out.

"I know you're upset," Catspaw said. "But you're so strong. You'll overcome this. I'll marry you to any goblin you name and give you anything you ask for. You know I'll always care about you," he added coaxingly.

Miranda's head came up slightly at this speech, and a dangerous look came into her eyes. "Will you really do that?" she asked quietly. "Will you give me anything I ask for?"

"Of course I will," said the goblin, forgetting Seylin's request. He was pleased to see her recovering so quickly.

"Then give me my freedom!" spat Miranda in a fury. "Let me out of here! I don't want to be around you for another minute, I don't want to be around goblins for another minute, and I certainly don't want to stay down here and marry one!"

"I can't do that," concluded Marak Catspaw helplessly, caught completely off guard.

"Oh, you can't!" cried Miranda in disgust. "You can't seem to do anything I want, can you!"

"You know you belong in the kingdom," Catspaw insisted reasonably. "You're the ward of the goblin King and always will be."

"I don't belong anywhere!" she cried. "You lied to me! You said you would give me anything! But you've always lied to me, haven't you? You said you'd marry me, too."

Catspaw stared at her for a long moment. Lying was a serious matter to a goblin King. "Very well," he said finally. "I'll give you what you asked for." He studied her distraught features with a worried frown. "Where are you going to go?" he asked.

"That's no business of yours," she hissed. "I'm not one of your people."

"Where are you going to go?" he repeated steadily. She wiped her eyes and reflected that he hadn't let her out yet.

"I'll go back to my family," she replied, looking away.

"That's a lie," he observed. She glared at him. How nice to be magical, she thought bitterly.

"I'll go watch the sunrise," she concluded more quietly. "I haven't seen it in months." And because this wasn't a lie, he didn't find the danger in it.

"All right," he said. She was calming down again. This would doubtless be for the best. He hadn't promised to let her out for good, of course. He could give her the freedom she had demanded for one day, under careful guard, and then have her brought back into the kingdom.

Whispering, he walked up to her and placed his paw on her forehead, where the golden Door character glimmered. Then he continued to stand there for another minute, his hand on her hair, regretting his choice of brides.

He was so close to her, she thought miserably. Close enough to kiss her. She wished with all her heart that she had a knife in her hand.

"I'll have Tattoo accompany you," the goblin King decided. "He'll get some things together for you to take."

Miranda jerked away.

"I don't want anything from you," she said in a low, deliberate voice. "I don't want to take a single disgusting thing of yours with me. I won't take your guards, and I won't take your money, and I won't take your rings," she added, voice rising, jerking them off one by one. "And I won't take your bracelets," she cried, ripping them off and flinging them at him.

Without realizing it, she pulled off the golden bracelet that Marak had given her, too, and the catch tore a jagged gash in her wrist. The blue butterfly, crushed in the act of flying away, fluttered awkwardly to the ground. Overcome with horror, Miranda watched it flop helplessly about. Then she dodged around Catspaw with an anguished cry and dashed out the door.

The goblin King gazed down at the scattered jewelry. "Guard, come," he called. The astonished Tattoo appeared at the door, trying to keep his silver face expressionless.

The King pointed after Miranda. "Follow her outside," he ordered. "Follow her into the daylight, but don't let her see you. I'll send your relief at noon."

With a shimmer, the goblin guard changed into a nightjar, a bird that flew at night. He swooped after the fleeing girl.

⌒

Miranda stood in the Hallow Hill graveyard on the edge of the forest, not far from the house where her family slept. The tall marble monument gleamed like a ghost in the pool of light from Kate's magical bracelet. She held the light close to read the inscription. *Miranda Richardson, b. October 9, 1836, d. April 6, 1854. In life, we are in the midst of death.*

It hadn't even been six months since Marak had worked the magic on them to make them think she was dead. With a chill, she remembered standing inside her house in the deep twilight, surrounded by their limp, silent figures. The entire estate, the whole village was there by special invitation, and every last one was asleep. The sleepers were dreaming a single dream. They were all at her funeral together. She had walked among them, watching the tears slide down their still faces, listening to their quiet sobs.

Not even half a year ago, she had left them, but there was no wreath or bouquet to show that she was missed. Only a handful of wildflowers lay at the base of the tombstone, their petals withered and dry. She bent to pick them up, her heart aching with grief. That would be little Charlotte, no doubt.

She sat in the nursery's deep window seat, a thick curtain between her and the rest of them. Outside, a cold rain drizzled down the glass, the hiss of the drops helping to drown out the shrieks and shouts that arose from the room. The girl was practicing the script character for hot water, *and she thought it interesting that this should be one word in goblin when it was two in English. She carefully traced over the golden lines on her magical crystal tablet, at peace with the whole world.*

"LET ME SEE!" howled a voice in her ear, and the small crystal square was jerked from her hand. Miranda sat up, tucking the metal stylus into her pocket, and pushed open the curtain.

"Look, she's scratching on her window glass," announced ginger-headed Jamie, parading around the nursery and waving it over his head. Charlotte and Toria marched behind him, giggling. He tripped over part of a castle and stumbled into an array of tin soldiers that his brother Richard had formed into ranks for the Battle of Waterloo. Their commander was not at all amused at this unexpected turn in the fortunes of war.

"Watch where you're stepping, you swine!"

"Nothing but an old piece of glass," caroled Jamie. "But she says it has writing on it. What's it say, Mere-Anda? What's it say in goblin?"

"Give it back, Jamie," she demanded in annoyance. "You know it doesn't work when you're looking at it."

"Oh, no! Just the little green goblins can see it! Tell us about them, if you're so smart. Tell us how they talk to you in goblin!"

But this Miranda couldn't do. She was forced into humiliating silence. The magic allowed her to mention the name of the language. It forbade her to talk about the people.

Jamie's procession came around the room again, and Miranda made a grab for the crystal square. The noise increased to a strident roar.

"What is going on in here?" demanded a young woman, bursting through the door. Her black-and-white uniform might have looked smart at the beginning of the day, but hours of bouncing wet babies, wiping sticky faces, and crawling under furniture for missing doll hats had taken their toll of starch.

"Simpson, my poor, afflicted sister is writing on her window glass again." Jamie brandished the offending object.

Simpson flicked a nervous glance at the silent girl. "Give it back to her" was all she said. Simpson was afraid of Miranda, and Miranda could tell. Most of the servants were. They didn't like her, either, although she was the only child who obeyed them. Marak had taught her that displaying good manners to everyone, from lords to scullery maids, was a sign of true distinction.

"I believe in goblins," said little Charlotte seriously, stopping at her older sister's knee. "I believe in goblins, and brownies, and fairies in bluebells, and pixies with dragonfly wings—"

Miranda stalked out of the nursery in disgust.

Her goal was the pleasant rug by the warm hearth in the music room, but she found herself face-to-face with her mother instead. Til, spectacular in a costly red gown with jet buttons, was accompanied by an ample woman with a comfortable face.

"Here's the little goblin linguist now," said the woman cheerfully.

"Yes, Miranda is so clever at her imaginary language," remarked the elegant Til. "She amuses herself with it by the hour. It's so beautiful, too! You must see a sample. Sometimes she has me quite convinced."

This was a bit much for the embattled girl. Her mother, having grown up in the kingdom, was effortlessly bilingual in goblin and occasionally ridiculed Miranda's efforts when no one else was there to hear. "You speak it even better than I do!" she said heatedly.

Til's smile froze for a second, and her eyes gleamed. Then she turned to the other woman with a lighthearted laugh. "Isn't it sweet how she includes me in her pretend games!" she purred. "Miranda, my pet, you're looking quite wild. You need to go to your room for a little rest. I intend to have a chat with Simpson this afternoon about the propriety of her nursery."

The girl, routed from the field of battle, went to her room and shut the door. Her mother's indulgent speech didn't fool her; she knew perfectly well what that talk with Simpson would mean. Only a prompt and permanent removal to her bedroom would give her the hope of any supper whatever. The room was damp and chilly, with no fire at this time of day, but at least here she could practice her goblin writing in peace.

Alone in the whispering darkness, Miranda traced her name on the glimmering tombstone. Pretend games, she thought wretchedly. That's just what they had turned out to be. All those hard years with only Marak's regard and her glorious future to sustain her, and in the end, she had nothing to show for it.

She couldn't face the shame of going back to her family. She imagined the trouble that would follow. "There's that goblin girl," people would mutter wherever she went. "We all saw her lying in her coffin, and then, one night, she came back."

The only thing to do is to follow my plan, she thought. After all, it's what I told him I wanted. Her eyes stinging with fresh tears, she laid the brittle flowers down at the foot of her tombstone and wandered off into the dark.

The elf lord paced the truce circle, restless, angry, and miserable. He had heard the marriage vows of his sober elves and sent them back to

camp, but he couldn't face their company tonight. He should be res-
cuing Arianna right now, but he had sent her away himself, after
swearing to her father that he would protect her. Overcome by grief
and despair, he wandered back and forth, almost incapable of thought.

A crashing of weeds, and footsteps sounded on the path. Only a
human could make that much noise in the nighttime woods. Nir
drew back into the shadow of the trees. He had nothing to do with
humans. A blinding flash of white light burst into the truce circle,
and he quickly turned away. An instant later, the light was gone, but
the human remained, stretched on the ground and gasping for breath.

At once Nir's magic concentrated on the prone shape, telling
him that this human was very important. He frowned in baffled
annoyance. What could a human mean to the elves? But he walked
toward it, drawn in spite of himself. His magic was never wrong.

The human was a woman. She was lying facedown in the grass,
sobbing, and her hair glowed with the color of dying embers. He
stared at her, puzzled. Important for what purpose? He couldn't
imagine what she could possibly be for.

"Why are you crying?" he asked her quietly, and Miranda held
her breath for a second, alarmed. But, of course: Catspaw had had
her followed. She should have known that she couldn't trust him
now, not after the other promises he had made.

"He promised to marry me, the heartless monster!" she sobbed.
"But he broke his word and left me with nothing!"

The elf lord recoiled in guilt and shame at the accusation, half-
expecting this phantom with the fiery hair to sit up and stare at him
reproachfully with Arianna's black eyes. This very important
stranger who wasn't even an elf. She couldn't be an elf, could she?

He knelt beside her and reached out to test her, barely brushing
her glowing hair. She didn't feel the touch, but he felt it, his magic
snapping through him like a plucked harp string. His fingertips

burned as if he really had touched an ember, and he knew what purpose she was to serve for the elves. What, but not why. It made no
sense at all! And it would lead to more suffering—suffering that he
would have to cause, as if he hadn't caused enough already. His
magic was so brutal, so thoroughly cruel. He watched her cry, angry
at the thought.

"You should have been at home with your own people," he told
her. "Your people shouldn't be out at night."

"My people?" muttered the miserable girl. "I have no people."

Nir sat down and considered the absurdity of this statement, thinking about his tiny band of elves. "No human can ever say that," he
replied. "Your people are everywhere. They cover the earth like ants."

"They're not my people," she sobbed. "They traded me away
before I was born. All my life, I was raised to be the King's Wife.
All my life! And now, on the night of our own wedding, he's marrying someone else."

Nir stared at the girl in complete horror. A human raised by
goblins? How ghastly! And now the foul beast had thrown her out
since he didn't need her anymore, just where Nir would happen on
her and his magic would find a use for her. If only that repulsive
creature had taken better care of her!

"You were his responsibility in any case," he said in disgust. "He
should have kept you down in the caves since you liked it there.
He shouldn't have let you out to roam the woods alone." Alone. He
concentrated. No, she wasn't alone. He raised his head very slightly
and detected the unnatural bird sitting in the branches about twenty
feet away.

The goblin bride's sobs died away to a confused sniff, and she put
out a hand to sit up. That white light stabbed out again with a painful
brilliance. Nir shielded his eyes. Swiftly, he touched the shining
bracelet on her hand, and the blinding light was extinguished.

Miranda gave a gasp. She didn't know what had happened; she only knew that she was in the dark. She sat up, frightened to see how black the night was, barely able to make out anything in the faint starlight. She located the shape of someone quite near her on the grass and drew back and peered at him anxiously.

"Who are you?" she wondered. "How could you talk about him like that? Didn't he send you to follow me?"

"Did he send me?" murmured the elf lord, flicking a glance toward the abnormal bird. "No, I'm no goblin." She stirred uneasily, her human eyes trying to make out something about him, and his attention was caught by the gash on her arm. "Did that monster bleed you, too, before he threw you out?" he asked in a cold voice. Miranda had forgotten the cut. She jumped as fingertips touched the gash in the darkness.

"Oh! No, I did that," she admitted. Then she cried out in pain as the fingertips seared across the wound like hot coals. She jerked her arm away and cradled her wrist, but she found there no break in the skin.

"I'm sorry," he said. "I know that hurt. The goblins must have special spells for that, but I don't know any healing spells. That's the only way I know to heal."

Miranda shivered. "How could you do that?" she asked in awe. "What are you if you're not a goblin?"

"You said he was a heartless monster," the quiet voice answered. "Then tell me what I am. I promised to marry a girl, too. But I brought her here and gave her to a creature out of her nightmares, and I watched that creature drag her away without lifting a hand to help her."

"You're the elf lord!" she exclaimed. "You gave him your own bride!" She thought about this in amazement. "You're two of a kind, aren't you?" she concluded with venomous scorn. "I haven't been taught the right words to describe you great lords."

In his misery, Nir felt the justice of this remark and found himself grateful for it. "I'm sure Arianna agrees with you," he murmured, looking at that angry, sightless face. He gave the goblin bird a wary glance. Time to act. "What were you going to do now?" he asked without particular interest, considering how to accomplish his goal.

"I'm going to kill myself," Miranda declared. Jerked out of his own thoughts, the elf lord stared at her in shock. "I'm going to wait until the sun rises, and then I'll drown myself. There's a lake about an hour's walk from here, and one side is a bluff straight into the water. I'll sit on the cliff and watch the sun come up, and then I'll throw myself in."

Nir continued to stare at her, outraged at the idea. This certainly made his task more bearable. "Why would you do such an evil and absurd thing?" he demanded. "It's ridiculous to use your death as some sort of futile punishment."

After all that she'd been through that evening, Miranda wasn't prepared to sit through a lecture. "I don't have to justify myself to you!" she snapped. "Go play with your silly elves!"

Her bracelet began to glimmer. Miranda saw a remarkable face looking into hers, a face possessed of a cold, splendid beauty. His black eyes gleamed with anger, and his look was calm and stern. He seemed very much like an avenging angel, and she cringed in surprised dismay.

He continued to gaze at her, implacable. "You couldn't justify yourself at all," he said severely.

"Oh, yes, I could," she replied, gathering her confidence, "and I'll do it the way you great lords do. My people think I'm dead; I can show you my tombstone. It's best for my people that I really be dead. As long as the people get what's best," she concluded bitterly, "it doesn't matter what happens to one insignificant woman."

"Child, I would have said," he remarked. "How old are you?"

"I'm seventeen!" she replied in indignation.

"Then you are a child," he concluded. "I was sure of it. That's justification for your foolishness, I suppose."

Offended, Miranda turned away, and he didn't speak again. Her battered feelings, her chaotic thoughts spiraled down into wretched ness. The force of her anger washed away, leaving her dull and tired. Nir studied her profile as her expression slowly changed to dreary misery, his own face cautious and calculating.

"You still have half a turn of the sky before the sun rises," he said. "But this great lord has to work a spell tonight. Will you do something for me? Do you see these white flowers?" He pointed at the small lilies springing up here and there out of the grass. "I need twenty-eight of them. Will you gather them for me?"

Miranda shrugged apathetically. She had always hated waiting for things and having nothing to do, so she began picking the lilies, searching for them by the faint light of her bracelet. He took them from her as she brought them and plucked them from the stems, pulling out their golden insides to leave a small hole at the back of each one. Twenty-eight, he thought to himself as she handed him a flower.

"I think that's the last one," she said.

"Do you?" he asked inattentively. "Wait a little, you can help me count them." He reached into his tunic and withdrew a small leather bag. Opening the top, he blew a quick breath into it, and the bag inflated like a child's balloon. When he let out the air, he was holding a leather bag about four times its original size. Miranda stared at it in surprise. It looked perfectly ordinary.

"Here," said the elf lord, and he piled the blossoms up in her hands. Then he climbed to his feet and plucked the flowers back one by one, examining them for flaws and dropping them into the bag. As he did so, he began to wander slowly toward the great trees, not watching where he was going. Miranda, walking beside him, counted the flowers out loud. She wished he would stop walking. It was hard to hold a mass of loose blossoms, walk, and count all at once.

"Twenty-eight," she announced as they reached the circle of trees. The preoccupied elf lord carefully tugged the bag shut and tied it to his belt, still wandering. Miranda walked with him, interested in the thought of the magic.

"What is the spell for?" she asked, curious, stepping close beside him to squeeze through the first ring of trees. She didn't know of any goblin spells that used flowers unless they were crushed like herbs.

"Do you really want to know?" murmured the elf absently, looking up at the dark crowns of the ancient oaks.

"Yes," she said. She had always liked magic. He glanced back down at her then.

"It's for you," he said. And the instant they passed the great trunks, his hand closed over her wrist.

Chapter Six

Miranda stopped, bewildered. "Let me go!" she cried, her tired brain wondering what this meant. She tried to pull away, but although the elf held her with only one hand, her jerks and tugs didn't even attract his notice. He had turned and was staring intently at the trees above them, his right hand held up in readiness and his whole body still.

As the goblin bird came swooping toward them, the elf made a quick movement, and there was a rustle in the trees overhead. A net of twigs and leaves arched swiftly around the flying bird, trapping it in a split second inside a living cage. Nir studied his handiwork. The bird was completely enmeshed. It would take hours to peck and claw apart the encircling twigs. But if it changed back into a goblin, the fragile branches would break under its weight and send it crash-ing to the ground below. The elf lord laughed, well pleased at the goblin's humiliating quandary.

Miranda didn't know what her captor was looking at, but his dark eyes shone, and his whole face lit up with the power of that tri-umphant, musical laugh. The inhuman beauty that had awed her before was now a terrifying force, just as incomprehensible and fear-some as the inhuman ugliness of the goblins. Miranda shrank back, and a lump rose in her throat. She felt instinctively that she had stumbled in fatal error across a sight not allowed to humans.

The elf lord glanced down at her with that laugh still shining in his eyes and walked rapidly away from the truce circle, pulling her with him. Momentarily overcome, Miranda walked beside him, unresisting. She felt in hurt reproach that Marak shouldn't have talked so casually about the pretty elves. Her impression of them had been quite different.

"Where are we going?" she demanded breathlessly.

"I'm taking you back to my camp so that I can work the spell on you," he answered.

"What will the spell do to me?" she asked.

"I don't intend to tell you," he said.

Accustomed to the straightforward goblins, Miranda found this statement astounding. Confident in their strength and insensitive in their feelings, goblins never bothered to conceal anything. "What do you mean, you don't intend to tell me?" she asked. "Why are you doing this?"

The elf was silent for some time as they walked, trying to make sense of the first question. At length, he gave it up as hopeless and went on to the second one.

"Why? I don't know," he admitted. "But you won't come to any real harm."

"I never do, with you great lords," snapped Miranda. "Your plots are so benevolent, aren't they? You lords do what's best for your own people. I'm not one of your people, so you won't care what happens to me."

This argument had worked beautifully on the guilty Catspaw, but the elf lord didn't look impressed. "There's truth to that," he said coldly. "But I only have to stop short of killing you to improve on your own ideas."

"Let me go!" said Miranda angrily, trying to pry his hand loose. "I'm sick of you great lords practicing your magic on me."

"You should be glad it's this great lord and not the other one," murmured Nir, watching for landmarks as they walked. "You were about to be enslaved by a monster and locked away under the earth. I'd think you'd welcome anything after that."

"Well, I don't!" she retorted. "At least the goblins showed proper respect. At least they were polite. None of them is half the monster you are!"

The elf stopped and turned then, handsome face set and eyes gleaming with wrath. "You think I'm a worse monster than he is," he exclaimed, "just because I won't leave you alone to kill yourself! Stars above! Illogical is the kindest word for your point of view."

Miranda took advantage of the halt to wrap her free arm tightly around a tree. "Let go of that," he commanded, but the order had no effect, and if he jerked her loose, the bark would tear her skin. He paused to think for a second, eyes narrowed. Then he touched her bracelet, putting out the light.

Total blackness. Before, she had been able to pick out shapes in the gloom, but in this dense forest, all detail was gone. Miranda blinked, but nothing in her field of vision changed to let her know if her eyes were open or closed.

In an instant, she was six years old again, and the panic that gripped her was absolute. She was nothing but a helpless child, tormented, trapped in the darkness. She held her breath to fight down the cry that tightened in her throat and shook her head to stop her mother's silky laughter. *Let me out of here!* She reached out her fist to pound on the locked door.

Nir studied her frightened face and wide, sightless eyes, catching her other hand in his as she reached out toward him. It was far from honorable, he thought in disgust, for him to use her human weakness against her. He thought about how it would be to stand here in the sunlight, his own eyes blinded by the terrifying whiteness of the day.

"Walk right beside me," he said, "and I won't let you stumble." He released her wrist and held the hand she had given him, tucking her arm under his to keep her close. "Not all the nights are as dark as this one," he added sympathetically, "and your eyes will adjust a little."

Miranda gave him no answer, occupied completely with the effort of the frightening journey. She found it exhausting to step and step into blackness. Her body was rigid, irrationally convinced that the next step would be out into nothing. Time passed, but how long or short, she couldn't have said. She lost all her bearings in time and place when she lost her ability to see.

The elf lord slowed and turned, speaking softly into the darkness beside them, and another man's voice answered his. Miranda's bracelet flared to a faint light, and she accepted the gift of sight with blissful relief. She looked up to see her captor and another elf man both studying her as they walked along, talking in some strange language. Deeply shaken by the walk, Miranda was completely cowed again by the elf lord's inhuman appearance. It was hard to imagine in her current state of fatigue that she had ever had the courage to argue with him.

The elf who had joined them was not nearly so frightening. Blond and blue-eyed, he was remarkably handsome, but he lacked the air of command that belonged to the elf lord as if it were a physical trait. He was staring at Miranda with open curiosity and a kind of humorous mischief.

They walked along slowly now as the two men talked. The trees began to space themselves more widely, their trunks thick and straight. Miranda heard the murmur of water nearby and realized that she was walking on soft grass. A wide clearing opened out. Overhead shone a sky full of stars.

"This is my camp," said the elf lord, stopping. "Hunter is bringing some things that I'll need." Miranda saw no buildings, tents, torches, or fires. She would have walked right through the clearing and never noticed anything special about it.

The blond elf Hunter walked off on his errand, but Miranda found to her dismay that she was quickly attracting an audience. Elves were drifting over to join them, their ageless faces noble and quite foreign, staring at her as if she were some new species of animal. Miranda stared back at them, anxious and uncomfortable, remembering Marak's stories of the elves' human slaves.

"Why did they even have slaves?" asked the girl. *"In the fairy-tale books, they're beautiful and good."*

"The lazy elves were just beautiful," he told her cheerfully. *"Some were beautiful and bad! Lots of elf lords didn't have slaves, but they had more and more toward the end. Whenever there was hard work to do, they made the humans do it."*

She frowned disapprovingly. *"I wouldn't work for an elf! I wouldn't care what they did."*

But now, standing in the darkness, surrounded by their alien magnificence, she was no longer certain of this.

Hunter returned with a folding stool and a small wooden tray. "Sit down," ordered Nir, pointing to the stool. Miranda glanced around nervously at the growing crowd of strangers and sat down without protest. She didn't want to find out, in front of this unsympathetic mob, if he intended to back up his commands with force.

The elf lord knelt at her feet and arranged on the tray the flowers that she had gathered, his curling black hair falling around the edges of his pale face as he worked. Miranda studied that strange face, his narrow, pointed ears, wondering in curious dread what the spell was for. If he wouldn't tell her, it must be frightful. Maybe he and Catspaw had argued, and he was doing something terrible in revenge.

Now he had all the lilies in four lines on the tray. He plucked hairs from his head and threaded one through each line of flowers. He picked up a string of lilies, and the blossoms remained evenly spaced along the hair, like white carved beads on a bracelet. Then he straightened up, still kneeling, and turned to Miranda. "Hold out your hand," he ordered.

Frightened, she clasped her hands firmly in her lap and looked for some means of escape, but the elves stood packed around her in a close ring, watching the proceedings with interest. The elf lord knelt back on his heels and stared at her, too, considering what to do next. It would be best to have her cooperation for this spell. He didn't want her damaging the lilies.

"You were ready to throw yourself into a lake," he remarked, "and now you look worried about a few flowers. Tell me, are you afraid of the silly elves?"

Miranda's head came up at that, and she glared at him, holding out her hand so he could tie the blossoms around her wrist. Nir kept his head bent and his eyes on his work. He didn't want her to see his triumphant expression. One by one, he tied on the strings of flowers, first to her wrists and then to her ankles, taking off Kate's bracelet and setting it on his tray without extinguishing its light. Then he caught Miranda's hands and pulled her to her feet.

"Look at me," he said, and Miranda looked into those beautiful eyes as he whispered the words of the spell. She felt in sudden panic that she should look away, but those eyes were all she could see. They seemed to pull her whole being into them, to join and become a patch of the night sky shining with the light of the stars. She stared at that sky, felt it arch over her and around her, felt the stars coming close to her sides. They were surrounding her in a brilliant net, making her their prisoner.

As Miranda stood frozen, as the elf lord said his spell, the strings of flowers began to spin. They spun faster and faster, glittering like water shaken under the starlight. Now the lilies gleamed like silver sparks that whirled and tumbled at her hands and feet, becoming small bright stars that shone with their own light. They faded in brightness as they slowed to a stop, a circle of seven silver eight-pointed stars around each wrist and ankle. The elf lord knelt again and drew a symbol with his finger on the top of her foot. Then he retrieved Kate's bracelet for her, watching the puzzled girl turn her arms and study her shackles of stars by its light.

Nir felt a pang of guilt as he considered the other spell he still had to work. This spell would keep her trapped in the nighttime, unable to move about in the day. He knew that the sun, hated and feared by the elves, was really the humans' moon, and to take it away from this poor child was to condemn her to a life of near-blindness. An unwelcome memory assailed him:

The small boy was crying, dazzled and frightened by bright light, standing in a ring of campfires belching up smoke and flame.

"What are you doing?" cried Father's frantic voice. "You'll set the entire forest on fire!"

A blond-haired woman knelt in the middle of the circle, her face haggard and stained with tears. "I had to." Her words tumbled over themselves. "I'm going blind. I'm going mad! Please, Ash, please. I can't live like this anymore!"

Nir winced, feeling the dreadful sadness, seeing the pain in that tear-stained face. I don't have a choice, he reminded himself. I have to do this for the elves.

"Stand still," he said to Miranda, and cradling her face, he spoke the elvish words of the spell: "Welcome, good friend, to the king-dom of the night." Then he kissed her brown eyes. Now those eyes would be locked away from the sun behind their own eyelids, and she would sleep through all the hours of daylight. That was elf magic, Nir mused with a little sigh. It was beautiful even when it was cruel.

Miranda was blissfully unaware of the awful spell he had just worked, but she couldn't feel more horrified anyway. When he told her to stand still, she did so. Even when he came very close and kissed her, she didn't draw back. No matter how hard she tried, she couldn't move a muscle. And the whole time that she struggled to make herself move, the stars at her wrists and ankles sparkled with a pale light.

Turning to his elves, Nir spoke in their language, and they broke up and drifted away. He absentmindedly took Miranda's hand and stood holding it as the elves walked off. Then he caught sight of her shocked face and lifted the hand he held to look at the sparkling stars on her wrist.

"Come with me," he said. "There's something I should show you." And he walked across the clearing toward the trees. Miranda found herself walking beside him, her hand apparently nestled trustingly in his. She tried to stop or make her fingers uncurl, but her efforts had no effect.

"This is the edge of my camp," said Nir, releasing her hand and watching the stars fade back to silver. "I'm going to let you try to leave now, but you should know that you won't be able to do it."

Miranda glanced about and saw no border of any sort. She took two steps away from him. Then she simply stopped and stood. Nir saw the stars begin to sparkle on her wrists and ankles as her hands balled into fists, her face becoming more and more appalled as she fought to make her body do her bidding.

"You're just wearing yourself out," he explained. "You can't take the next step. The Seven Stars Spell forces you to obey reason-able commands and keeps you from causing harm to us or to your-self. And because of the character I wrote on your foot, it's also keeping you in camp. It's almost dawn," he added, looking up at the sky. "Time for the morning meal."

He led her away again and found her a comfortable place to sit. Miranda didn't notice where she was, and when he left her, she didn't realize why he left. She could think of nothing but her own battles within herself. How could she see so clearly what she needed to do and then just not do it? When he returned and put a piece of bread into her hand, she didn't even glance up. She was reliving the terrifying feeling of being unable to direct her own movement.

Nir wasn't surprised that the human girl wouldn't eat. If she had been raised to be that monster's wife, he must have fed her for years, just as Nir himself had given food to Arianna. He frowned, upset, thinking of Arianna taking her food from that unnatural paw.

"You need to realize that your food will have to come from others now," he pointed out. "He's not feeding you anymore. He's feeding his wife." But she didn't acknowledge that he had spoken.

The elf lord considered what to do while he ate his bread and bowl of stew. Perhaps, he thought uncomfortably, she felt that it was humiliating to take food from an enemy, a stranger not from her own race. Certainly none of his maidens would have accepted food from a human man. And explaining matters to her was out of the question. That would be bad enough when the time came, he was sure.

Nir finished his stew and set the bowl aside moodily. He couldn't think of any satisfactory way out of the dilemma. But he didn't intend to let her starve. She would have to give up her self-destructive plans. He touched the stars at her wrist that held her prisoner. "Eat," he commanded.

I won't do it, Miranda decided; I couldn't eat if I tried. But her hand obediently closed around the bread. She found herself taking a bite, chewing it carefully, and swallowing. She couldn't help it. She couldn't stop. No humiliation she had ever faced from her family, no cruelty of her mother's had been as awful as this: to be ordered around like a cart horse by magic. She covered her face with her hands and burst into distraught tears.

She's crying again, Nir thought angrily, and this time it's my fault. He thought about the things he had done that night, deeply ashamed of himself. He and the goblin King were squabbling over a pair of children the way dogs fought over bones. Neither one of them, he concluded in disgust, was interested in the children themselves, they both just wanted to use them to gain some advantage. And this human knew it, even if Arianna hadn't; she kept talking about the great lords and their plots. Maybe she had known somehow that a few hours of freedom would be all she would ever have. Death would have been her only escape because she couldn't defend herself. Now she was trapped in another lord's plot, and even death was forbidden.

But at least this time, he reflected, she wasn't with the barbaric goblins. The elves knew her for what she was, a child who still needed care. It didn't matter what his magic had planned for her in adulthood; right now he could look after her as a civilized person should. Nir felt relieved at the thought. It made him seem less ruthless.

"Don't cry," he coaxed, putting his arms around the poor girl and smoothing that glowing red hair. "You wanted someone to do what was best for you. It's best that you eat, and it's best that you stay safe in camp. Don't cry anymore."

His mild commands had no effect. Furious over his presumption, Miranda wanted to jerk away from his grasp, but she couldn't do it. It seemed as if crying was the only thing she could control. Nir, listening to her, struggled with his own unhappy thoughts. These two things echoed through his life from his earliest childhood: a human woman crying bitterly and his own voice begging her to stop.

Miranda's sobs began to subside. She was too tired to keep on crying. The night had been so long and horrible. She felt that it was years since it had begun.

The elf lord continued to stroke her hair, admiring its unusual beauty. "When will you be eighteen?" he asked.

Miranda heard the question in a doze. "October ninth," she

answered automatically. With some time and effort, Nir calculated that into elvish.

"The first autumn moon," he translated, "a month and a half away." That was very soon, he thought gloomily, and he wished his magic made more sense to him. First betraying Arianna to the goblins, and now this: it was no wonder that he rarely had the heart to dance with his elves.

"Time to sleep," he said, looking up at the brightening sky, and Miranda stumbled after him as he guided her through an elf's preparation for sleep. It was unlike the process in a house or in the goblin palace, and she found it very awkward. Then he led her to the tents, set up under the thickest cover of trees where the least amount of sunlight could disturb them.

He glanced down at the hand he held as they walked along together. The stars sparkled and faded, sparkled and faded, as she tried in her exhaustion to resist. It seemed so pointless to Nir.

"Why do you keep fighting the spell?" he wanted to know. "The things I'm asking of you aren't harmful or wrong."

"You're not asking anything at all," observed Miranda sleepily. "That's why." But he didn't understand her argument.

The elf lord unrolled a mat at the opening of a tent and sat down on it, making room for her to sit beside him. The low tent formed a triangle at the ends. The two flaps at the front end were rolled back and tied, and the flaps at the back end were partly open, letting through the early morning breeze.

Nir tugged off the slippers that Miranda wore and hung them up on hooks at the edge of the tent roof. Then he scooped her feet up, laid her ankles across his lower legs, and began briskly rubbing her feet with a tingling cream. There was nothing particularly unusual about this. It was a normal attention for an elf man to pay to a woman or a child, and the little children did it for each other. But the reserved Miranda had never in her life dreamed that a stranger might take such an outrageous liberty. She felt thoroughly embarrassed and shocked. She glared at his bent head as he worked, and the silver stars lit up again.

"Don't you want your feet cleaned?" Nir asked as he rubbed them, perplexed. "Feet are important. They need to stay healthy. There, you're finished," and she could pull her feet away. "The left-hand pallet is yours, and the right-hand one is mine. You can use Arianna's cloak; she left it hanging on her side. She won't be need-ing it anymore," he added unhappily.

Miranda looked into the tent and saw two pallets lying side by side. She realized in deep offense that they were hardly inches apart. "I'm supposed to sleep here?" she gasped. "I can't possibly! There must be somewhere else I can sleep!"

The elf glanced at her in some surprise. He was unwrapping the leather straps that cross-gartered his lower legs and rolling the straps into neat coils. "Where else would you sleep?" he wanted to know. "You're too old for the children's tents. I brought you into camp myself; you're no one else's responsibility." He took off his own soft boots and removed the felt inner boots, hanging both pairs up under the edge of the roof.

"But I just can't," Miranda protested, overwhelmed at the thought. "You can't expect me to. It's not decent!"

Decent, mused the baffled Nir, cleaning his own feet. He had grown up speaking English and elvish, but he hadn't spoken so much English in years, and sometimes she used words that genuinely confused him. But looking at her shocked expression, he realized what was wrong. Of course, he should have expected this since she came from the repulsive goblins. He remembered his argument with their horrible King, and it was his turn to be offended.

"You are a child," he told her coldly and emphatically, "and regardless of what you think, we're not monsters. No right-thinking man could even contemplate kissing you at your age. It's not that it wouldn't be decent," he continued, looking for the right words. "It would be—sickening, disgusting," he concluded firmly.

Miranda went straight from being alarmed to being insulted. She crawled into the tent and threw herself down on the left-hand pallet as far as she could be from his side of the tent. Facing into the sloping wall of cloth, she felt him lay over her the cloak that had belonged to Catspaw's wife. How awful, she thought miserably, that she should have to be reminded of her. After a minute of rustling, silence reigned in the little tent, but she could still hear the elf's quiet breathing. She didn't care what he said, it wasn't decent to keep her in here. It was sickening and disgusting, too.

After a few minutes of stormy thought, Miranda noticed that the tent wall before her wasn't black. It was very dark green. She glanced at the cloak that covered her. It was green, too, a different shade. She sat up in excitement, studying her hands and dress, and looked out through the end of the tent at the world outside. Color was pouring into it as dawn came in earnest. The long night was finally over.

"The sun's coming," she said eagerly, turning to the elf lord. He lay under his own green cloak, its hood pulled over his face. His black eyes, squinting already in the light, peered out at her from its shade.

"That's true," he agreed, watching her quietly.

"I want to see the sunrise," she said. "I haven't seen it in so long. Please let me go watch it. It won't take a quarter of an hour."

Nir looked up at her excited face, his heart sinking. The first thing she asks of me, he thought, and it has to be the sun. "You're tired," he said. "You need to rest." His eyes were hurting as he watched her against the glare of light from outside. "Lie down for a little while and wait for the sun."

Miranda lay down, still optimistic. "May I go?" she persisted. "Mayn't I just go out for a few minutes? This is such a pretty patch of forest, and I want to see it in the daylight."

To see in the daylight. Nir mused over this. He pulled his hood so that it shadowed his eyes again, and he still had trouble seeing her in the blinding light of the morning.

"Just wait," he said sadly. She was looking at him with such hope. He couldn't bear to crush that hope now. In a few more minutes, the sun would come close enough, and the spell would do its work. There was no need to tell the excited girl that she would never see the daylight again.

Miranda lay restlessly waiting, thinking about the day breaking outside. She couldn't imagine that he wouldn't let her go. He seemed odd, but not really unkind. She looked into those eyes shining out from the shadow of his hood and tried to think of an argument that would make him relent. Then her eyes closed of their own accord, and her restless movements ceased. The eager expression faded out of her face and left it peaceful in sleep.

Chapter Seven

Marak Catspaw quitted the anteroom littered with bracelets and rings and retraced his steps, walking down flight after flight of stairs. The King's Wife Ceremony rooms were deep underground, where no frantic enemy could effect a rescue. He came to the low tunnel and unlocked the King's Lock that he had placed on the short, iron-bound door.

The bare room beyond was a dismal welcome to his kingdom, he thought with regret. The stone walls of the primitive chamber were unpolished and undecorated, and no furniture provided a distraction. It was such a small space that even he found it confining. To an elf bride, it must be suffocating. Arianna had crawled into a corner and sat curled up in a defensive ball. His mother was kneeling by her side.

Kate stood up. "How is Miranda?" she asked worriedly. She looked terrible, her face drawn and white and her eyes red from crying. Catspaw cursed the elf lord from his heart.

"She'll be fine," he said. "Mother, tell the women not to fuss over Arianna. Just have them do the tests, change her clothes, and put her hair up in some simple way. And when she leaves the chamber, lie down on the couch. I'll send you to sleep as soon as I see her."

Kate's anxious expression eased somewhat. She had hardly been able to bear the thought of witnessing the hideous wedding. "Thank you, Catspaw," she said gratefully, and left the room, going into the chamber where the goblin women were waiting for Arianna.

The King knelt down by his pitiful bride. The petite girl had her back to the corner and her arms around her knees, and she was staring straight ahead into space. She hadn't been crying, although her dark eyes were glassy. Perhaps she was too far into shock. She didn't look at him, but when he drew close, her breath came quicker, in shallow gasps.

"Arianna," he said, and he put a bouquet of purple flowers into her hands. The elf girl gave a little cry and clutched the flowers like a drowning man clinging to a rope. He watched her run her trembling fingers over the large, waxy trumpets.

"Arianna, these flowers live down here in my kingdom, and you can, too," he said. "Tomorrow, I'll take you to see a whole field of them. It isn't as bad here as you think."

The young woman didn't respond. Her terror was almost tangible. Catspaw considered the futility of trying to reassure her. What could he say? *Don't be frightened?* Why shouldn't she be? Everything that she had probably never wanted to happen was happening all around her. *I won't hurt you?* That would be a lie. Before another hour was up, he would slash open both of her hands.

In the end, he didn't say anything. He just put the golden shackles on her, gave her the magical drink, and sent her in to the women. The King's Wife Ceremony would doubtless be the most horrible event of her life. The best thing he could do was to get her through it as quickly as possible.

Overall, Catspaw thought the ceremony went very well. He was preoccupied, concentrating on all the difficult magic, but he was impressed by his bride's courage. Arianna didn't make a single sound the entire time, not when she walked across the shifting letters that proclaimed her freedom from any other marriages and not when he painted on her forehead the symbol that would seal her underground. She didn't gasp when he cut her hands open to mix her blood with his own and form the prognosticating scars, and Charm could have told him that she was one of only thirty-two King's Wives who hadn't screamed when the golden snake coiled itself around their necks to begin its guardianship of a new King's Wife. But then again, Arianna never opened her eyes, either. Seylin and Richard had to hold her elbows to guide her from place to place.

After it was over, Catspaw brought her to the small King's Wife Room to recover. She huddled on the couch where he had put her and cried bitterly, holding her scarred hands to her breast. The worried Catspaw gently uncurled the hands, one after the other, to study her palms. A straight, silvery slash now crossed each one, but they had healed beautifully during the ceremony. There was nothing wrong with them that he could see.

"Show me you can use them," he told her again and again, until some part of her overwrought mind became aware of the request. She bent the hands and closed the fingers, and the goblin King felt relieved. Some elvish King's Wives persisted in a hysterical belief that their hands were permanently crippled, and because the problem was only a mental illusion, it couldn't be cured.

But the poor girl didn't stop crying, and nothing he said seemed to help. She wept as if she had lost everything at one blow. Eventually, he carried her over to the bed in the corner of the room and covered her up with a blanket. Then, very carefully, so that she wouldn't notice the magic and fight it, he sent his wretched wife to sleep.

Marak Catspaw sat beside her for a long time, thinking about how much he had looked forward to his wedding. Miranda would have been so pleased that the ceremony was over, so happy to be a King's Wife at last. He wondered where she was and who she

would wind up marrying and how he would feel when he per-
formed the Binding Spell that married her to somebody else.

He stretched out beside his unconscious bride and put an arm
over her. The slender elf girl cringed away from him in her sleep.
Her whole body was still trembling with shock. Tired and dejected,
the King closed his eyes and fell asleep with a sigh.

Arianna awoke from a ghastly nightmare into an even worse one.
She lay perfectly still, remembering where she was, studying what
she could see of the square cave. The goblin King was sleeping, his
breath stirring her hair and his terrible paw-hand stretched across
her body. She remembered the stories she had heard as a small girl
about the hideous goblin monster, Lionclaw, who had used his paw
to slash elves to ribbons.

But Arianna didn't shiver or shove the paw away. Such a movement would wake him up, and at all costs, she mustn't do that. Very
gently, very carefully, she wove whispered words around the enemy
King, something between a spell and a fervent wish. She felt his
body relax from sleep into a further oblivion, and then she cautiously
crept from the bed. On the couch lay her elf clothes. She tore the stiff
goblin dress off and hurriedly changed into them. In a very short
time, she was out the door. It wasn't that Arianna intended to escape.
She knew she couldn't do that. She just meant to be as far as possible
from her terrible husband when he awoke. It would take him a little
while to find her.

Out here, the light was almost blinding. Twisting tunnels met
her bewildered view, and she chose passages with no particular plan.
Some led into small rooms full of sacks and boxes. Others led to
steps. Finding that she was on the lowest level of the caves, she began

to climb. The farther she went, the shinier the walls were, and the more the light hurt her eyes.

Now she was dodging monsters, creeping behind them, ducking into rooms and alcoves to avoid them. The ranges of steps were broader, and the hallways were wider, decorated in bright colors of stone. Arianna opened a door and shrieked. She had walked into a nest of goblin young. She backed up and then ran, hearing their growls and squeals as they poured out of the room to follow her.

Giddy and short of breath, she dashed up a flight of stairs and found herself face-to-face with a whole crowd of goblins. She turned, but more monsters were coming up the stairs behind her. Her stomach cramped, and she clutched the wall, sick and dizzy. Deformed bodies pressed around her in a mob, and she closed her eyes to avoid the sight. The babble deafened her, and her knees buckled. She sat down abruptly on the stairs.

A curious noise came to her through the gathering confusion in her brain, and she felt that snake from last night on her shoulders again. This time Arianna peeked at it. Slitted golden eyes met her gaze not four inches away: the metal snake was staring straight at her. She promptly closed her eyes again. Now she heard it speaking in a loud, clear, slithering hiss, stringing together words that she didn't understand. The babble quieted, and she heard a bumping, rustling noise as the crowd drew away. She laid her head on her knees, trying not to faint.

After a few minutes, she became aware that she was feeling stronger. She wasn't as lightheaded and sick. The crawly feeling was gone, and so, apparently, was the snake. Then she heard an unfamiliar voice.

"The stars are beautiful," it said.

Arianna was so astonished that she opened her eyes and sat up. The ghastly mob had vanished. Only one goblin stood at the bottom of the stairs now, about ten feet away. He was man-shaped and silver-skinned, with black hair and blue eyes. Odd markings covered his face.

"The stars are beautiful," he said again.

Arianna drew in a shaky breath and looked around, grateful that the crowd was gone. She gave a start at the sight of a golden coil on her bare arm. The snake! But when she felt it, nothing was there. It was one of the goblin King's enchantments.

The bizarre silver man still stood at the foot of the stairs. Arianna eyed him warily. His black cloak was mud-stained and ripped in several places, and he had a few leaves stuck in his hair. It raised her spirits to see them in that lifeless place. He was shifting his weight awkwardly from foot to foot as he watched her. It dawned on her that he looked nervous.

"The moon are beautiful," he stated seriously. "*Is* beautiful," he added in an embarrassed undertone.

That was it, she realized in relief. This goblin knew a little of her language. He was just trying to say something polite so that she would know he meant her no harm. But he was obviously supposed to watch her until the goblin King could take custody of her again. Her temporary respite would soon be over. She put her head on her knees and closed her eyes, gathering her courage.

There was a long pause. Then she heard steps coming near. She cowered, but they retreated, and the goblin spoke again.

"Water is"—he hesitated—"is good."

Arianna opened her eyes. He was still at the bottom of the stairs, but now a metal cup was on the step beside her. She picked it up. Cool water. She drank thirstily.

"Thank you," she said to the man.

Then *he* was coming. She could hear his loud, heavy steps ringing on the stone. He appeared at the foot of the stairs with another black-draped monster and quickly came to her side. She shut her eyes and dropped the cup, flattening herself against the wall. Another wave of nausea rolled over her.

Catspaw assessed the condition of his bride. Her breathing was uneven, and she looked unwell. He laid his paw on the elf girl's forehead to work a strengthening spell.

"My people didn't mean to distress you," he told her. "They're very curious about you, and they didn't realize that they would make you ill by coming close. What you're feeling is a normal aspect of your elvish magic. We call it the fear sickness. It will wear off in a few days."

The girl ignored him, keeping her eyes closed. The goblin King reminded himself that he shouldn't expect anything else at this point. He turned to give an order to the two guards who stood on the landing below. Then he stopped in surprise.

"What are you doing here, Tattoo?" he exclaimed.

Tattoo delivered his report to his monarch, feeling uneasily that it did not present him in the most flattering light. He related the conversation between Miranda and the elf in the truce circle and his own capture up in the tree. Marak Catspaw was absolutely furious.

"Call Seylin," he ordered the other guard, and soon the handsome adviser appeared. Tattoo delivered his report again, even more uncomfortable this time.

"Why did he do it?" demanded Catspaw angrily. "It's perfectly obvious. He intends to use Miranda to take revenge on me because I claimed his fiancée. You saw how he had Arianna hidden, hoping I wouldn't notice her. He meant to trick me into claiming one of the five inferior choices; then it would have been too late to change my mind."

"Maybe he felt sorry for Miranda," proposed Seylin. "Maybe he wanted to be sure she couldn't carry out her suicide attempt."

"He knew she couldn't kill herself. He knew she was under guard. And he attacked that guard, in violation of the treaty. He was waiting for him!"

Seylin turned over the facts in his mind. "It doesn't make sense," he reflected.

"It does make sense," snapped Catspaw. "That elf is being vindictive. You saw what he did to Mother just because she'd been the goblin King's Wife. I still mean to honor my part of the treaty, regardless of his behavior. We're sending him the first spell book tonight, but make sure it contains no military magic. Deliver it yourself and insist on Miranda's return. I want her back in the kingdom as soon as possible."

"Certainly," responded Seylin. "Goblin King, I think you're scaring your wife."

Catspaw turned to study the girl who sat beside him on the stair. Arianna was looking from one to the other of them with anxious eyes. Of course, he thought. He had been speaking in goblin. She couldn't understand what they were saying.

"Don't be alarmed," he said to her. "I know I sound angry, but I'm not angry at you. We were consulting about a kingdom matter." The elf's expression didn't change. He might as well not have spoken. She had the fixed, desperate look of a wild animal caught in a trap.

Marak Catspaw irately considered how pleasant his life had been just one week ago and how much of a mess it was in now: a guard attacked, his ward stolen, and brides switched on his wedding night. He had been lamenting not long before how boring his reign would be because the goblin King lacked any real opposition. Now he was beginning to have the uncomfortable feeling that he had found a real opponent at last.

Chapter Eight

Miranda woke up confused, unable to place where she was. She opened her eyes to find herself in a little tent and a man sitting beside her, watching her with interest. Alarmed, she lay quite still and glanced around anxiously. She wished that he weren't so handsome. He made it hard for her to think. Something was wrong, but she couldn't tell what it was.

"Good evening," he said. "You slept well."

"Evening!" echoed Miranda. "I want to see the sunrise." That was what was wrong: it was already darker than it had been seemingly just a minute before.

She closed her eyes as one awful memory after another besieged her. Today should be her first day as a King's Wife, but she would never have the prestige and acclaim she had worked for. Her future was dead, just as dead as her guardian, as dead as she ought to be.

"You don't look a thing like an elf," commented Nir. "No elf has brown eyes like a deer's, and you're not small like our women are, but you're beautiful anyway. I didn't know that was possible. I thought the only beautiful humans were humans who looked like the elves."

"Blame it on Marak," she muttered. "He was always working spells on me when I was young."

The elf lord considered this information. "Did the goblin King give you your red hair?" he wanted to know. "No elf has red hair. I've never seen hair like yours."

"I don't have red hair!" exclaimed Miranda, dislodged for the moment from her sorrow. She opened her eyes to find the elf study, ing her in surprise.

"Of course it's red," he replied. "Why argue about such a thing?"

Miranda closed her eyes again, depressed beyond words. It was already growing dark. The elf lord continued to look at her, in no hurry to leave the tent. It was still too bright out to suit him.

"What's your name?" he asked.

"Miranda," she replied.

"Miranda!" he exclaimed in horror. "That's ghastly! Nothing but a goblin's trick!"

This unexpected outburst goaded her out of depression again. She had never been one to dwell on misfortune, and it was apparent that she wouldn't get the chance now. She sat up and began folding the green cloak that had served as her blanket, determined to make herself behave sensibly. She didn't want this stranger to discover how hopeless and forlorn she felt.

"It's a perfectly normal human name," she pointed out reason, ably. "Miranda is in one of Shakespeare's plays. It's a Latin word, I think."

"It's elvish," Nir informed her coldly, turning away to roll up his own cloak. "It's the elvish word for the goblin King's Wife."

"No, it's Latin," contradicted Miranda. "Or Spanish; I can't remember which. My brother's tutor told me it means 'seeing.'"

"'Seeing,'" echoed Nir unhappily, thinking of those brown eyes peering blindly about in the nighttime. "I don't think Seeing is a good name for you, either. In elvish, *mir-an-da* means 'protected by the coils of the magical snake.' In other words, the goblin King's Wife. I'm not about to let my elves call you such a horrible name. You remind me of a fox with your red hair. I think I'll call you Fox."

The one nice thing about having lost everything she had ever hoped for was that she no longer had to smile and pretend to be

pleased. That was good, she decided grimly, because she wasn't feeling the least bit gracious or charming.

"Fox? That's an insult!" she cried. "Foxes are a thieving nui-
sance, and to call a girl a female fox is a very bad name."

"Why?" asked the elf lord.

Miranda frowned. "I don't know. I just know that it is."

"I don't know why it should be," commented Nir. "Foxes are
clever, and they shine like little fires in the woods. They play and
dance just like the elves, and they have red hair like yours."

He hung his cloak up on his side of the tent and retrieved and
tied the belt of his tunic. Then he crawled to the tent opening,
unrolled the mat, and put his bare feet on it, crisscrossing the leather
straps again around the lower legs of his breeches. Miranda hung up
her cloak and turned to look at the simple pallet. It didn't even have a
pillow. How could she have slept so soundly without a pillow?

She crawled awkwardly from the tent to find that she had an
audience. Two beautiful little children stood in front of her, their
eyes round and sober as they stared. Miranda stared back, embarrassed, her hair a tangled mess, sweaty and miserable from having had
to sleep in her clothes. Her damp dress was a mass of wrinkles, but
the elf lord's simple green tunic and breeches showed no wrinkles at
all. Lacing his boots, he looked as if he had been awake for hours;
his pale face wasn't sleep-worn, and his black eyes were bright.
Miranda found this irritating. Even if the elf had said that she was
beautiful, she found it trying to live among a people who made being
beautiful seem so effortless.

The elf lord looked at the children's serious expressions as he finished lacing his boots, and his face lit up with one of his rare smiles.
Indicating Miranda, he made a comment in elvish, and the little girl
giggled something back. They spoke for a minute as he climbed to
his feet and reached down to help up Miranda. No stars glittered

about her wrist this time as he held her hand. She was overcome, as she had been before, by the captivating force of his smile.

The children scampered off, and he knelt again to roll up the mat at the front of the tent. Miranda looked around uneasily. All about her in the twilight, elves were coming and going, emerging from tents, or sitting and talking with their neighbors. They were all dressed in green; they were all terribly attractive; and they were speaking a language that she couldn't understand. They also seemed to be entirely at ease with one another and pleased with one another's company.

Miranda had thought that the elf lord held her hand as a way to force her to walk with him, but she realized that holding hands must just be an elvish habit. A man and a woman or a boy and a girl would be holding hands as they walked by, and five young women went by in a chain, talking happily together as they walked toward the river. She was startled to see several men keeping company with girls who couldn't have been more than fifteen at the most, brushing their hair for them by the tents or walking along talking to them. Her human sensibilities made her feel embarrassed by all the close contact. The scene before her was perfectly charming and graceful in its artlessness, and she felt instinctively that it had nothing to do with her.

Shy and uncomfortable, she tried to summon her dignity. When it came to meeting strangers, she knew only the two extremes: humans had invariably either mocked her or disliked her, and the goblins had been fawning and deferential. Unfortunately, she was already quite sure that these elves weren't going to fawn over her. After all she had suffered, she felt that it was particularly painful to face a crowd of people she didn't know.

Without really wanting to, she moved closer to the elf lord, and when he stood up again and walked toward the river, she walked by his side, trying not to look as lost as she felt. *Who invited you?* she heard her mother's voice say in her mind, but the elf lord didn't drive her away. He seemed to expect her to accompany him.

"I've sent Kiba to tell her mother to make you some clothes," he said. "But they won't be ready tonight; she has to make the cloth for them first. You'll have to wear those goblin things until tomorrow."

Still able to see distances in the deepening twilight, Miranda studied her surroundings with interest. They were in a beautiful valley. Tall, straight trees grew in thick green turf that reminded her of the truce circle, and small flowers of different shapes and shades nodded at her feet. A little river, about ten feet wide and somewhat deep, ran along nearby. They walked through the wide clearing, or small meadow, where he must have worked the spell on her last night. Here was a profusion of wildflowers, but she was surprised that the grass was so short, forming something like a dense, soft carpet.

She looked up eagerly, her eyes taking in as much of the waning light as they could. The cloudless sky was a clear indigo, and the first stars were already out. She could see that the river, glimmering in the fading light, made a loop around the edge of the meadow. Near the middle of the loop, it became wide and shallow. Trees resumed on the opposite side, and a band of tall, forested hills cut off the remaining colors of the sunset to her right. To the left, the forest sloped up gradually into a more distant line of wooded hills.

No other elves were nearby. They were in the shadowy forest. Nir had brought her there as a kindness, knowing that her human eyes would enjoy the bright light. His own eyes found it rather uncomfortable still.

"Now is the time of day when we elves go bathing," he said. The river had carved out a flat stone bank, and he knelt down on the stone to wash his face. Miranda wondered at the remark. She hadn't seen any way to heat water, and the tents were too small to bathe in.

"Bathe where?" she wanted to know. And then, when he looked around in amazement at the question, she said, "You mean they bathe right in the river?" She thought about this, rather shocked, while the elf considered, not for the first time, how little sense humans seemed to have. "But you can't mean that they bathe out in the open where everyone can see them," she insisted. "That wouldn't be decent!"

Decent again. At least this time Nir understood what the word meant. "It's decent," he assured her patiently, dipping a wooden comb in the water and pulling it through his hair. "The women usually bathe together and the men bathe together, or they go off by ones and twos, married couples, for instance. But no one bothers anyone else, and they're still wearing their underclothes anyway, that way they're always just as clean as the elf is."

Miranda was astonished that a man would mention such things to her, but she kept her face expressionless. If elves discussed them, she would, too, so as not to be thought naive. "Ugh," she remarked with distaste. "It's a wonder they don't die of pneumonia, walking around half the night with wet things on."

"But they're not wet," said Nir. "Elf clothes have the Drying Spell on them. As soon as they come out of the water, they're dry. See?" He splashed some water on his tunic, and the dark stain quickly faded out.

"Do you want to go bathing?" he persisted, walking back up to her, his washing finished. "I can show you where the women bathe."

Miranda found this a bad idea on many different levels. "No," she said quickly. "I don't want to get into that cold water."

"Cold?" echoed Nir. "In the summertime?" He was surprised into a musical laugh, and once again, Miranda found herself afraid of him. The elf lord was quite beyond human at such times, like one of those pagan gods who walked the earth disguised as a man. She understood now why Daphne had run from Apollo. She ran away herself, hurrying past him to the riverbank and kneeling to wash her face.

Nir handed her the comb as she came up the bank, and they

walked back to the forest together. She jerked the comb as rapidly as she could through her hair, grimacing at the many tangles, while the elf lord reflected that humans made the most graceful tasks seem ungraceful. He didn't realize that she was hurrying because he was watching her. Miranda thought his attention impolite.

He left her to collect their evening meal. Two elves had laid piles of food out on a sheet, and they appeared to be cooking the flat, cir- cular bread on some sort of rock. It was the men who went up to take the food and then brought it back to share with a woman or a girl. Only the little children went up on their own. Miranda found this sort of servile role odd for a man, especially for the elf lord. She cer- tainly couldn't imagine the goblin King waiting on anyone.

"Thank you," she said stiffly as the elf lord came to sit by her side, handing over her breakfast wrapped up in a cloth. She unwrapped it to find half a piece of bread, a strip of dried meat, a carrot, and five radishes. Not quite breakfast in the goblin kingdom, where she would have had whatever she ordered, no matter how elaborate. Lately, she had been favoring apple tarts.

Kate's bracelet lit itself with a faint gleam as the evening became night. It wouldn't light with its usual brightness anymore, and it reminded her abruptly that she was in the dark. Miranda shuddered at the thought.

"I slept the whole time the sun was up," she said. "It was an enchantment, wasn't it?"

Nir looked away. "Yes, it was the Daylight Spell," he replied, "the one I worked when I kissed your eyes."

"But why?" she demanded. "I already can't leave your camp, and I have to do what you say. What harm would it have done to let me see the sun?"

"If you could see it, you'd think of nothing else but the next time you could see it again," he answered. "You'd stay awake in the day while we were asleep and sleep in the night while we were awake. The elvish world doesn't have the sun any more than the goblin caves have the moon. You have to learn how to live in our world now."

Miranda abandoned her awful breakfast, rolling it back up in the cloth. His pretense of her being some sort of guest was pointless, so she didn't have to act the part. She was only a slave here, she reminded herself, and there was nothing she could do about it. Very well: she didn't intend to waste her time and self-respect in absurd struggles. Marak had taught her not to put off unpleasant things.

"What are my duties?" she demanded.

"Duties?" asked the puzzled Nir.

"My work," continued the girl firmly. "What did you bring me here to do?"

The elf lord felt a stab of guilt and dodged the question. "Among members of a civilized race," he answered, "children do no work. I would never order you to drudge and toil at your age."

"I am *not* a child," asserted Miranda with some heat, and Nir felt quite taken aback.

"Of course you are," he said. "The fact is obvious. I don't understand why you keep challenging it."

"I am a grown woman," declared his human captive with dignity. "I don't care to be treated like a child. I don't need anyone looking after me, either. I am perfectly capable of taking care of myself."

The elf lord looked at her, expressionless. He said, "That's why you would be dead by now, I suppose."

"Thank you for breakfast," replied the furious Miranda. "Please excuse me. A great elf lord must have much to do." She stood up and walked away, and she was very relieved to find that he didn't order her to come back.

She went on a walk and surveyed the dim stretch of forest, bumping into the invisible camp border several times. The dark didn't make her so nervous tonight because she could hear the lyrical conversation of elves coming from all directions. Her faint bracelet provided only a short ring of light around her, and trees and people emerged from the blackness with eerie suddenness. Unable to form a complete picture of her surroundings, she was struck by odd details instead: the lacy patterns of twigs and branches, the shadows that fanned away from her into the dark. She found herself reaching out to touch tree trunks and bushes as she passed, stroking the rough bark, feeling the cool, pliant leaves. Nearby, an exquisite voice began to sing, and Miranda paused to listen, enthralled.

When she looked around again, she discovered that she had acquired an entourage. The elf children stood in a little crowd at her heels, as charming and disconcerting as lovely ghosts. She stared at them in dismay, realizing what a spectacle she must seem, and they stared at her curiously and a little anxiously, as if she might charge at them, or possibly start shouting. Then a golden-haired girl smiled bravely at her, and Miranda smiled back, completely conquered. There was just no way that she could resist an elvish smile.

The children crowded around close to her then, talking all at once. She couldn't speak elvish, and they couldn't speak English, but it didn't really matter. She sat down on the ground so that she would be eye to eye with most of them, and then she pointed at them one at a time.

They told her their names, with their friends or older siblings helping out to such a degree that she found it hard to understand a word. Kiba's name she already knew, and her little brother turned out to be Min. Tibir was the oldest boy, possibly about ten. The littlest boy, Bar, could on no account be induced to speak, but so many children spoke for him that it was some time before she could learn his name.

Then she tried to tell them hers, *Miranda*. They went into fits of laughter, delighted to find an adult who didn't know her own name.

Sika, they told her, and when she looked puzzled, they touched her hair, and Tibir pantomimed sharp ears and a bushy tail. So that was it, thought Miranda, more than a little annoyed: *Sika* was the elvish word for "fox."

Nir watched his human prisoner from a distance, pleased to find her getting on so well. Then he went to look for Kiba's mother to discuss his orders for the clothes. As they talked, Willow walked up and stood respectfully, waiting to be acknowledged. He was on guard duty in the forest to the south of the camp.

"The elf goblin is here to see you," he announced, "and he's brought a big wooden thing with him."

"A big wooden thing?" wondered Nir. "You may bring him into camp."

After a few minutes, Willow returned with Seylin, who was towing a large desk with the Carrying Spell. He lowered the desk to the ground.

"Elf lord," he said, "I've brought the first of the elvish spell books. This one has healing spells in it, so I thought you'd want to see it right away." Nir took the book from the goblin, his eyes betraying a gleam of excitement. "And I brought copying materials, too, as requested. We weren't sure you had a comfortable place to write, so I've brought one of our writing desks for you to use."

The heavy desk was made all of a piece with its bench attached, and the writing surface had room for two books to be opened on it side by side. A little sensitive at the arrival of the goblin, which reminded him of Arianna's horrible ordeal, Nir genuinely appreciated this thoughtfulness. It was true that his camp wasn't well set up for writing.

"Thank you, friend goblin," he replied. "I look forward to learning the spells." Dismissing Willow, he sat down at the desk, laying the spell book on it, and examined the blank book and writing materials. "And how is Arianna?" he asked reluctantly. He wasn't sure that he really wanted to know.

"Oh, she's fine, as well as could be expected," answered Seylin. "We persuaded her to eat a little this afternoon." The elf didn't look up at this encouraging report. He trimmed the tip of a quill with his knife, dipped the pen, and started writing in the blank book. Seylin still lingered. He had the air of a person not yet discharged of his mission.

"Elf lord," he asked, "is it true that the human girl, Miranda, is in your camp?"

"Not a terribly useful name for her, is it?" remarked the elf. "Yes, she's here. Why would it matter?"

"The goblin King has been concerned about her," replied Seylin cautiously. "Miranda is his ward; he considers her a goblin subject. She was distressed last night, so as a kindness, he let her return to her human home under guard. But he wants her brought back into the kingdom as soon as possible."

"Why would he want her to come back?" asked Nir. "He has another Miranda now."

"Oh, Miranda's very special," answered Seylin. "Her parents were both raised by the goblins, and the old King lavished great care on her, weaving enchantments through and through her. She's a strong human bride who will be very important in the genealogies; her blood will be an asset to the high families for generations." He paused. "May I see her now?"

Nir continued copying for some time after this speech ended. He didn't know why it should make him so angry. After all, they had gone to a lot of trouble over her, and there was no reason why they should think that she would matter to anyone else.

"Of course you may see her," he said finally. "Ama," he called to a young elf woman passing by, "please tell Sika to come here."

Miranda walked up a short time later, studying the writing desk with curiosity. Then she caught sight of Seylin and stopped. As Nir glanced up, she gave him an indignant glare. Traitor, said the glare.

"Miranda, I'm glad to see you're well," said the handsome goblin in a friendly way, stepping toward her. She reminded herself that he had known all about Catspaw's new bride and hadn't bothered to warn her.

"How kind of you," she replied coolly. "I really can't imagine why you're here."

"I've come to take you home," answered Seylin. "I know you were upset last night, and I certainly don't blame you, but you must realize by now that you belong with us. You won't be happy anywhere else."

"Being happy has had little to do with my life so far," responded Miranda. "Now that Marak is dead, I don't expect it to again. I have no intention of returning, and what's more, I have no need. Catspaw gave me my freedom when he broke our engagement."

"The King did what he had to do," Seylin replied smoothly. "But you're still his ward, and you owe a debt of gratitude to his father. It's time for you to honor that debt and come home."

"Come home to what?" demanded the girl skeptically. "To take over Kate's English classes?"

"No, to get married," replied the goblin. "Catspaw says you can have your choice of any man in the high families, but I think the best match for you is Tattoo. Sable would be so pleased to have you as a daughter, and you know you're fond of them both."

The pain of all that she had lost struck Miranda like a stinging blow.

"Marak didn't raise me to be Tattoo's wife!" she said with icy fury. "So Catspaw did what was best—well and fine, but I don't have to kiss his cheek for it! I won't come back now and curtsy to him and marry one of his lackeys. I was raised to be a King's Wife—a King's Wife, Seylin! And I won't be anything less!"

"Now, that's a fine plan," remarked the goblin with weary patience. "And just how do you intend to accomplish it? Wait around here with your nose in the air living off the goodwill of the elves? They're not interested in a human, no matter how grand her destiny is."

Miranda had no answer to this, and they both knew it. She turned away from him, fighting back tears. "I'd be dead by now if I had my choice," she said bitterly.

"Don't take it so badly," advised the goblin, putting an arm around her shoulders. Then he jerked back with a sharp cry of pain.

"What's the matter?" she asked. Seylin was staring at her wrists in avid fascination.

"Miranda!" he gasped. "It's the Seven Stars! The Seven Stars! I can't believe it!"

The puzzled girl looked down at her wrists and touched the circles of stars. "What do they have to do with this?" she wanted to know.

"Everything," answered Seylin ruefully. He paused to think and then gave a sigh. "I'm afraid the elf lord's been having a nice laugh at my expense."

Nir glanced up at that, and it was true that his eyes were suspiciously bright. "I didn't realize that your King would still be concerned for her welfare," he said. "Please assure him that he has no need to worry. The stars keep her perfectly safe."

"They certainly do," agreed Seylin sadly. "Especially safe from goblins. You can't come home anymore. And you would have been happy with us, I know it."

Miranda hid her astonishment at this unexpected victory. "Marak didn't raise me to be happy," she replied. "He raised me to be a King's Wife." And she turned on her heel and walked away.

Most of the elves were in the little meadow now, dancing to the music of pipes, harps, and a sweet-toned violin. Feeling bewildered, Miranda wandered down to watch them. The white stars were thick in the black sky overhead, and the graceful dancers were mysterious and alluring by their faint light. Miranda let herself be captivated by the bewitching spectacle and forgot about her grief for a while.

She felt better, she realized. She had stood up for her honor and refused the comfortable life that the goblins had planned. But this was certainly no place for her, either, with nothing to do. These elves were even stranger than the goblins.

She mulled over what she had learned from Seylin's conversation. The elf lord hadn't enslaved her after all. He had been so angry about her suicide plan, so insistent that she was a child who needed care. He had clearly just done what he thought was the responsible thing to do. She felt grateful for this, and she supposed she shouldn't have been so curt and uncivil to him. He had given her a second chance to think things over.

Well, she had done it, and there was no avoiding the obvious conclusion. She would have to go back and face her family and find a new life among human beings. That would be hard, but Catspaw was right: she was strong, and she would survive. Marak had raised her to be both brave and practical. There was no sense putting it off.

The elf lord was copying his spell book when Miranda approached. Looking at his pale face, she felt a wistful pang. She would never see anything like him or his elves again, and she was sure that she would never forget him.

Nir glanced up at his prisoner's purposeful expression. Then he put down his quill and waited. He already knew what she was going to say.

"Thank you for saving my life," she began. "You were right about my killing myself; it would have been evil and absurd. You were right, too, that I should have been at home. I'm ready to go back to my own world now."

"Your world, Sika," murmured the elf lord. "And what world is that?"

"The daylight world," she answered, thinking of the warm sun overhead, the greens and browns of the trees, a pale blue sky with clouds of white and gray and lavender. She couldn't wait to see the sun again. That would make up for a great deal.

Nir winced at the happiness that shone in her eyes.

The little boy lay in his tent in the predawn hush, listening to her argue and beg. "I don't belong here," she said, her soft voice pleading. "Ash, let me go back to the daylight."

Father's voice followed hers, quiet and sad: "Will the daylight hunt for you? Will the sun bring you food?"

Nir shook off the memory with an effort. "You told me that you had no people," he pointed out.

"I didn't think I did," she said, rather embarrassed. "I thought I was too good for them, I suppose. I'd been raised all my life to think of myself as something extraordinary, someone set aside for a special destiny. Marak told me that, and I believed him." She sighed. "I thought he could read it in my face."

"The goblin King is right," remarked the elf. "You aren't ordinary, and you have a special destiny. I'm glad that you were raised to know it. It may be the only thing that brings you comfort in your life."

Miranda stared at him, taken aback. She couldn't imagine what he might mean. "I don't care anymore," she assured him. "I'm ready to go back to my family whether I'm ordinary or not. Would you please remove the magic now?" She rubbed her hand over the stars at her wrist.

The elf lord looked at them, too, and rubbed his own finger over the stars. "I can't remove them," he said quietly, "and neither can anyone else. Only time can take them away."

This shook Miranda at first, but she rallied, determined to be logical. "Even if they're permanent," she pointed out, "they don't have to keep me here."

"It is true that the stars can let you leave camp," he agreed.

"Then you can just do that," proposed the girl. "And if they keep protecting me from harm at home, then that would be a good thing."

Nir studied her moodily for some time, still rubbing his finger over the stars. Once again, he saw no way out of his dilemma.

"You don't understand," he said at last. "I'm not concerned about the magic. I would let you leave if I could, but I can't let you go. You're too important to the elves."

Miranda stared at that unearthly face, at those beautiful, unreadable black eyes. He could read her own expression easily enough. She looked absolutely horrified.

"Important how?" she demanded. "Why should elves care about an ordinary human?"

Nir angrily considered the suffering he was causing. "Not ordinary. Extraordinary," he corrected.

Miranda hesitated, trying in her shock to frame an argument to refute him. She didn't know what to say. After all, Marak had raised her to be extraordinary.

"But I don't have to be," she pleaded at last, in defiance of both great lords.

"You already are," he answered. "That's what my magic tells me."

There was nothing more to say. Miranda just turned and left. Tired and numb, she wandered away and dropped down on the grass by the river, listening to its soothing rush and gurgle in the darkness. The tangle of trees closed around her, cutting off the light of the stars. Miranda stared up at the pale undersides of leaves caught in the bracelet's weak light. Its faint reach was so short, and the night was so immense. Blackness, all around her. A world without the sun. She couldn't go home because she was extraordinary. She was where she would always be.

You have to get used to it, gloated a silky voice in her mind. *You'll live your whole life in the dark.*

Miranda flinched, trying to dodge the memory. Would she never be free of her mother? Unbidden, her mind went back in time. She was standing in total darkness, pounding on that locked door, begging to be let out.

"You're cursed," purred that voice. "You'll never see daylight again. You can't imagine the things that live in the darkness. They'll be your only friends."

The little girl was hysterical, wailing and screaming, with no dignity left at all. Anxious, whimpering, late into the night. Waking up to find that he had come. Pulling her pillow over her head. Afraid to walk down the hall in the darkness. Afraid to face him again.

She heard the bedroom door open and felt him sit down on the bed. "How's my little girl? Miranda? What's wrong?"

Sobbing, Miranda threw herself into his arms, telling him of her childish treason. In broken sentences, she confessed all her sins against him. But here was no icy contempt, no harsh disapproval. She was cradled in warm arms, safe from the darkness.

"I shouldn't cry," she bawled helplessly. "You aren't raising a crybaby."

"It's all right," he consoled her. "Sometimes crying is good."

He waited until she had cried herself out, and then he had her tell him what had happened. His calmness steadied and comforted her. Whatever he might have thought of Til's behavior didn't show on his face.

"Your mother can't curse you," he explained. "You're protected against that."

"But she knew my future," Miranda protested tearfully. "She did. She said so!"

He held her away, studying her face. He had never looked so wise.

"She didn't know your future," he declared finally. "I do. I'm not raising my little girl to be trapped in the dark like a ghost. You have a special destiny, and that's why I teach you so many things. I'm raising you to be a King's Wife, and that's what you're going to be."

"A King's Wife?" She thought about that and felt a spark of hope and courage. "Just like in the stories? I'll marry a prince and live happily ever after?"

"Just like that," he promised, smiling. "Except that he'll be a King." And he tucked his little girl back into bed.

"You're a King," she remarked hopefully as she settled onto her pillow.

"And about fifty years too old for you," he chuckled. *"You'll have to wait for the next King. Sleep well, Miranda. I'll stay here to watch. You're going to have nice dreams."*

Miranda found that she was crying. All her love and faith in Marak and all his love and faith in her had turned out to be for nothing. She would never make him proud, and there would be no living happily ever after. In the end, it was her mother who was right.

A hand touched her arm in the darkness, and she jumped in alarm. The elf lord stood beside her.

"There's nothing to be afraid of," he said. "Nothing comes into an elf camp but elves and those creatures the elves bring. Not even a fly or an ant can come in. Nothing can hurt you here." Miranda could have pointed out that her mother still had an uncanny ability to hurt her, but she couldn't speak because of the lump in her throat.

"It's time for the morning meal," he noted. Miranda just shook her head. He took her hand, and she stood up, the stars on her wrists and ankles lighting in protest.

"You don't have to eat, but at least come spend time with us," he said, and the silver stars winked out.

Later that morning, she sat at the opening of the tent for as long as she could to see the colors return to the woods. Squinting through the bright light, Nir watched her and wondered how the daylight world looked.

━━━◯───

Seylin stood outside the goblin King's bedroom door and gave a gentle call in his thoughts. If the King was asleep, he could wait until morning to hear the bad news. But after a minute, Marak Catspaw emerged, wearing a shirt and breeches of dark blue elf cloth that Irina had made for him. Seylin wasn't surprised. His monarch always dressed like an elf at night because the stretchy cloth was so comfortable to sleep in.

The King motioned for silence, and they tiptoed to a small study. Catspaw closed the door and sank down wearily into a chair. "She couldn't sleep," he sighed. "Or rather, she wouldn't sleep. Finally I used magic on her, but she fought me for a long time. I'm impressed at her strength. She has a lot of magic, and she isn't afraid to use it. She's resting now, but not very well. Where's Miranda?"

"Still at the elf camp," said his chief adviser slowly. "I couldn't bring her home."

"What do you mean, you couldn't bring her home?" demanded Catspaw. "I'll go tomorrow, then, and _I'll_ bring her home."

"In the first place, she refused," observed Seylin. "She says that you gave her her freedom." When his King made no comment at this indirect reproach, he continued, "And in the second place, he's used the Seven Stars."

"The Seven Stars!" Marak Catspaw sat bolt upright and stared at him. "Adviser, you're mistaken! There can't be an elf left alive today who knows that spell."

"This one does," replied Seylin. "The stars are in place and in force. They burned me badly." He gingerly pulled up his sleeve to reveal a line of nasty wounds and blisters. "That was from one touch," he observed.

Catspaw leaned forward to look at the damage, frowning with concern. "Seylin, you should have healed those!" He left the room to retrieve a jar of salve.

"To be honest, I tried on this area," confessed Seylin when he returned. "You can see that it didn't do much good. Besides, I thought you should see them."

Using a generous amount of salve, the goblin King healed the burns. Like most magical tools, the salve increased in strength with the magical power of its user.

"That criminal!" he exclaimed. "He has complete control over her now, and he knows there's absolutely nothing I can do. But why? To use the Seven Stars—that's the most bizarre thing I've ever heard of!"

"I've been puzzling over what he wants with her all the way back," admitted Seylin. "I can't think of a single precedent for it. Of course, there's no precedent for Miranda herself."

"He means to use her against us, that much is plain," declared the King. "She's a weapon now. Maybe he wants to force us into a situation where I have to choose between her life or a guard's."

"You don't suppose," said Seylin cautiously, "that he could intend its original use?"

"No, I don't, and neither do you," his ruler replied. "That could only mean he's insane." He sat in sober thought for a few minutes. "There's no way to break the spell, we're sure of that?"

Seylin shook his head. "The stars give him control over her until he dies."

"Now, there's a tempting thought," said Catspaw grimly.

He said good night to his lieutenant and tiptoed to his bedroom, but he found the door half open. He heard a slam, and Seylin hurried back into the room.

"She's gone!" exclaimed the King.

"She's overpowered the guards," said Seylin. They went to the doorway of the royal rooms. The two guards lay in untidy heaps on either side.

"Look at Mongrel," directed the King. "You can tell he was completely unprepared. I told you," he said admiringly, nudging the unconscious goblin with his toe, "that Arianna's not afraid to use her magic."

They both spoke the Tracking Spell, spotted the small footprints, and followed the running track. It led them down many flights of stairs, through the echoing grandeur of the empty Throne Room, and out of the palace entirely, into the gigantic cavern that contained the ornamental gardens. It finally ended in the part of the artificial forest that represented winter. The elf girl lay curled up on the snowy white stone at the foot of a slender metal tree. She was sound asleep.

"I brought her here today," said Catspaw softly, reaching up to touch the delicate crystals that hung from the silver branches. "I suppose it reminded her of home." He studied his sleeping wife with a puzzled frown. "She's a strange girl," he remarked.

"You could carry her back," suggested Seylin, but the goblin King shook his head.

"She's finally resting well," he observed. "I don't want to risk waking her up. I'll stay here with her. Go tell the Guard to post men at the edges of the grove to keep everyone away in the morning. And lend me your cloak," he added without much enthusiasm.

As Seylin walked off, the goblin King stretched out on the hard stone by his wife. He shifted uncomfortably. It was going to be a miserable night.

Chapter Nine

Miranda awoke suddenly as the enchantment released its hold. She felt damp and sweaty. With a sigh, she rolled over to find the elf lord already awake. Sitting cross-legged on his pallet, head bent beneath the sloping cloth, he was cutting his arm with his own knife and then healing the cuts. She watched him sleepily for a minute, not particularly surprised. The goblin pages had done it, too. It was the only way to practice healing spells.

The elf lord gave her a wary glance, trying to assess how she might be feeling. She had been so upset that morning, and she was so unpredictable, ready to argue over the most ordinary things. This was something Nir wasn't used to. None of his elves argued with him at all.

He cut himself again and carefully healed the cut. Miranda picked up the knife that he had set down and examined it curiously. The handle appeared to her ignorant eye to be some sort of antler or bone. It had a pebbly texture and varied in color from gray to white. The blade was quite remarkable. Single-edged and about seven inches long, it was of no metal she had ever seen. It was white and shone like satin.

She fingered the blade thoughtfully, but when she wanted to test the edge, she found that she couldn't, and the stars at her wrists lit briefly. Nir glanced up in time to see them and took the knife away.

"If you want to know whether it's sharp or not, just watch me," he said, cutting himself again. "It's an elf knife," he continued as he stopped the bleeding. "This one was my father's. We still don't know how to make them. I hope we can learn from those books the goblins are bringing us."

Miranda picked up the knife again. It was very pretty as knives went. Nir paused to watch.

"It's said that the last elf King's Wife killed herself with a knife just like that one," he told her. "No one knows how she could have done it."

"What is it made of?" she asked, not particularly interested in elvish history. "It doesn't even feel like metal."

"That's because it's not," he answered. "We never use metal if we can help it. No metal, and no fire; they belong inside the earth, like the goblins. I don't know entirely what the blade is made of, but deer bone makes it white. I can guess that because the Slaughtering Spell powders most of the bones, ready for making knives like this."

Miranda watched him as he studied his arm with a frown, prepar-ing to make another cut, and she thought about all the times she had done the same. As long as the stars lasted, she wouldn't be cutting her-self again, and she felt a little relieved that this man would never know what she had done. He would be horrified by it, she was sure; he would doubtless identify it as yet another sign of her childishness.

And Miranda decided that he would be right. There was some-thing immature about hurting oneself in the hope that someone else would come along to stop the pain. It belonged with begging for presents, with daydreaming about a glorious future. It belonged to her past. She was done with hoping for better things to come; she was ready to face life as it was. At least this man didn't try to entice her with stories about how wonderful things were going to be.

When it was time for the evening meal, the elf lord once again brought her food. Miranda supposed that he was just treating her like a child, but her dignity didn't object to being waited on. She reached out to take it, but he held the napkin away as he sat down beside her.

"Tonight you need to ask me for your meal," he said. "You need to ask like an elf. *Ninda*—'bread,'" he explained, and he held up her half of the flat circle.

"*Ninda,* please," said Miranda doubtfully, studying the bread he handed her. She didn't think *ninda* was a very good word for it.

"*Dunabi* means 'please,'" he corrected. "*Shar,*" he continued, holding out a radish.

"No, you can keep those," said Miranda, and her face lit up with a smile. Nir looked at her, rather taken with it. She hadn't smiled at him before.

"I've hunted for your share, and I don't want anyone else to eat it," he observed. "In the wintertime, you'll be glad to have these."

"*Shar, dunabi,*" she said, shrugging, and he handed her the vegetables. As they ate, he pointed out things to her, saying their names.

"Why do you want me to speak elvish?" she asked.

"Because I don't allow English in my camp," said Nir. "You live with us now, and you have to learn to be like us."

Already depressed about the darkening night, Miranda felt that this was rather too much. "Do you know how many years I spent learning goblin?" she demanded angrily. "Days and nights of practicing, drilling, reading, writing. Years and years, while my whole family laughed at me!"

"What a sorry waste of your time," remarked the elf lord sincerely. "Igira is finished making your clothes. She still needs to fit them to you, so she'll take you back into the woods where you won't be disturbed."

"Into the woods to change clothes!" At the sight of her horrified expression, Nir's eyes grew bright.

"I assure you," he said, "that it will be perfectly decent."

Igira was an amiable woman, blond and blue-eyed like her daughter. "She doesn't speak English," observed the elf lord, "but I don't think you'll have trouble understanding each other. During this fitting, I order you to carry out her commands as you would mine." This really wasn't an order to Miranda but an order to the Seven Stars. Miranda glared at him for it, but when Igira took her hand to lead her away, she had no choice but to go.

It turned out to be a good thing that Nir had invoked the stars. Miranda had gone through countless fittings in her life, but never one in the semidarkness out in the open woods. Igira helped her undress, absolutely astounded at the quantity and variety of clothing she hauled around, and Miranda wasn't in the least happy about parting with it all.

Elf women wore only two garments, an under-dress and a dress. Igira pulled the dark brown under-dress over Miranda's head and went about adjusting it. It had a scoop neck and no sleeves, and it extended to her knees. It was unlike any garment she had ever worn. The cloth was knitted in some way, and so it was very elastic, staying close to her body. Miranda felt as if she were wearing a giant sock.

Igira made sure that the top fitted snugly. As she pinched material between her fingers, a strip of cloth came away as if it had been cut off, but the cloth left behind stayed whole. Miranda surveyed one side after Igira had cut some cloth out of it, but she couldn't even find a seam.

When the under-dress fitted to her satisfaction, Igira brought out a knitted belt. She wrapped this around Miranda right below her breasts, pulling the bodice of the under-dress tight and anchoring the belt under each arm. She had Miranda hold the ends over one another for her. Then she produced a thin leather lace and quickly laced them together.

Next, Igira pulled the dark brown elf dress over Miranda's head and began to fit it to the girl just as she had fitted the under-dress. Not as stretchy as the under-dress, and more substantial, it had no collar and no sleeves. This felt strange: Miranda wasn't used to having her arms bare to the shoulders. It had no fastenings, either. The simple round neckline stretched just enough to pull over her head. Snug to the waist, the dress widened out into a full skirt, the thick, heavy material draping and rippling gracefully as she turned. It didn't extend much past the knees.

Miranda had seen the elf women walking and dancing in their short dresses, but she hadn't really thought about wearing such a garment herself. It was a drafty arrangement after all her petticoats. She took a few experimental steps. The under-dress, hugging her legs, felt strange in contrast to the loose folds of the dress. She expected it to begin creeping up, but it stayed where it belonged, and the dress slipped easily over it. She could move much more freely, and nothing about her new garments caught at her or dug into her: life in a pair of socks was very comfortable.

The elf woman gathered up the pieces of cloth and picked up the myriad garments that Miranda had worn. Then she led the girl back to camp. The elves gathered around to admire the simple brown dress that suited her brown eyes and auburn hair, the form and shape that made her into a member of their world. The women walked beside her, smoothing or twitching the dress approvingly, and the men called out comments as she went by. It was just as well that she couldn't understand elvish because most of it was teasing. "Here comes the morning star!" they said, referring to her bright bracelet. "It's the fox with her paw on fire!"

The sensitive elves had been horrified by the goblins, depressed about Arianna's loss, and reserved and uncertain over Miranda's own appearance in camp. They had sensed their lord's concern and dismay over her, and they had attentively observed all the arguments that had taken place, arguments ordinarily being rare in an elf camp. Now they felt that they had achieved a victory. Their lord had kept the poor, unhappy girl that the goblins had wanted back, and he had changed her into something like an elf. They surveyed their new companion and found her pretty, and so they were ready to celebrate her transformation, as wholeheartedly pleased with themselves as if they were the ones who had personally dragged her out of a wretched captivity.

Igira sat Miranda down on the grass. The minute she did so, several women came over and began combing Miranda's hair. Miranda didn't know what to do about the unwanted grooming, so she just endured it with a shocked face. The women exclaimed over the fascinating color, lifting tresses and watching them glisten in the light. They were very happy. They had been wanting to get their hands on that unusual hair ever since her arrival.

Motioning for Miranda to extend her feet, Igira pulled off the girl's slippers and propped her ankles up on a thick log. Then she cleaned her feet just as the elf lord always did while several more men and women drifted over to watch. They passed the goblin slippers from one to another, laughing over them and making faces as they knocked on the hard soles.

With elf hands in her hair, elf hands on her feet, and elf hands passing her property about, Miranda decided resentfully that she couldn't call herself her own. But Igira, glancing up and catching her eye, gave her a friendly smile. Then, as she worked, she told her enthralled audience all about the excruciating clothing that the goblins had forced the girl to wear.

Igira walked away into the darkness and returned with a small white pot. Reaching into it, she plastered some warm, wet goop onto Miranda's feet, shaping it carefully until it looked as if the girl were wearing dark slippers. At last, when the stuff was thick and even enough to satisfy her, she motioned for the girl not to move.

Miranda was just wondering whether this was some outrageous joke when the elf lord appeared out of the dark and sat down beside her. Her hair-combing crew broke up and left at his approach, leaving Miranda glad of his company.

"What *is* that?" she demanded, pointing at the cold, soggy slippers.

"Those are your felt inner shoes," he told her. "They have to dry on your feet, so you're going to have to stay still, but you can watch me give a magic lesson. That will take everyone's mind off you."

What Miranda watched, she decided, didn't resemble a lesson. It was more like a riot. Elated over Miranda's rescue and thrilled with the healing spells, the elves turned cutting themselves into a new form of entertainment for the pleasure of making the cuts disappear. They inscribed messages and drew pictures on their arms; they played highly unsafe forms of catch-the-knife; and Hunter staged a mock swordfight with a companion that gave both of them plenty of cuts to practice on when they were done. A young man pretended to cry, holding out his hand for his shy fourteen-year-old fiancée to heal. Miranda thought that the whole undignified display was perfectly ridiculous.

"I've never seen grown men carry on like that," she said in amazed disapproval to the elf lord when he returned to sit beside her. She had a vague feeling that he should share her disapproval, if only because his own dignity was so remarkable. But the handsome and stately lord just watched his elves with a pleased smile.

"I have," he commented. "Many times."

When the inner shoes were dry, Igira peeled them off and handed them to her. They were something like the felt that she knew, but there was a springiness to them that normal felt didn't have, and they were amazingly tough. Nir helped her up, but she had to walk barefoot to the shoemaking elf. Her goblin slippers had completely disappeared.

Galnar was the oldest man in the camp, but Miranda had no idea of that. He didn't look particularly old; he just looked kind. His hair was so blond that it was almost white, and his green eyes and shrewd smile reminded her painfully of Marak. He had exhausted his fun with the healing spells and was playing his violin softly to himself when Miranda walked up with the elf lord, ready for him to make her shoes.

Elf slippers were made of just two pieces of leather, the large one wrapping under the foot and the smaller one covering the top, and in order to get a good fit, the leather was stitched with the foot already inside it. Miranda stared breathlessly as the curved bone needle, unguided by any hand, flashed through the leather almost faster than the eye could see, pulling the pieces tight around her feet. She was sure she felt the stab of that needle at least a dozen times.

When the Stitching Spell was over at last, Miranda took a few steps, surprised to find that her new shoes, with no hard soles, let her feel the ground beneath her feet. They were more like gloves than shoes, she decided. Then she realized with an unpleasant shock that she had almost a death grip on the elf lord's hand. During the spell, she had squeezed it so tightly that now it was slippery with sweat. Uncomfortable about this, she tried to free herself, and the stars at her wrists began to sparkle. The elf lord noticed them and let her go.

"That's the first time you've been glad of a hand to hold," he said quietly. Miranda was too embarrassed to reply.

The goblin King had come to the end of a trying day. It had started long before dawn, when he had had to sleep on the cold stone of the metal grove beside his runaway wife. Not that that had done much good, he reflected. Even though he was sure he had been unable to do more than doze, she was gone again when he awoke. This time, her lengthy, wandering trail had ended in the green banquet hall's jam closet.

By that time it was morning, so he had roused her from her nest behind the pickle barrels and jars of brandied fruit and had kept her with him all day, walking through the valley under the waters of Hollow Lake. He was sure that she had enjoyed visiting the flowers, but he couldn't persuade her to say a single word. Now he was exhausted from the long nights and hard days, and he was sure that she must be exhausted, too. With her penchant for roving, she was sleeping much less than he was.

If the day had been a trial, he couldn't complain about its ending. He was lying in his own comfortable bed with his nomadic wife beside him. She sat on the bed with her legs folded under her and her silky black hair around her shoulders. Slowly, gracefully, she was combing out the tresses, watching him all the while.

The First Fathers of the elves, he knew, had endowed all the members of their race with beauty, but there was almost as much difference between the attractive elf commoners and the stunning elf nobles as there was between an average human and an elf. Arianna was spectacular even for an elf lord's daughter, he was sure. Sometimes her beauty made his head swim.

What he wouldn't give, he thought drowsily, to have his arms around her now. Watching her comb the smooth black locks, he felt his worries slipping away. Someday soon, he would take her in his arms and feel that cloud of soft hair around him. What a day that would be, he thought blissfully, closing his eyes with a sigh.

A second later, he opened them again.

"That was an excellent sleep spell," he said coldly. "A subtle and powerful effort. I would have woken up to find you halfway across the lake valley, I suppose. If you don't stop these nonsensical peregrinations, I'll lock our bedroom door with a King's Lock, and you'll find your magic of very little use to you then."

With a cry, Arianna flung down the comb and retreated from the bed. The goblin King propped himself up on his paw to look for her. She had taken refuge behind a brocade-covered bench and was peering at him over its top.

"Honestly, Arianna!" he exclaimed. "What sort of behavior is this? Sometimes I feel as if I've married a bird or a squirrel instead of a woman. I should be luring you to my side with lumps of sugar!"

No answer. The elf girl laid her arms across the top of the bench and rested her head on them, still watching him.

"But you can speak," he pointed out. "You spoke to me in the truce circle. I'll make you a bargain. If you'll start speaking to me again, I won't lock the door."

He saw her hesitate and glance longingly toward it. After a moment of thought, she shook her head. The goblin King was pleased. This indication of further resistance was in itself more cooperation than she ordinarily gave him.

"All right, I'll make you another bargain," he said. "Come lie down now so that we can get some sleep, and I won't lock the door."

Arianna emerged from her corner and slipped into bed next to him, pulling the blanket over herself so gracefully and gently that he wouldn't even have known she was there if he hadn't been looking at her. She really was like a wild creature, he mused. No wonder he never woke up when she left.

Propped on his paw, he studied his apprehensive wife. He stroked her black hair, marveling at its softness, and played with the strands around her face. She stared at him anxiously, not moving a muscle, and when he took her hand, she didn't resist. But when he raised the hand to his lips, she gasped and tried to jerk it away.

Marak Catspaw gave an irritated sigh. While she might look like a woman to him, it was obvious that he still looked like a monster to her, something that might decide to bite off a finger and chew it up for a snack. The goblin King found himself once again cursing the villainous elf lord.

"Arianna," he said with soft bitterness, "I know you won't be able to believe this, but I had a fiancée, too. She was a human girl, taller than you are, and quite lovely as humans go, with red hair that was even more remarkable than yours. She liked me, and she liked to talk with me; we had read the same books, and we enjoyed discussing them. She used to smile at me, and even kiss me, and as incredible as it sounds to you, my fiancée wanted to marry me. The night that I married you, she shed tears."

The elf girl listened to this disclosure with an astounded expression, and Marak Catspaw relented.

"I won't lock the door," he promised. "Even though you can't leave my kingdom, you aren't a prisoner here. You're the King's Wife, and you can go wherever you like. You don't need to overpower the guards, either. They're posted to stay at the doors until you or I give them an order. If you leave, they won't try to stop you, and they won't follow you. But you need to sleep now, not go wandering. You're wearing yourself out, and your health is important."

Still holding her hand, he settled himself beside her and began to work on a sleep spell of his own. She detected the magic at once and began to fight it, tensing herself up with the effort. Very well, he thought, that wasn't going to work. He could force her into unconsciousness by sheer magical power, but she would continue to oppose the spell. She might not move for several hours, but she wouldn't get much rest, either.

Catspaw began to send her dream images instead, scenes from the forest outside the goblin caves. He imagined for her the stars from the top of the Hill and the quiet lake far below, its dark surface patterned by the rising moon with a thousand silver wrinkles. As he sent her the whisper of night breezes, the quiet drift of clouds, he felt her start to relax. Her breathing slowed, becoming even and regular. The tired girl shut her eyes.

Now he sent her the image of a leaf being blown from a tree. He followed it in his mind, tumbling through space, skimming effortlessly along on the river of wind. It dipped and flew, spinning high into the air, until it disappeared into the empty sky. The goblin King's eyes closed, too.

After a couple of minutes, Arianna blinked and cautiously looked around. Withdrawing her hand carefully from his, she maneuvered out from under the blanket. With a bewildered frown, she studied the goblin, touching the tawny fur on the back of his paw to find out how it felt. Then the elf girl slipped noiselessly from the room.

Pulling open one of the gold double doors, she surveyed the black-draped monstrosities beyond. The two soldiers stared at her, and there was no mistaking their apprehension and unease. The diminutive girl walked past as if she didn't notice them. These hulks were no match for her; she would try the King at his word before she knocked them to the floor. But the guards stayed where they were, and she could feel their eyes follow her as she walked away. The goblin King hadn't lied to her after all.

Arianna was beginning to learn her way through the strange square passages of the palace. In spite of her fatigue, she felt her spirits lift at the stillness around her: even in this dreary underworld, she felt the hush of the falling night. Goblins, like humans, lived their lives in the blaring, blazing hours of the daytime. They huddled in their compartments around her now, their thoughts vague and incoherent in sleep.

Feeling momentarily safe, free from her sleeping giant, the girl paused to lean out one of the great empty windows high above the valley fields. She didn't look at the lights below that made her squint with their brilliance, crossing the valley in a gross and clumsy parody of a star-filled sky. Instead, she looked up at the rich, green, incandescent lake water that trapped the lamplight and reflected it downward like a vast but indistinct mirror. No moonlight or starlight shone through that watery mirror-sky, but strange currents of pale green and turquoise wandered across it, barely revealing themselves, like a breath misting on cold glass. The goblin world was quiet now, and she felt the soothing peace of it, herself a child of quiet. After the long day of listening to her husband's staccato growl and rumble, the silence seemed like an exquisite song.

Why did he want her to talk? What could she say to him, an enemy, that could possibly please him? He tried in his lumbering way to please her, she could tell, but his words meant nothing. Arianna had that most troublesome and temperamental of magical gifts, the ability to feel a person's thoughts. And she knew that when this alien King looked at her, he wasn't speaking about what was on his mind.

Not yet, he was thinking as he talked to her of plants and flowers. *Later. Soon. And then*— But here Arianna's gift failed her, as this gift almost always did. Only a handful of goblins and elves who had ever lived knew precisely what went on in the minds around them.

While the goblin King roared and rumbled his meaningless phrases, Arianna focused all her magic on his *then*. What plan had this unnatural beast concocted for his foreign bride, whom he kept ostentatiously by him as he governed his hosts of malformed eyesores? There had been terrifying whispers in the elf camp about what a goblin King did to produce a bride worthy of his status, and she was sure she understood his plan. He would continue the magical operations on her that he had commenced on the very first night.

Arianna shrank within herself as she thought of that ghastly time, when he had transformed her, little by little, before a screaming, chanting mob. Every new spell he had worked had robbed her of some of her beauty, as had plainly been his intent. No doubt he meant her to be a showpiece, an exhibition of his magical skill and vision. She uncurled her hands to study the white lines inscribed in her flesh and rubbed the garish snake around her neck. On her forehead flashed a bright letter for all to see. *The goblin King's Wife,* it said—a mark of ownership, like the symbols that humans seared into the sides of their cattle.

What had saved her that night? What had stopped him from carrying on this transformation until she looked as frightful as he did himself? Undoubtedly she had begun to fare badly, and he had been afraid that the procedure would cost too much. He was sincere, at least, in his worries about her health. Perhaps she wouldn't have survived.

And now his shadowy *not yet* haunted his thoughts and hers as she instigated obstructions and delays. She knew that her attitude baffled him: her strategies were limited, and his plan would triumph in the end. But life was a finite space of time: each moment, she came closer to her escape. And each moment that she stayed herself was one she counted as a victory.

"Arianna!"

She turned from her window to find an intruder there. That oddest of all oddities, the goblin who looked like an elf, was a little distance from her in the hallway, his handsome face puzzled and concerned. He had stopped in surprise, doubtless wondering at finding her there. Then he stepped forward, composing his face into cheerful normality, murmuring something calm and reassuring.

Arianna continued to stare at him, unmoving. Then she put out her hands. At once, a large white owl hung in space where she had been. It hovered for an instant, wavering, beating the air with its soft, silent wings. Then it launched itself through the great empty window and floated off into the night.

Chapter Ten

Equipped with proper elf shoes and clothing, Miranda felt more comfortable, but she was far from contented. The next night, she went bathing with the women in the cold river water, but they didn't allow her to take a dignified bath. Instead, they played tag, splashed one another, and splashed her, too, and insisted on washing her hair.

Concerned that she had no work to do after the evening meal, she looked for some useful activity to join. But the elves didn't do anything useful, they just fooled around: dancing, singing, playing with their children, coming and going on walks. She noticed a pair of hunters leaving to bring back a deer for the band's daily stew, but it was clear that they enjoyed hunting too much to call it work. Only the elf lord, copying spells and practicing them at his writing desk, was performing a task that Miranda could approve of.

She sat down near the edge of camp, dejected and annoyed. It didn't matter that the elvish life was so lovely, she thought. They really should engage in some honest labor. They could be plowing a field right now or cutting down some trees to build a house. Marak had been right about the lazy elves. They needed taking in hand.

Just as she was concluding this arrogant thought to her satisfaction, Hunter and another elf man walked up behind her on their way back into camp. With lightning skill born of long practice, they had half her hair in an untidy braid before she knew what they were doing. When she reached back to smack their hands away, they were already walking past her, talking together in low voices as if she weren't even there. This was exactly the sort of thing, she fumed, that she should expect from the silly elves. Rummaging in her small store of elvish, she found the right word for them.

"Turturla!" she yelled. Children! The men laughed and turned to look back at her, answering in bursts of graceful elvish as they continued on their way. Nir heard the exchange and smiled to himself. Then he paused in his writing to think about it. It was the human prisoner's first attempt to speak elvish to an elf. That was very good, he mused: a real step forward. Of course, it had been an insult, but that didn't really matter. One had to start somewhere.

That does it, decided Miranda in disgust, standing up and brushing herself off. I don't care if I am important to a bunch of pretty children who have no manners with strangers and nothing to do but play stupid pranks. I don't see what I'm supposed to add to their world except be made the butt of jokes. I want to know what I'm doing here, and I want to know it now. And if I don't like it, I'll find some way off this stretch of ground if I have to dig under the camp border with my teeth.

She marched resolutely off to the elf lord, thinking of all the things she wanted to say. She walked up to his writing desk, ready to do battle, her face looking like a thundercloud. But the elf lord closed his spell book when she appeared beside him and turned to her with a smile. It was the first time he had ever smiled at her, and he won the battle before she could say a word. She forgot that she was angry. She forgot everything. She just stood and stared at that smile.

"Sika," he said, "I'm bored with writing, and I'm tired of learning spells. Let's go on a walk." Then he stood up, stretched to take the writing cramp out of his arms, and reached for her hand. No stars lit up in protest this time. The dumbfounded girl was quite incapable of protest.

They climbed up the side of the nearest hill together, the elf lord's hand guiding her as she struggled to find her footing. Not far from the top, they came out of the trees and stopped above a short cliff. The whole elf camp lay below them, the bend in the river gleaming in the light from the stars.

The elf lord walked along the cliff edge and then sat down where a broken slab of rock angled up to provide a comfortable backrest. He looked at the small figures of his elves dancing in the meadow below. Miranda sat beside him, listening to the faint music.

"When I was little," he told her, "I was raised by a human woman who lived with my father and me. She always talked about being in the dark. Elves move camp each season, but we moved all the time, and I got the feeling that we were trying to escape the dark, as if it were a frightening place. But dark is really a shade, isn't it, like dark red or dark green. Do humans see everything in dark colors?"

"I can't see colors at night," answered Miranda. "Everything's black, except that the moon and stars are white, and a little light shining on the river is white. The sky is dark, and the ground is even darker. That's why we call it being in the dark."

The elf lord looked deeply shocked. "No color at all?" he echoed in dismay. "Do you mean that the whole scene in front of you now looks just like a goblin's cloak? That's far worse than I had imagined!"

Miranda considered this, looking around. "What do you see?" she wanted to know.

"I see the leaves of the trees, all different shades of green, tossing in the wind, and the patterns that the elves are making as they turn and dance in circles. The sky is a dark blue-green, going on and on forever, and the stars hang in it like globes of fire—yellow, red, orange, pale green, blue, and white like ice. The big round disk of the moon is dark blue. Only the thin rim is bright." He paused. "A silver-gold rim, I'd call it. I don't know your word for that color." At the astonishment on her face, he grimaced. "But to you, it's all just black."

"It's a curse," Miranda said softly, as if she were talking to herself.

"My mother did it. She told me I would live my whole life in the dark." Even though this was a statement, her voice had a question in it, and Nir felt bound to answer it.

"I'm sorry," he murmured. "That was a true curse." This was not what she had hoped to hear. Nir watched her unhappy face, feeling guilty.

"I know what it means to be cursed," he said quietly. "My magic is like that: a blessing to the elves, but a curse to me. It's very powerful. It does things on its own that I don't expect, and it tells me to do things, too, and sometimes they're very hard for me. I have to do them, and I usually don't understand their purpose until later. Often I never understand."

"Then why do you do them at all?" asked Miranda.

"Because they need to be done for the elves so that we can survive. They're always the right thing to do."

"How do you know that they're the right thing," pursued the girl, "if you don't know why you should do them?"

Nir shrugged and looked away. "I can't even tell you that."

Miranda studied the man, feeling intrigued. He hadn't revealed much about himself before; their talk had been relatively formal. It occurred to her that he didn't like to speak about himself. He was reserved, just as she was.

"I still don't know your name," she admitted, rather embarrassed about it.

"You do know my name, Sika," he replied with a smile. "You use it at least once a night. My father gave me his name and his father's name, *Ash,* which means 'lonely' or 'alone.' But my people call me Nir, which is as good a translation as my language has for 'great elf lord.'"

Miranda felt even more embarrassed and quickly changed the subject. "Did your magic come from your father?" she asked. "Goblin magic is passed down."

"No," he replied. "I don't know where it came from. But then, I know nothing of my relations; perhaps my grandparents were like me. My father was gentle and playful, a perfectly ordinary elf, hardly magical at all. The only extraordinary thing about him was the love that he had for my mother."

"That's sweet," said Miranda with a smile.

"Sweet?" Nir looked at her in surprise. "Well, perhaps it was. In any case, he was baffled by my magic. Even as a child, I knew things that he didn't know. I was so different from him."

"Set aside for a special destiny," said Miranda with perfect understanding. She was enjoying the conversation. She hadn't ever met a man who was like her: dignified, reticent, troubled by a difficult past. Catspaw and Marak were both confident and talkative, comfortable with themselves.

"What's the worst thing that your magic made you do?" she wanted to know. She doubted he would answer the question, but after a second's hesitation, he did.

"The worst thing," he reflected. "I'm not sure. Bringing Arianna here to give her to the goblins was a horrible thing to do, but that wasn't the worst thing that my magic did. It killed my wife, Kara, and I didn't know in time to stop it."

"You were married?" exclaimed Miranda in astonishment, her feeling of empathy vanishing abruptly. She certainly had no experience to match this.

"Kara and I were married for years," he replied. "She was Hunter's sister. They were the first elves I found. Kara was heartsick that we never had any children. I didn't mind, but she said that I should have a son to be lord after me, and because she was a commoner, she thought that I shouldn't have married her.

"When I made trips to gather elves, I usually took my wife, but one time, my magic told me to leave her behind. She was sure that my magic was getting rid of her, and she said that she didn't mind, that she was glad to go. But she cried and cried. She couldn't bear to say good-bye, and I couldn't find any way to reassure her. When I left, she walked beside me, crying, until she was in danger of not making it home to camp before day. Then I stopped and kissed her and ordered her to go back, and I never saw her again. Hunter told me she was dead in our tent that evening. My magic must have killed her somehow, but I never would have left if I had known."

What a terrible burden to live with, thought Miranda in amaze-ment, even worse than losing Marak and all of his promises. "Was Kara as beautiful as Catspaw's wife?" she asked, and then regretted the question. Of course she was, you fool, she told herself. All elves are beautiful.

"No," said Nir. "Arianna was more beautiful, but that didn't mean I loved her more. An engagement can seem short or long. I only had to wait five months for Kara, but I thought I'd go mad. I had already waited four years for Arianna, and I could have waited another four. I would have been happy not to marry her if I'd known she was happy with another elf. The thing that haunts me," he said moodily, "is the thought of that monster kissing her lovely face."

The statement reminded Miranda of the depth of her own mis-fortune.

"It haunts me, too," she said, feeling wretched. "When Catspaw kissed me, I never would have believed that he would kiss anyone else."

"He kissed you?" asked Nir, thoroughly shocked. "You don't mean that, surely, not a real kiss. Just a kiss on the forehead, perhaps. You're too young to know the difference."

Miranda gave him a scornful look. She might not have been mar-ried for years, but that didn't mean she was a complete baby. "Catspaw kissed me many times," she replied crisply. "And, yes, I *do* know the dif-ference. Not," she concluded in a sad undertone, "that they meant any-thing, in the end."

The elf lord was beside himself with moral indignation.

"That freak-eyed pervert!" he declared angrily. "Kissing you like that! Taking advantage of his guardianship to ruin your childhood! No wonder you wanted to kill yourself when he didn't keep his promise of marriage. No wonder you keep insisting you're not a child!"

The stupefied Miranda just stared at him. "But I liked it when Catspaw kissed me," she said.

"Of course you did," he remarked, eyeing her with pity. "It made you feel important to the revolting beast. You can't possibly understand his abusive assaults."

"No, that's not fair to Catspaw," insisted Miranda, quite upset. "He was always very thoughtful, and I truly did want to marry him."

Nir looked at the expression of pain and confusion on the beautiful young face, and his heart went out to the poor girl.

"It's all right," he consoled her. "We won't talk about it anymore. You shouldn't have to think about it." He put a comforting arm around her, sighing as the startled Miranda tried to pull away and the stars flashed their warning.

"You see," he observed, touching the stars, "how badly he damaged your nature. You're afraid of every touch, even when the women comb your hair. You can't tell the difference between ordinary kindness and some sort of dangerous, twisted attention. You're always trying to decide what's decent. It's the saddest thing I've ever seen."

"I'm not afraid of anything," said Miranda blankly. The stars winked out.

"If I'd known about this before I put the spell on you, I don't think I'd have had the heart to do it," he continued. "That explains why you were so frantic. You must have been terrified! I know you thought that I was a monster, too, but you know I wouldn't do a thing like that, abusing a defenseless child."

Miranda looked up at him. His face was only a few inches above hers, looking at her very kindly, his black eyes sad and sincere. She thought that he was undoubtedly the most attractive man on the face of the earth, and what she wanted more than anything in the world, she realized, was that he would kiss a defenseless child. The kiss wouldn't be a thing like Catspaw's kisses, she was positive of that. It would be worth an entire lifetime of darkness.

"I'm so sorry for you," he said earnestly. "You've had such a tragic childhood, and now I've trapped you in a world that looks like a goblin's cloak. I just wish there was some way I could make it up to you."

It was time for the morning meal, so they walked back to camp. Nir thought, not for the first time, that humans made a tremendous racket in the woods. Miranda wasn't paying attention to anything. She thought she floated.

The bread that went with their everlasting deer-meat stew had berries embedded in it. Nir tried to teach her the word for that, but his quick-witted pupil was rather slow tonight. She was probably still upset, he concluded. Of course she was. That monster!

Miranda decided, watching him, that he looked even more noble when he frowned.

The next evening, the elf lord announced to his band that he had learned why the human girl was so afraid to be touched: the goblin King had tortured her for his own sordid pleasure. She didn't even understand this, he went on wrathfully. She had been taught that this treatment was normal. They would all have to be particularly patient with her so that she could learn to trust people again.

Miranda didn't understand what he said, but she knew that it concerned her, and she could tell that the other elves were appalled. Even the children stared at her in horror. But Galnar came to sit beside her. Smiling, he pulled out one of his deer-bone pipes and began to play. And Hunter threw himself gracefully down on the ground before her and produced a pair of shiny sheep's knucklebones.

He and the boy Tibir spent the next couple of hours teaching her to play the ancient game. They played it elf-fashion, wherein both bones had to land on the wrist or the back of the hand to score. Miranda proved hopeless at it, having none of their dexterity, so Hunter thought up elaborate handicaps to make the play even. This entertained the three of them much more than a regular game of knucklebones would have.

The elf lord was amazed at the change in his human captive. She began trying to speak elvish, she gathered flowers with the women, and she played games with the children in the meadow. He took her on long walks, explaining elf life to her, and she asked endless questions. She smiled readily now, and from his work at the writing desk, he often heard her laughter.

It all went to show, he thought to himself, what a little kindness could do.

⁓

It would doubtless have pleased Nir to learn that the goblin King had not yet kissed his new bride. Such a perverted assault was out of the question: Arianna was far too distressed. Marak Catspaw tried to treat her with consideration, but he made no progress at all. He held true to his promise not to lock their door, but he had to locate her several times a night. She turned up in all sorts of odd places and became the talk of the kingdom. The sophisticated ruler found his wife's strange antics embarrassing.

Marak's scheme to raise a bride for his son now turned into a real liability. Catspaw was the first goblin King in history who had not been properly educated for dealing with a reluctant spouse. He felt upset and annoyed by Arianna's mysterious behavior. Over and over again, he had to remind himself to be patient.

As the days went by, Arianna began to decline. She was sleeping very little and eating even less. Her beautiful face became worn, and she was no longer lively and graceful. And one morning, when Catspaw found her sleeping in a corner of the tailors' storeroom behind a blockade of bolts of cloth, the golden snake around her neck awoke.

"Goblin King," it hissed, "your wife is losing strength. Soon she will become very ill. Twenty-three King's Wives have become ill in this manner, and six of them have died. See to this matter at once."

The irate King called in his chief adviser and informed him of the ominous warning. "What should I do?" he demanded. "Why does she keep running off like this? Where is she trying to go?"

"I asked her that the other day when you were in court," said Seylin. "I pointed out to her that she couldn't escape. 'I know,' she answered. 'But at least I'm safe for a little while.'"

"Safe from what?" asked Catspaw.

"That, she wouldn't tell me," replied his adviser. "But it's obvious. She's safe from you."

"What does she think I'm going to do?" wondered the King. "Maybe Sable will have some idea. Arianna's talked to her, I know. Guard, come!" he called, and Tattoo walked in. "That's another thing, Seylin. She talks to you, Mother, and the elves, but she won't talk to anyone else. She hasn't said a single word to a normal goblin."

"She's talked to me," interrupted Tattoo, and then immediately wished he hadn't. In the surprised silence that followed, he could hear his commanding officer's voice: *A door guard protects the King's counsel and respects the King's privacy. Never mention what you hear, and never speak unless you are addressed.*

"What did she say to you?" asked Seylin with interest. The King said nothing, but his icy glare spoke volumes.

"Oh, not—not much," stammered the unfortunate Tattoo. His silver skin couldn't blush, but the tips of his ears darkened. "Just a couple of words—'thank you'—or maybe one word—I can't remem‑ ber, is 'thank you' one word in elvish or two?"

"Get out," ordered Marak Catspaw emphatically, and Tattoo rapidly obeyed. He stood outside the door, listening to his sovereign's raised voice. "She spoke to *him*? She spoke to *him*! And all the time, she watches *me* like a rabbit!" Meanwhile, the miserable young gob‑ lin called himself every name he could think of and wondered how he would break the news to his mother when they kicked him out of the Guard.

"That's just it," explained Seylin. "For some reason, she's terri‑ fied of you. It has nothing to do with goblins in general. She doesn't seem worried about anyone else."

"Then I'll confine her to bed," decided the goblin King, "but I'll stay away from her so she can rest. And we'll have the elves sit with her in turns and try to get her to talk. Maybe she'll tell them what's wrong."

The poor worn‑out elf girl watched in tears as he worked the magic that kept her from leaving her bed. It wasn't hard after all to be patient with her, he decided with grudging compassion. He explained as kindly as he knew how that he was only trying to make sure she got some sleep and that he himself wouldn't disturb her unless there was some good reason. Then he left her alone with his mother and went off to court.

Kate sat in an armchair by the bed with a book of Keats's poems, keeping a worried eye on their patient. In spite of her mani‑ fest state of fatigue and the silence in the room, Arianna still wasn't resting. She was shifting nervously from place to place on the bed, trying to find some weakness in her invisible prison. The air hummed and crackled as she tested her limits with magic, trying to batter her way out with spells.

"I understand how you feel," volunteered Kate, trying to distract her. "When I first came, I hated to be locked up, too. I used all my magic to try to break free."

Arianna stopped her efforts and looked at Kate, her face white and her black eyes glittering as if she had fever. "Were you really the old goblin King's Wife?" she asked. Her voice was husky from lack of use.

Kate smiled and held out her hands, revealing the scars. Arianna studied them, glanced down at the scars on her own palms, and then buried her hands in her lap. "Yes, my husband died just a few months ago," said Kate. "I miss him terribly."

The elf girl was silent for some time, thinking about this. "I don't understand why he didn't treat you like a normal goblin King's Wife," she said finally. Her soft voice sounded bitter.

She must know, decided Kate, that I can go outside. She thought about how hard it had been for her in those early days to know that Emily could leave the kingdom. "I was like you at first," she explained, "but not long after I came here, I saved my husband's life."

"I wish you hadn't!" said the elf girl fervently. "Or I wish I could do something like that, too. Now I just have to wait." Her feverish gaze swept the room as if she were looking for executioners. "I almost wish it were over," she confided. "I think it's almost worse than the change."

"What change?" asked the puzzled Kate.

But here the patient seemed to feel that she had said too much. She went back to her magical escape attempts and spoke no further. At last she must have concluded that the effort was hopeless. She stopped and bowed her head. Then she crept over to the side of the bed where Kate was sitting.

"Do you have any idea," she whispered, "or did he ever say . . . anything . . . about what I'm going to look like?"

The astonished Kate met her tortured gaze and finally understood.

"Oh, good heavens!" she exclaimed. "You can't think that my

son would—would—" But her command of elvish seemed to have vanished. She dropped the book of poems and started to her feet. "This is horrible! I have to tell Catspaw!"

"No!" shrieked the elf girl, making a grab for her. She was stopped at the end of the bed. She lifted her magic hand, whispering words, but Kate, on her way through the door, made a quick gesture of her own. Kate wasn't aware of the duel, and she was entirely unaware of the danger, but it was a very good thing for her that her magic was military.

Left alone, Arianna was in the grip of her greatest fears. Once the goblin King knew that she understood his ghastly plans, he would realize that it was useless to wait for her to accept them. Then he would doubtless begin the work at once. Half crazed with panic, caught in a trap, she reached out with all the magic she had. She called for help to save herself from him, and everything in the room that belonged to her world responded. All the objects that had once been living plants sprouted and started to grow.

From the linen bedsheets sprang up a tall, thick stand of flax, burying her within its reedy depths. A bowl of fruit on the bedside table exploded into activity, young pear and apple trees jostling each other for room, and the grapes erupted into a snarl of vines that uncurled like a nest of green snakes. From Kate's book shot up a pine tree, already bearing cones, and a pressed rose between two pages sent out a thorny cane. The crackle and rustle of rapidly forming leaves joined with steady thumps and bumps as ripe apples hit the ground, split open, and rose up as young saplings of their own. A pine cone burst, scattering its seeds with a report as loud as a gun shot.

Deep in her nest among the flax stems, Arianna heard that peculiar metallic sound, and the golden snake once again faced her. "What are you doing, King's Wife?" it hissed quietly. Its elvish, she noted, was flawless.

"I'm making sure he can't find me," she whispered back, too

caught up in her battle with the goblin King to see it as an enemy, too. The snake surveyed the dense mat of living plants as well as it could: a mesh of grapevines, weaving itself together above their heads, was rapidly blocking out the light.

"You are the first King's Wife to practice agriculture in the King's bedroom for the purposes of defense," it hissed proudly. "I see no danger here." And it collapsed into sleep once more.

Marak Catspaw and his mother hurried to the door. He turned the knob, and they both stood and stared. A dense, dark thicket of young trees blocked their way, twined with prickly, rose-covered canes. The impromptu forest rustled and stirred in the continued effort of growth. With a hum, a young grapevine whizzed past the doorway, unrolling large green leaves in its wake.

"Mother, get out of here!" exclaimed Catspaw, and she turned and fled. Then he held up his lion's paw. "Stop!" he commanded loudly. The noise ceased, except for the occasional thud of a juicy pear. But a very formidable barrier faced him.

The goblin King began to make his way into the dim, green depths. Something solid cannot be turned into nothing at all: Catspaw had to change each plant into something else. One by one, he touched tree trunks, changing the saplings into wisps of fog. He changed rose canes into ice and broke through their shining cylinders with a tinkling crash. He had to work very carefully because Arianna might have masked herself under an illusion. He tested each separate plant before destroying it to make sure that it wasn't his wife.

Slowly and laboriously, the goblin King made a tunnel-like pathway to the bed. Then he vaporized the heavy knots of grapevines. He parted the flax plants, and there was the elf girl, curled up like a field mouse in hay.

Before she could make a move to escape him, Marak Catspaw seized her right hand and held it to his paw, draining away her magical strength. Arianna cried out and struck at him: the spell hurt, and the more resistance it met, the more painful it became. It was a shame, he thought grimly, to fulfill her worst ideas of him like that. But he couldn't risk her killing anyone who might come to the door, and in her current state, she almost certainly would.

Her magic gone, Arianna rocked back and forth in pain, cradling her throbbing arm. Catspaw altered some flax reeds, dispersed their foggy ghosts, and sat down beside her on his ruined bed.

"You have to tell me what you're afraid I'm going to do," he said urgently. "You think I'm going to change you. Into what?"

Interpreting the injury to her arm as a threat of further retribution, the elf girl was finally frightened into speaking. "The goblin King is angry that he can't marry another goblin," she burst out. "He's angry that he has to marry an elf. So he cuts her and burns her and bends her bones until she looks worse than the ugliest goblin."

"That's not true at all," said Catspaw, very surprised. "I wouldn't do a thing like that except for revenge, and I would never practice revenge on my wife."

"They told me you would do it," cried the terrified girl, "and look, you've already started!" She uncurled her palms to reveal the scars and held them up as evidence.

The goblin King gathered both shaking hands into his human one. Her magic hand was very cold, and he began rubbing it to bring the blood back.

"No, I haven't," he said reassuringly. "Someone lied to you about what I was doing. Those are just part of the wedding ceremony."

Wedding? Arianna didn't contradict him, but the statement seemed absurd. Her exhausted brain couldn't begin to apply that term to the disgusting spells he had worked.

"Every King's Wife has those lines," continued Catspaw. "They give an indication of our future. You'll have a long life." He traced the line on her left palm. "And so will I." He traced the other one. "You've seen several elves here, Arianna. No one has changed them into anything else."

"Those others don't have to be married to the goblin King," she whispered. "The King of all that's ugly wants his wife to be as ugly as he is."

"Just because I look different from you doesn't mean I want you to look like us," said the goblin. "If I did, I would tell you. Why should I lie? I haven't done a single thing to change your appearance since the King's Wife Ceremony, and that took place weeks ago."

Arianna looked up at him, solemn and reproving, her black eyes larger for the purple shadows beneath them in her pinched white face. "You're waiting until a better time," she accused. "I see it in your thoughts."

The goblin King mused over this, impressed and interested by her claim to be able to mind-read. "You see me wanting to deform you?" he asked. "I'm not, so that can't be right."

Arianna hesitated. "I see you waiting," she confessed. "Always, when we're together, you think, 'Later, not yet, soon.' Always! It's in your mind every time you look at me!"

As he took this in, the sophisticated King became perturbed and indignant, perhaps because his thoughts had been so woefully misunderstood, or perhaps because he now had to explain them. "I'm not thinking about deforming you," he retorted in exasperation. "I'm thinking about kissing my wife! When I'll be able to hold you, put my arms around you— Might I point out that I'm your husband?"

The elf girl's stare went blank. "You wanted to *kiss* me?" she exclaimed.

"It's something married people do, I believe," he remarked severely.

Arianna gazed at him in complete amazement. "Then when you were thinking—all that time—" She made a sound between a breath and a sob. "You just wanted—you wanted—" But now she was quite overcome. She gasped and whooped, and her shoulders shook until tears spilled down her cheeks. She couldn't manage to stop for some time. Relief and something that might be mirth showed on her face, but the goblin King felt very anxious about her. He never could quite make up his mind whether the exhausted girl was laughing or crying.

"I wish you had just said so!" she told him finally, rubbing her hand over her streaming eyes. "Besides, you can't be thinking that. I'm too young to kiss."

Poor little elf, she looks so tired, he thought worriedly, and he put his paw around her. "You're not too young," he countered. "You're too tired, too upset, too sick. And I don't want to make you any worse."

Arianna leaned her aching head against his chest, thinking about this. Catspaw looked around, marveling at the destruction she had wrought. The bits of floor and walls that he could see through the leafy, exuberant growth were shattered by invading roots.

"Your magic isn't gone forever," he said. "It will come back in a week or so. I know you miss your forest and your plants. I'll bring you a small tree, and you can keep it in a pot. It won't live very long down here, but it will survive for a few months."

"No, don't," said the elf girl softly. "A tree shouldn't have to die in this terrible place. I wouldn't want to watch it."

"I'll bring you a branch, then," he promised, holding her close. "A fir branch. They smell nice. I'll bring you flowers, too, the finest flowers I can find. I'll start searching right away." He reached out and snapped a rose off a nearby stem. "Here, this is for you."

Arianna cradled the rose in her scarred hands with the ghost of a smile on her face. "That search didn't take you very long," she whispered.

A second later, she was fast asleep.

Marak Catspaw spent the day watching over his wife, but his thoughts were far from kind. He called his two lieutenants into the wreckage of his bedroom and held a whispered consultation. Not that he needed to whisper. Arianna was sleeping so soundly that shouts wouldn't have waked her.

"The elf lord sent this poor girl here thinking that she was going to be mutilated," he hissed furiously. "No wonder she kept leaving—she never knew when I might decide to scarify her, or slice off a couple of toes! That elf is a sly, scheming menace. He deliberately tried to sabotage my marriage."

"There isn't an elf King now because of a failed marriage," remarked the white-haired Richard. "If you lost your life, Marak, the goblins would be as bad off as the elves."

"Exactly," declared his sovereign. "I think that lord has some plot in mind. Arianna and Miranda are both part of it."

"But how can that be?" objected Seylin. "Arianna didn't say that the elf lord told her you would deform her. She could have learned it from camp gossip, and he might have had no idea. He didn't know that you would choose her to be your wife, either, and he certainly didn't know about Miranda."

"Adviser, you're thinking like an elf," said the King impatiently. "He knew perfectly well I would pick Arianna, unless he thought I was simply a fool: he knew we were interested in an aristocrat and intended to look over the whole band. She was his own fiancée; he spent half his time with her. Do you actually suggest that he never talked to her about what would happen?"

"He could well not have," replied Seylin. "Elves hate to talk about unpleasant things. And if I'm the one who thinks like an elf, I should know."

"It doesn't matter in any case," said Catspaw. "If he could abandon her without making sure she understood what her new life would be like, then he doesn't deserve to be a leader, but I think that Arianna 'knew' just what he wanted her to know. And he undoubtedly had learned about Miranda as well. He had obviously done some spying. Remember, he knew that I was unmarried before we told him."

"Tattoo was clear on that," noted Richard. "The elf had it all planned. He walked Miranda to the edge of the truce circle, nabbed her the minute she was out, and trapped the guard within seconds, as neat as you please. He's a cunning one, all right."

"Cunning *and* vindictive," added Catspaw. "Don't forget what he did to Mother, right under all our noses. He's afraid to take on a man in a fair fight, but he doesn't mind mistreating women."

"What do we know about his plans for Miranda?" asked Richard.

"We have no idea what he has in mind," replied Seylin. "The Scholars studied the problem for days and came up with nothing."

"This is a military situation," declared the King. "Richard, I want that camp watched day and night. And I want to find out how Miranda is and what he may have told her about her purpose there. A goblin can't enter the camp, but Sable could do it."

"If you're right about him," observed Seylin, "then you're putting Sable in danger. And goblin spies would violate the treaty."

"He broke it first," interposed the military lieutenant. "He attacked one of the Guard on goblin lands and took the King's ward hostage."

"We'll make sure that Sable has an innocent reason to enter camp," decided Marak Catspaw, "and we'll send her when we're sure he isn't there. Don't worry, adviser. I swore when I signed the treaty to act in the best interest of the elves, and I fully intend to. Whiteye proposed to become King of the two races, and the idea strikes me as sound. They lack a real leader. I'm the one who can best take care of their needs."

"The elf lord would never agree to that," protested the astonished Seylin.

"No, he wouldn't," mused Catspaw. "I'm seeing more and more reasons why that elf needs to go."

Chapter Eleven

Miranda was alone, practicing her constellations. Nir was teaching them to her the elvish way, having her form them on the ground with pebbles and then look for them in the sky. Even elves had to learn constellations. They knew where every star was by instinct, but they had to learn the names and patterns.

"Miranda!" The soft voice came from the trees nearby. She looked up from her pebbles in surprise. Who would use her goblin name?

"Sable!" Miranda hurried over to the elf woman. "What are you doing here?"

"I'm bringing the elf lord another book," said Sable, handing a bulky spell book to the girl. Then she dusted off her hands and pushed back her long black hair. Miranda found the book surprisingly heavy, so she sat down with it in her lap. Sable sat down beside her, spreading the full skirt of her silk gown out to cover her feet.

"Nir isn't in camp right now," Miranda told her. "He's out hunting, and I don't know if he's finished with the other book."

"I know he's not in camp," said Sable, looking around carefully. She switched into goblin. "The King's worried about you."

Miranda felt insulted by both the language and the comment. "How kind of him," she snapped. "I think of him constantly as well. I'm not speaking goblin to you."

"Speak what you want," replied Sable in goblin. "But you're a prisoner here, and the King wants to know why. You're his subject; the elves have no right to hold you."

"Nir took me in after Catspaw threw me out," declared Miranda. "I would have killed myself if Nir hadn't stopped me, and I'm not a goblin subject anymore."

"Don't lie to yourself," said the black-haired elf impatiently. "The King didn't throw you out, he released you for a little while under guard because he thought letting you have your own way would calm you down. The elf lord trapped your guard, dragged you to his camp, forced you to undergo spells, and imprisoned you here. And the question is: Why? What do you know about it?"

Miranda considered this information unhappily. She hadn't known about the guard, but she knew the rest was true. She didn't like to think about it. The elf lord she had fallen in love with didn't go around attacking people. He was kind and wonderful.

"I'm important to the elves," she said. "Nir's magic says so, and he has to do what his magic says. I don't know why I'm important, but I can tell he feels sorry for me. That's all I know. He isn't like a goblin; he doesn't just blurt everything out. He's an elf. He's refined."

"Refined." Sable's tone was acidic. "I can tell he's an elf man who doesn't drop your food on the floor. The King thinks he may have real harm in mind for you, some sort of plot or revenge."

"I don't think that's true," replied Miranda. "Nir worries about me. He thinks Catspaw abused me because he kissed me before I was eighteen. I don't know why he was so angry over a few kisses."

"It's really just an elf custom, the eighteen rule," answered Sable uneasily, sounding as if she were trying to convince herself. "Elf women have a terrible time with childbirth. If they went into labor before they were fully grown, even magic wouldn't save them. And the elves live so closely together, sleeping in little tents, coming and going through the forest. If their society weren't structured by the eighteen rule, there would be complete chaos. As it is, a woman's a child one night and married the next: no stolen kisses, jealousies, dangerous friendships, or chaperones. She learns to love her fiancé over years of childhood, without the pressure to grow up too soon. I have to admit, I'm an elf," she sighed. "It still makes sense to me."

"I think that's why Nir hasn't told me anything," said Miranda gloomily. "I know he thinks of me as a child. But I like it here. Everyone's so nice to me, they treat me just like an elf. There's only one difference that I can think of. I'm dressed in brown, and everyone else is dressed in green. Maybe brown is just for humans."

"Elves wear brown in the winter, green in the summer," said Sable matter-of-factly. She paused to study Miranda. "He had you put in brown because you'd look terrible in green," she said cynically. "That kind of thing matters to an elf."

Nir heard from his people that Sable had been in camp and had spoken goblin to the human girl. He was worried and suspicious about the intrusion. He learned what he could of the visit from Miranda, but he knew she didn't tell him everything. The Seven Stars didn't control her speech. She was free to keep her secrets.

"Sable helped me understand some things I didn't know about elves," volunteered Miranda as she sat on her pallet that morning. "She explained why elf women marry at eighteen and why you were so angry at Catspaw."

Nir, coiling his belt and stowing it in the corner of the tent, didn't glance up at this statement. He privately wondered why anything that obvious would need an explanation.

"And she explained why you had Igira make me brown clothes," added Miranda sadly. "Because I would have looked terrible in green."

"She said that?" murmured Nir as he settled himself on his pallet. "You should have asked me. I would have said that your clothes are

Clare B. Dunkle

brown because you look beautiful in brown. I don't understand that woman. She's even more horrible than that poor little goblin girl who looked like an elf. She's an elf who acts like a goblin."

"I don't think that's her fault," Miranda pointed out. "Sable was horribly mistreated. She told me she'd never known kindness until she lived with the goblins. Marak taught her magic himself, and he made sure she learned to read and write. She didn't even know elvish when she came. It was the goblins who taught it to her."

"The old goblin King was very clever," said Nir with his eyes closed. "He knew that elf women have more children if they're happy, so he made sure they were happy, and he knew the children would be more elvish if he developed the character of the women. It makes the elf blood last longer down in those caves."

"Oh, you make it sound so awful!" cried Miranda in distress. "Why can't you say anything good about the goblins? Sable loved Marak like a father, and I don't see what's wrong with that. Marak cared about his elves, he really did."

"I did say something good about the goblin King, I said he was clever," remarked Nir a little heatedly, propping himself up on an elbow. "If you'd asked him, Sika, he'd have told you what he cared about. He cared about their blood. He cared about it when he took it out to look at it, and he cared about it when he strengthened it through teaching and good breeding. We elves care about the deer, too; we put spells on the land to keep them healthy and make them bear more does. But the deer don't thank us, and they don't love us. We consume them, and that's just what the goblins do to us."

Miranda stared at him, astonished at the hostility in his voice. He studied her shocked expression. "You have to understand something," he said. "We have always been the goblins' prey. I signed a treaty with them, but they won't honor it. My magic knows that already. The elves are in danger now, and I don't know what to do."

"Why would you be in danger?" demanded the girl. "Catspaw isn't evil. He wouldn't hurt innocent people."

The elf lord continued to study her, amazed at how severely they had crippled her thinking. She herself had suffered terribly in their schemes, and she didn't seem to blame them at all.

"We're a temptation to the goblin King," he replied. "A whole band of unprotected elves—that's like putting a bag of gold before a human! Whether he's evil or not, he won't be able to resist. He's either thought of the possibilities we offer, or he's a fool."

"The possibilities of what?" asked Miranda in confusion, and Nir gave up the attempt.

"Never mind," he sighed. "You lived with them too long. I can't make you understand."

If the elf lord was worried, he kept his troubles to himself after that, and Miranda wasn't worried at all. The man she loved couldn't be planning harm and revenge for her. Instead, he spent lots of time teaching her things and talking to her. She was positive that he enjoyed her company.

One night she walked up to the writing desk to ask him to go on a walk. "Look at this, Sika," he said excitedly, holding out his hand.

On the ground by her feet a wide circle of glimmering white bumps appeared, rising silently from the dark earth. When they had burgeoned to a height of four inches, plump mushroom caps formed, unfolding like tiny umbrellas.

"A dancing ring!" exclaimed Miranda, and then she blushed over such a silly statement. But the handsome lord didn't laugh at her. He just looked a little puzzled.

"They're not for dancing, they're for eating," he explained seriously, plucking one of the gleaming white mushrooms. "When I think of all the nights I went hungry! I would have loved to have known a spell like this."

He took her to watch the crescent moon rising over a small lake. Miranda thought about food as they walked along.

"We eat bread all the time," she pointed out. "I've seen sacks of flour in camp, but I didn't think the elves farmed."

"No, the elves don't farm," answered Nir, smiling at the thought. "An elf with too much hard work to do is a very unhappy elf. The First Fathers arranged our lives so that we could play and be beautiful. Beauty and hard work don't belong together."

This didn't come as a surprise to Miranda, but she was more for-giving of the idea than she once had been. After all, she thought appreciatively, there was something to be said for beauty.

"We buy our bread," said the elf lord. "I think we always have. We buy the flour from whoever mills it nearby."

They came to the lake and sat down on an outcrop to rest. The stars shone out above them and below them as well, reflected in the calm water.

"Where would elves earn money?" Miranda wanted to know.

"We enchant a few springs and pools on the perimeter of our land, putting spells on them for health and beauty. Humans come to drink the water, or the women wash their faces in it to improve their looks. Human men don't seem to care how awful they look," he mused. "I don't think they ever wash in the water. But in gratitude for the help, the humans throw in a little money."

Miranda thought about this, gazing at the mirrored skies of stars. There was a pool near the Hall that the servant girls washed their faces in on Midsummer morning. She knew that they always threw in a penny. "I thought that was just superstition," she said with a frown.

"It is if there aren't elves nearby," answered Nir. "Those en-chantments don't last forever. I renewed them on a pool the other night when I was out hunting. The water probably hadn't been any-thing but plain water for at least a hundred years, but I found lots of money in it anyway. You'd think the poor humans would have noticed. It seems so sad," he sighed. "To be so ugly or sick that you'll keep desperately throwing money away even when it obviously isn't helping."

"I wouldn't worry," said Miranda reassuringly. "The ones I knew who threw money into a pool didn't take it too seriously. It was just an old custom."

"Then it's stupidity," countered Nir with a shrug. "That's one way we earn our bread. And Galnar's taken his violin to village fairs. He doesn't do it to earn money, of course; he does it because it's fun, but he comes away with lots of money, and he has to be careful not to take too much. Humans will pay an elf musician every penny they have. As long as he plays, they won't stop dancing, and when he stops, they want more."

"There's a nursery rhyme about that," laughed Miranda. "We say it to the children when they're small."

Nir smiled to see her laugh. He wondered if she had ever laughed for the goblins. "I'm not surprised," he commented. "It would be an experience never to be forgotten for a human to dance to elf music, and certainly something to tell the children. Why haven't I seen you dancing? You've probably hurt Galnar's feelings."

"Oh, I don't know how to dance," said Miranda carelessly.

The elf lord stared at her, speechless from shock, but Miranda didn't even notice. Telling an elf that she didn't dance was like telling a dwarf that she thought precious stones were ugly. Nir could hardly believe it. To be almost a woman, and never to have danced! He blamed the goblins, of course. They'd raised her so carefully to be that monster's wife, but they'd never given her the chance to laugh or dance.

The next night, Miranda was lying on her stomach, making grass whistles with little Bar, when the elf lord appeared beside her.

"Come along, Sika," he said, reaching down a hand. Miranda climbed to her feet and dusted off her dress.

"Are we going for a walk?" she wanted to know. "I'd like to go back to the lake again; it was so pretty to see the stars twice."

"No," said the elf, "we're not going for a walk. Tonight we're going to dance."

Miranda was alarmed at the thought, and the stars flashed out their light for the first time in weeks. Nir eyed the stars critically as they walked along together. Sometimes, he decided, the spell was a good thing.

"But . . . I don't know how to dance," faltered Miranda in distress.

"I don't know what you mean," replied the elf lord. "No one knows how to dance any more than they know how to breathe. You just breathe, and you just dance."

They reached the meadow and joined the dancers, and the astounded girl learned that this was perfectly true. She danced immediately—she danced the whole night—without knowing how. Perhaps it was because of the Seven Stars, or perhaps it was because of some charm in the music. Perhaps it was simply because she was out with the elves, the changeling girl lured into their play. Miranda's feet flew. She held hands, broke, whirled, and grasped hands again. All around her were faces alight, eyes shining with joy, and her face was a mirror of theirs.

Miranda forgot the darkness, her dignity, and her uncertain future. She forgot who she was, where, and when. She could have been a dancer in any age of the world, on any grassy field in any land. She faded away from herself and took her place in something greater, a beautiful, harmonious plan. She was a part in a pattern still whole and unbroken, before it had broken apart. It should have stayed whole. The pieces should have stayed in their dance. They didn't even have to know how to stay. They had had to be taught how to break.

As the two of them walked back to the forest for the morning meal, Nir wondered what she was thinking. *That was fun* or *I liked it?* Or, a little better, *I didn't want to stop?* He knew she could never be an elf, but how much of her could feel like an elf? How much of her could belong to that world that wasn't really her own?

Miranda looked up, her brown eyes very thoughtful, to meet his attentive gaze. "I never knew dancing was so important," she said. And while she watched, startled, the elf lord laughed, completely happy—happy for the first time in months.

⌒

Marak Catspaw was strolling with Arianna in the ornamental gardens of the palace. They passed the lamplit fountains and flower beds filled with creations that the dwarves had made from precious stones.

The elf girl gazed at the colored rocks carved to look like living plants, their stiff, cold forms a travesty of nature. "Oh, I don't like it here," she sighed.

"I know," said Catspaw sympathetically. "What would you change if you could?"

A little color came into Arianna's thin cheeks as she thought about this. "I'd open up the cave so that the stars could shine in," she declared. "I'd throw away these rocks and grow real flowers. I'd bring in rain and wind and snow, and foxes and deer."

The goblin King contemplated this untidy wilderness in his pleasant, orderly kingdom. It made him feel a bit gloomy. "And you'd change me for that elf lord, I suppose."

Arianna considered the suggestion. "I don't know," she murmured.

"You don't?" asked the astonished King.

"You're ugly, and he's not," she pointed out in justice. "But you don't scare me anymore, and he still does."

That blackguard, thought Catspaw grimly to himself. Of course. I should have known. "What did he do to you?" he demanded.

"Nothing," answered the elf girl. "Nir was always very kind." She stopped, hoping that he would change the subject, but he didn't. "It's just that he wasn't like us," she went on slowly. "He was always so worried and sad. He didn't control his magic; it controlled him. We never knew what it would tell him to do—even he didn't know.

"He was kind, but his magic wasn't," she confessed in a low voice. "I was afraid about marrying him. They said that he actually killed his own wife."

The goblin King held his peace and smiled reassuringly at her, but that evening he broke the news to his lieutenants.

"Richard," he said, "Miranda is definitely in danger. We have to get her away from that madman. Ask Sable to risk contacting her again to tell her about the goblin spies near camp who can help her. The dwarves have been modifying the old elf prison; she can stay there until she's free of the stars."

"Until?" asked Seylin sharply. "The end of the stars means the death of the elf lord. You know how important he is!"

"I think, adviser," said Catspaw in an even tone, "that you should know how important Miranda is. She meant the world to my father, and she means a great deal to me. When that vindictive elf enchanted the goblin King's ward, he placed his life in balance with hers. Which life do you think I value more?"

Chapter Twelve

The elves moved to their autumn camp, a thick patch of pine forest nestled against steep bluffs that blocked the biting wind. A brook came springing down the nearly vertical slopes, jumping the rocks in waterfalls and rapids. At a level with the tents, it became calm water and gurgled along its way again.

The elves were still wearing their sleeveless green clothes, but now they wore their green cloaks as well. Igira had made Miranda a new outfit in preparation for winter. The dress had long sleeves and a longer skirt, but her legs were still bare. In the winter snows, the women wore brown leggings, but it wasn't time for them yet.

Miranda wasn't used to being outside in cold, wet weather. She had enjoyed walking in the summer rains, but the autumn rains were another matter. She wore her winter clothes while the elves wore their summer clothes, and she still found the lengthening nights uncomfortable.

Soon after they had settled into their new home, Nir went hunting, and Sable hurried into camp.

"Miranda, you're in danger," she said. "We've learned that the elf lord is insane, that he killed his own wife. He controls you completely with those stars, and there's no telling what he means to do."

"That's not true!" protested Miranda. "Nir didn't kill Kara, his magic did. He was terribly upset about it."

"What difference does it make if he or his magic killed her?"

inquired the elf. "He thinks that he's kind and good, but the people around him suffer. The Guard is watching the camp, and they've noticed that you can go outside the boundary with the women. The next time you go, the Guard will help you escape."

"Nir always orders me to stay near one of the others," observed the girl.

"Then point her out, and the Guard will capture her. You can follow her back to the kingdom."

Miranda shook her head. "I won't do it, Sable. I know you're not lying, but I don't believe that Nir would hurt me." She hesitated. "I might as well tell you the truth. I love him, and I want to stay here."

"You love an elf man?" exclaimed Sable. "Miranda, you're nothing but a slave! You don't mean a thing to that lord!"

"That's not true," replied Miranda steadily. "He feeds me and hunts for me; he shares his tent with me. He spends more time with me than he does with anyone else."

"Charming," said Sable coldly. "But that will stop in another two weeks, when the full moon comes back. You don't understand. To the elves, you're a child right now, so you have to live with someone. You don't have a fiancé to live with, so the elf lord is keeping you with him. But as soon as you're eighteen, you'll be a woman: you'll live like a widow and have a tent of your own. Then the elf lord won't have to worry about you anymore."

Miranda felt stunned. Nir couldn't just cast her aside. After all, she mattered to him. No, she reminded herself, heart sinking, he had said that she was important to the elves. She just wanted to think that she was important to him.

"Why can't I stay in his tent?" she asked in dismay.

"You'll be ready for marriage at the full moon," said Sable. "If you stayed in the elf lord's tent, that would mean you two were married, and he's not about to marry you. Elf men never marry human women. They can't even have children together."

Miranda thought about that, and her world became a bitter, cheerless place once more. It wasn't that she expected Nir to marry her. She had just thought that he would always spend time with her. But of course—he was just looking after her, taking care of a homeless child. It was like him to be that considerate.

"I understand," she sighed. "I know I'm a slave. But I don't believe he's insane, and I love him. I want to stay here."

"Did you know that he's turned you into a weapon to kill goblins?" demanded the elf. "If you held a goblin's hand long enough, you'd burn right through the bones. You need to give up this pretty dream, Miranda, before his 'magic' kills you, too. Try to find a reason to leave camp."

Nir returned from the hunt to find the human girl in tears. "That goblin elf was here again! What did she say to you?" he demanded.

"Nothing that matters," Miranda assured him. She tried to smile, but her eyes were miserable, the way they had been when she had talked about being cursed. Nir was too upset to stay and look at them.

He stalked out to the south guard post. Hunter stood there, whistling quietly, having just relieved Sumur. Nir felt his skin crawl and mentally located the unnatural rat crouching in the bushes nearby. How he hated goblins!

"We need to hunt again tomorrow night," he said. "I won't be able to take my next turn. Tell Sumur that he and Willow can hunt for us at the three-quarter moon." He felt the rat sit up in its hiding place at this news, its whiskers quivering with excitement. "I can't stand it!" he exclaimed passionately. "It makes me positively ill. Don't tell me you can't feel that!"

"Feel what?" inquired Hunter, looking around.

"That!"

A great, twisted shape erupted from the bushes directly in front of the blond elf. Hunter had a confused impression of round eyes and long floppy ears before the creature loped away through the trees.

"Oh, that!" he gasped once his heart restarted. "Of course I noticed *that*."

"This forest is full of goblins now, night after night," said Nir grimly. "The treaty means nothing at all. They've talked to Sika again, and now she's crying. The goblin King must have realized why she's here, and he means to turn her against me. If we give that monster another month, the elves will be finished. I have to find out what to do!"

"Just out of curiosity," said Hunter, "why is the human girl here?"

But the elf lord wasn't listening. He stood motionless, eyes closed, rapt in the deepest concentration. After a minute, his right hand grew incandescent, brightly skeletal. The bones shone as if they were made of light, the skin that covered them glowing dusky pink.

Nir opened his eyes with a joyful laugh. "I can stop them!" he cried. He reached out to clasp Hunter in an ecstatic embrace, but the blond elf stepped back nervously.

"Good—good for you," he stammered, eyeing the luminous hand.

"We'll be rid of these monsters once and for all," Nir continued in excitement. "I tell you, Hunter," he added, shaking a finger at the elf, "they'll see who they're dealing with!"

Hunter shied sideways and then turned to see the boulder that he had been leaning against transform itself into a spiky mass of deep blue delphiniums. "I say," he said anxiously, "do you mind terribly not waving that hand at me?"

"Did you want something?" asked Nir with absentminded good humor. "I'm sorry. It'll have to wait." And he disappeared between the trees in the direction of the retreating goblin guard.

The night was cold and blustery. Depressed, Miranda retreated to the elf lord's vacant tent and curled up on her pallet, reading his spell book by the light of her diamond bracelet. She didn't know all of the words, but the goblin that she had learned was not a sorry waste of time after all. The magical characters shared by the two races apparently had the same meaning.

Lying on her stomach, she paged through the big old volume. *A spell for preventing worms in deer. A spell for preventing cough in humans.* Wonderful, she thought dully. I'm one of the livestock. *A spell for producing apples in winter.* Not that they'll cook those apples into anything tasty, she reflected. Their food is simply terrible. *A spell for traveling by cloak.* By cloak? Mildly cheered, Miranda thought of climbing onto one and using it as a flying carpet. *A spell for keeping humans inside the boundary.* Her heart fell into her toes once more. She shut the book and pulled her own cloak around herself, closing her eyes.

Much later she became aware that someone was shaking her. "Sika, wake up," said the elf lord's soft voice. "I need your help."

Miranda sat up, blinking. It was dark in the tent. It was always dark, she thought sadly. The only thing that brightened her endless night was the elf lord's stunning appearance. He knelt by her, his beautiful black eyes shining in the light of her bracelet. "Sika, I need your help against the goblins."

She stumbled after him through the windy forest. Her cloak whipped behind her and caught on passing bushes. "Against the goblins?" she asked, her brain foggy with sleep and misery. "What do you want me to do?"

"Nothing that will harm you," he replied, walking rapidly and guiding her awkward progress.

Miranda thought about what Sable had told her. "Nir, I don't want to help you fight goblins," she told him worriedly. "Why should I?" But the elf lord made no answer.

They came to a perfectly round hill rising out of the woods. The night was moonless, and clouds hid the stars, but Miranda could make out a line of tall, straight ash trees climbing the hill in a curve. Nir led her along a path that lay at their roots, spiraling up the steep slope. The whole dark forest spread out below them.

"Now, do you see the water shining over there, under the stem of the Leaf?" he asked.

Miranda shook her head. "I don't see any stars," she told him "The clouds are in the way."

"Oh, of course they are." He stood in thought for a moment. Then he lifted his hand, and the night sky went into turmoil. The clouds boiled like froth on a kettle, churning in wild undulations. They split apart and slid rapidly away, revealing the white glitter of stars.

"Now, you see the stem of the Leaf," he continued as if nothing of importance had happened. "That water beneath it is the brook that passes our camp. I want you to walk back to camp on your own, following the brook upstream. Don't you think you can do that?"

The shock of Sable's message, the heavy sleep, and this magical upheaval in the sky had a strange effect on Miranda. The elf lord no longer looked friendly and familiar in the weak light of her bracelet. He was an inhuman, inexplicable presence in the dark, and he frightened her.

"Nir, I don't want to," she faltered, drawing back. "I don't want to help you do something evil."

"They are the ones who are evil," declared the tall elf decisively. "They have no business here in my forest. I want you to walk back to camp. That's all I ask."

The girl shivered in the black torrent of wind that was pouring over the brow of the hill. "Is it true that you've turned me into a weapon that can kill goblins with my bare hands?" she asked.

The elf touched the stars at her wrist and looked down at her.

"Yes," he said. "But it doesn't matter. That's not something I'm asking you to do."

"You could," she insisted, and her voice was thin. "You could
order me to kill them, and I would have to!"

"Sika," he said, "the goblins mean to destroy us. All I'm trying
to do is to keep that from happening. Why do you listen to them?"
His voice was pleading. "Why can't you trust me?"

Miranda looked up at that pale, perfect face and thought about
how much she loved him. "Can I really trust you to do what's best
for me?" she whispered. "What I need, and what I want?"

He looked at her in silence for a few seconds. Then he stepped
away. "No, you can't," he said sadly. "I want you to walk back to
camp now." And he turned and disappeared into the night.

Miranda's first feeling was panic. She had never been left alone in
the dark. Even if she couldn't see very far, she could always hear
voices talking and laughing in the gloom. Usually some sort of
music was playing as well. It filled up the darkness and made it safe.

Now she was all by herself on unfamiliar ground, and she could
hear nothing but the rushing of the wind. It was an alarming sound,
empty and powerful, with no sympathy for one lonely human.
Miranda looked at the white pinpricks of stars, the black forest
below her, the strange hilltop she stood on, with its ghostly procession of trees. I don't belong here at all, she thought desperately, and
she started down the path toward the distant elf camp, stumbling,
running. Then she stopped abruptly.

Why does he want me to walk this way alone? she asked herself,
very troubled. How will my taking a walk on my own help him to
fight goblins? Maybe he knows that the Guard will come out to greet
me and try to take me back. Maybe he's waiting nearby, and he
means to kill them.

She sat down at the foot of one of the ash trees, in a drift of slippery, crackly dead leaves. What should I do? she thought miserably. Catspaw didn't marry me, and I've turned my back on the goblins. I'm important to the elves. I can't imagine Nir hurting me, but he admits that I can't trust him. Maybe his magic is making him do something cruel.

Marak, what should I do? she asked the darkness. I thought you knew everything, but now you're lost and empty, like the wind. I never wanted to be anywhere but with goblins while you were alive. Now I can kill goblins with my bare hands, and they're supposed to be the ones who are evil.

"I told Cook I was learning goblin," announced the little girl, "and she said goblins are evil fairies who steal little children and boil the meat from their bones."

"Did she really?" asked Marak. He glanced up, an angry gleam in his eyes. "And is this woman still on the staff?"

"Do you have any idea," Til demanded furiously in return, "how few really good servants will come out to this wilderness? That woman is a treasure. All my guests are jealous. Mrs. Hempstead actually complimented her turtle soup."

Marak considered her dispassionately for a moment. Then he bent over his little girl once more. "Miranda, goblins aren't fairies, and they're no more evil than anyone else. And they would never boil children. That's revolting."

Young Miranda had not really understood that it was revolting and had harbored secret hopes that the goblins might do something about her brother Richard. "Are you sure?" she asked in disappointment.

"Yes," said Marak. "I am the goblin King, and I rule all the goblins."

Miranda stared at her strange guardian, deeply impressed and terribly excited. "Oh, I wish I could tell Cook!" she exclaimed.

"All right, you can," promised Marak with a chuckle. "You tell Cook that you know the goblin King, and he wanted you to tell her that goblins aren't evil fairies and that boiling children is a disgusting idea. And I'll tell you what," he added carelessly, fishing a coin out of his pocket, "give her this and tell her it's a present from the goblin King."

The next afternoon Til had company down for the week, and Cook was deep in the middle of preparing a meal for twenty guests. She and her girls were filling meat pies when an intruder wandered into the kitchen.

"I know the goblin King," announced Miranda.

"Do you," grunted the busy woman, flicking her eyes critically over the child. Miranda behaved well, but the servants didn't like her. She had a poise that no little girl should have, and her eyes watched them coolly as if she knew secrets.

"The goblin King wanted me to tell you that goblins aren't evil fairies," declared the young messenger, but her audience did not reply. "And the goblin King says," Miranda continued, "that boiling children is a disgusting idea."

"He can have an opinion, I suppose," muttered Cook, reaching for a giant bowl of filling.

"And he wanted me to give you this," added Miranda, holding up a coin. Cook stopped and stared at it. Then she wiped her hands and reached for it. The girls came over to gawk at it, too. It was solid gold.

"It's a present from the goblin King," said the little girl sincerely, and Cook's face turned irritable again. She tucked it into her apron pocket and went back to work without a word. Miranda felt distinctly disappointed.

"May I have a tart?" she asked.

"No," snapped Cook. So the child turned with a sigh and wandered back out of the kitchen. As the door shut, she heard an outburst of excited, disapproving chatter. Then she heard a muffled bang.

Til was quite bitter over it the next time Marak came to visit. "Quit and gone in the middle of an afternoon, and the rest of the kitchen staff, too!" she shrilled. "Strange creatures leaping out of aprons and popping like fireworks, and my hunting party completely ruined! Mrs. Eliot will tell everyone, and I'll never live it down."

The goblin King just laughed until he cried.

Miranda laughed, too, savoring the memory. No, Marak's goblins weren't evil. The elf lord was beautiful, but she would never help him hurt a goblin. She wouldn't go back to his camp. Sable was right, and he himself had confirmed it: he didn't care what happened to her. He had given her no order, so she was free to do as she liked. She would go back to the goblin kingdom.

But you love him! protested a part of her brain as she studied the stars to try to find her way. I do, she confirmed, feeling a painful stab of grief, but I'm not going to help him do his killing.

Miranda set off along the pathway that spiraled down the hill, the straight sentinel trees making her uneasy. She hurried toward the forest that began at the foot of the slope, and the ragged tangle of woodland blocked out the stars as she made her way into its depths. But here was something new: a clear path in the underbrush right at her feet. Miranda welcomed its tidiness in that leafy chaos. A few more feet, and an ash tree loomed ahead of her. Starlight shone down on her again. Another ash tree past that one, and another, in a gentle curve. Miranda stopped in confusion. She was climbing back up the hill.

This time she walked slowly into the dim forest, turning around frequently to keep an eye on the hill behind her. The thick boughs of trees closed in over her, and the forest swallowed her up. She crept along, making a direct path for herself, gauging the angles from trunk to trunk. The next trunk was straight, with an ash tree's diamond ridges. Stars broke through the vine-hung gloom. She was walking up the hillside path once more.

Spirals played in patterns inside the girl's dazed and desperate brain. This spiral could loop around on itself, she decided. Very well, she would abandon the path and escape its devious tricks. She went sliding and scrambling right down the face of the hill. She felt it level off, saw the uneven edge of forest ahead of her, and ran under its branches. The next thing she knew, she had run right through the black fringe out into starlight again. She was climbing the steep hillside before she could even stop.

The elf lord found his human huddled at the foot of the bottommost ash tree, her face a study of bewilderment and distress. He knelt down by her side and put his arms around her.

"I'm sorry that upset you," he said. "It was wrong to frighten a child like that, but I didn't know how else to test this spell."

Cold and miserable, Miranda nestled into the warmth of his arms. "That's all I am to you, aren't I?" she said. "Just a child."

"Of course you are," he said kindly. "I'm not like that fur-handed monster."

"But I'm only a child for two more weeks," she said with a sigh. "Then you won't have to take care of me anymore."

Nir was puzzled by her unhappy expression. "I thought you wanted to be a grown woman," he pointed out.

"Not anymore," she whispered. "I'm glad I still have two weeks."

"I don't blame you for feeling sad," he said sympathetically. "At the very end of your tragic childhood, you've finally found someone to take proper care of you. It's too cold for you here. I'll take you back to camp."

Miranda let him help her up and lead her through the endless shadows. "I wasn't going back to camp," she confessed wretchedly.

"I know," he replied. "I'm sorry for tricking you. You can see that I don't trust you, either."

⟡

The next night, Nir left camp to go hunting. He didn't hunt deer, but he found exactly what he was after. As Sable came slipping through the trees, he stepped out to confront her.

"Stop!" he called. She yelped in fright, but she stopped. "You'll tell me what I want to know," he said with stern satisfaction, walking up to her. "You're an elf, so you don't have a choice. What did you tell Sika—Miranda—last night that's made her so unhappy?"

"I told her that the goblin King has arranged for her escape," retorted Sable, turning away from him and staring at the ground. "I tried to convince her to take advantage of it."

"You tried?" echoed Nir in some surprise. "Why did she need convincing?"

"She loves you," muttered Sable reluctantly. "She wants to stay with you."

"The human girl *loves* me!" exclaimed the elf lord incredulously, and he gave a triumphant laugh. "That's dealt a nice blow to the goblin King's plots for her, hasn't it? Tell me, how did you try to convince her?"

"I told her what you elf men are like," snapped Sable, "that you have no feeling at all for her, that you're just waiting until her marriage moon to throw her out of your tent. I told her how dangerous you are, that you're insane, that you even killed your own wife."

The elf lord's face went white with indignation and fury. "How dare you say such things! How dare you bring harm to your own people!"

"The goblins are my people, not the elves," replied Sable. "I'd never live among people like you who have no feelings for others."

"What would you know about the feelings of elves?" cried Nir. "Fine! You'll have what you want. Look at me," he commanded, putting his hand on her head, and she looked up at him for the first time. "And listen," he said in a low, firm voice, looking into her eyes. "I tell you that you are not an elf. You are a goblin instead. Go back to your King and say that the elf lord tells him that his spies won't plague me much longer. I'm giving him fair warning: if I catch him meddling with Sika again, I'll murder any goblin I find. Now get away from here. And don't let me see you again."

Sable shook all over, seeming to shrink before his eyes. When he released her, she staggered backward and fell onto the damp ground. Mindlessly, automatically, she crawled away from him, but her eyes never left his face. Torn between grief and disgust, Nir watched her go, the elf that wasn't an elf. Then he turned and walked back to camp.

Hunter was waiting for him by the tents.

"Some tracker you are!" he scoffed, his blue eyes bright. "I caught my quarry long ago, and she's already flayed and carved."

"So's mine," sighed Nir. "Please gather the others. I have to talk to them."

Miranda was sitting by Galnar, listening to his violin. Half the camp was dancing to the music, but she was too unhappy to dance. Before Sable's warning, she would have wandered the camp boundary to watch for Nir to come back from hunting. She wouldn't let herself do that anymore, but she was still impatient for his return. She had only two weeks to spend with him before it was too late.

The elves all gathered under the shelter of the bluffs and listened to their lord. Miranda couldn't understand his rapid elvish, but she heard different names mixed into it, and a thrill of excitement went through the crowd. She wandered over to Hunter, who stood to one side.

"What's he saying?" she whispered. Hunter turned with a bewildered expression and leaned toward her, cupping his hand around his ear. "You heard me!" she whispered. "I know you speak English." He smiled indulgently at her and patted her on the head. She glared at him. Elves are so silly, she thought.

Nir finished speaking, and the assembled elves dispersed, heading off on different errands. The lord walked up to his friend and his prisoner. "Hunter, Sika is your responsibility in my absence," he said, "but she can stay alone in my tent. Sika, follow his orders as you would mine. That is to say, reluctantly," he added, a smile lighting his dark eyes.

"In your absence?" asked Miranda anxiously.

"Yes, I have to leave tonight," he said. "There's a spell I need to work. I'll be back at the full moon."

"The full moon!" gasped Miranda. "No! That's too late! Take me with you," she begged.

"I can't, but I'll be back soon," he promised. Soon, thought the stricken Miranda. As soon as I'm a grown woman, and you stop worrying about me. My last two weeks, gone. She wandered away from the men as they talked, and crept into his empty tent.

Miranda didn't let herself cry. She lay facedown on her pallet, overwhelmed by misery. She wished she were asleep, unconscious, dead. She heard Nir crawl into the tent and felt him sit down next to her, but she didn't move.

"Sika, you asked me last night if you could trust me to do what you want," he said. "I don't know the answer. I have to do what's best for the elves, but I'll make you happy if I can."

"Catspaw told me the same thing," she muttered, "that he would give me anything to make me happy, anything. But he wouldn't give me the one thing I wanted, and neither will you."

"You can't be sure of that," he replied. "Tell me what you want. I'll give you anything that's in my power to give."

Miranda felt again the despair of Marak's death and the loss of her tidy future. Her dignity, her hard work, even her perfect man-ners—nothing in her life had any meaning.

"Very well," she said with bitter fatalism. "If you really want to know, I want you." A lump rose in her throat at the pitiful hopeless-ness of it all.

"You want me?" said the elf lord softly. "That's good. That's in my power to give."

Miranda was just breaking into tears when she heard him. She sat up slowly, wiping her eyes. "But," she began. "But—you can't, you know. Elves don't marry human women."

"This elf does," replied Nir with a smile.

"But you don't want to marry me," she insisted helplessly.

The elf lord looked puzzled. "Maybe humans think backwards," he remarked thoughtfully. "You're telling me things that you couldn't possibly know without asking questions about them first. Telling me

I can't marry you. Telling me I don't want to marry you. How do you know that, Sika? Have you asked?"

She stared at him. "Do you want to marry me?" she whispered.

"Of course I do," said Nir. "Why do you think we're always together?"

Miranda's world had fallen apart a couple of times, and she had tackled the wreckage with vigor. But her world hadn't gone from horrible to splendid in a second. She didn't know what to do. Marak had raised her to do her duty for the admiration that it would bring. He had taught her to defend herself against cruelty and disappoint-ment—and not to trust anyone but him.

"Do you love me?" she breathed.

"Yes," he answered. "Not that I understand you very well. You're so different from us. The elves all belong to me, but you don't. I suppose that makes you very appealing."

Miranda thought about this in complete amazement. The elf lord was remarkable, inhumanly handsome, unlike anyone she had ever known. It had never occurred to her that she might be unlike anyone he had ever known.

She wanted to prove to herself that this was really happening, so she reached out and took his hand. She could feel her face beaming with joy, and she didn't know what to do about it. After a lifetime of hiding her emotions, she felt exposed by her own happiness. She didn't dare to look at him. He would surely see what she was feeling.

Nir leaned his head against hers and looked at her hand holding his, wondering what she was thinking. "This engagement has seemed very long," he reflected. "I'm glad it will be over soon. I'll finish my magic, and we'll dance on the night of your marriage moon. We can survive until then, don't you think?"

Miranda looked up, and he smiled at her. She smiled back and felt a lightness sweep over her, as if her heart were a little flake of ash that had just flown up the chimney. But a second later, she came back down to earth with a thump. She remembered that he was leaving.

"I want to come with you," she said. "You took Kara on your trips."

"And so I would you, if I could," said Nir, "but this is a difficult trip: constant walking, constant magic, too cold and hard for a delicate human who can't see in the nighttime woods."

Miranda thought about Kara and remembered what Sable had said about elf men and human women. "Maybe your magic is getting rid of me," she exclaimed in distress.

"No, it's not," said the elf lord reassuringly.

"But I—I probably—well, maybe certainly—can't have children, either."

Baffled, Nir studied her anxious expression. "Sometimes I don't understand you at all," he remarked. "Please worry about something that makes sense to me, like whether or not it's going to rain tomorrow. Don't worry about whether or not you're going to have a child years from now. That seems very strange." He put his arms around her and held her close. "I have to go."

She walked with him to the boundary. "Can't you kiss me goodbye?" she begged.

"No," he said, smiling, "but I'll kiss you hello." And then he walked away. She stood at the edge of camp and watched him disappear into the blackness, the stars at her wrists and ankles sparkling as she struggled to follow him. How pointless, she thought bleakly. How completely irrational. Her new guardian came to stand beside her.

"Hunter, he's gone!" she exclaimed in despair.

Hunter thought up several witty replies to this but looked at her face and decided against them. "You're right," he concluded. "But you'll be glad he's gone. I'll feed you better."

"How's that?" Miranda asked absently. "You're not a lord."

"That's just it," the blond elf assured her. "No special privileges for Nir. He says that's what ruined the elves in the first place, excess and caprice at the top. But I always eat better than everyone else. A little excess and caprice at the bottom never hurt the elves."

"Elf food is terrible anyway," said Miranda. "I don't see what difference it'll make."

"Not elf food!" insisted Hunter. "Just Nir's food. No, you take it from me, all dried deer meat is not the same. It may look the same, it may smell the same—"

"It may taste the same—" said Miranda, smiling.

Hunter drew himself up indignantly. "Oh, go ahead, mock a serious subject!" he declared. "That's all you humans think about anyway, making silly jokes." Miranda laughed, which had been Hunter's goal all along. He was very pleased with himself. He was sure the elf lord could still hear her.

Miranda went to the tent alone that morning, happy that the spell would shortly force her into sleep. She awoke with a start, knowing even before her eyes opened that something was wrong. Then she heard the shouting.

She scrambled out of the tent. Elves were screaming, running, frozen in confusion, stunned, and terrified. But the shouting was in English. She ran toward the sound.

Just beyond the boundary stood sixty goblin soldiers, the finest and most hideous of the King's Guard. In front of them stood the goblin King, shouting for Nir.

"Come out of there, elf lord!" he called. "Don't make me wait all night. We're not here to hurt your elves, I promise. We're just here to kill you."

Chapter Thirteen

"Catspaw!" shouted Miranda, running up to face him across the boundary line. He could have reached out and touched her if it weren't for the magic that kept them apart. "Catspaw, get out of here with your Guard! You're frightening the children."

The goblin King smiled down at her, but his eyes were very cold. "I'm not just frightening the children," he growled. "I'm frightening them all. Every last one of them—except my sensible Miranda. Where is he?" he continued, gazing at the cowering elves with cruel satisfaction. "I don't see the prettiest elf anywhere."

"He isn't here," she said. "He left last night."

"Of course he did," said Catspaw, nodding grimly. "But don't worry, we'll find him." He turned to his Guard. "He's not here," he called in goblin. "Mongrel, hunt his trail."

"How dare you break the treaty like this!" she cried as the gangly, droopy-eared goblin came forward and began sniffing along the boundary line. "Nir gave you his own bride, and you've gone back on your word!"

"I'm not breaking the treaty," said Catspaw. "He broke it first. Last night your elf lord attacked Sable as she came to see you. He sent her back with a warning to me that my spies weren't safe, and then she died right in front of me, her heart stopped by magic. Treaty or no treaty, do you think I'd let him live after that?"

Miranda stared at him, speechless with shock. Nir, arms around

her, telling her he loved her, and Sable, collapsing in death as a brutal warning against spies. "That can't be possible!" she exclaimed.
"It can't be! Sable's dead?"

"She's as good as dead," answered the goblin. "Someone has to
stay with her and work the magic to make her heart beat while the
Scholars search for a counterspell. I'm almost positive it won't help,
but I had to try something."

"He wouldn't have done that!" insisted Miranda. "Nir wouldn't
have killed Sable!"

"Oh, yes, he would," replied Marak Catspaw. "Your pretty
elf enjoys attacking women. You should know; he dragged you
away and worked magic on you by force. Mother was the first, in
the truce circle, no less. He got a hand on her by fraud and left her
devastated."

"He attacked Kate?" gasped Miranda. How could anyone hurt
Kate?

"Sable is the third goblin subject that he's treated this way," said
the King. "Who knows how many of his own people have suffered?
Sable was afraid of him from the start, and so was Irina. Sable only
came here at all because she was worried about you."

Miranda's world was crumbling into ruins again, something
that she was growing used to. "There has to be another answer," she
declared. "You can't kill him, Catspaw. The elves need him to do
what's best for them."

"They don't need him at all," said Marak Catspaw. "They need
me." He looked around serenely at the terrified, fascinated elves. "I'll
make sure they're safe, well, and properly taught. We should have
ruled the elves after the death of their King, just as Marak Whiteye
proposed. If they'd agreed to that, there would still be thousands of
elves instead of this tiny band."

"King Fox and the chickens!" scoffed Miranda.

"You sound just like they do," Catspaw retorted. "It's a good thing Father can't hear you. How many elves have I harmed, Miranda? How many did Father harm? All the elves hate us, except for the ones who actually know us. And poor Arianna! They told her I would cut her and bend her and scar her up until she looked worse than the ugliest goblin. You can't imagine how terrified she was. It's the saddest thing I've ever seen."

"But Catspaw, you can't kill Nir," she insisted helplessly. "I love him."

The goblin King flexed his lion's paw and studied the big claws. "So I've heard," he remarked dryly. "That's not why I'm killing the elf lord, but that's the reason I'll enjoy it."

"But you said you wanted me to be happy!" exclaimed Miranda. "Nir's going to marry me."

"No, he isn't!" laughed Catspaw. Then he paused to study her face. "There are only two explanations for this," he continued matter-of-factly. "Either he's lying to you as an exceptionally cruel form of revenge, or he's insane, which I'm inclined to believe anyway."

Mongrel came trotting up, ears flapping. "I've found the trail," he wheezed in his high, whining voice.

"Good," said the goblin King. "We'll finish this in no time. And I do want you to be happy," he added, turning away. "The minute he's dead, those stars will fall off, and you can come back home where you belong."

Miranda hurried along the boundary line, keeping up with his long strides. "Catspaw, Catspaw, please!" she begged. "You said you'd do anything for me!"

"I did it already," he answered. "Father didn't raise you to be imprisoned by a mad elf."

Think, think, Miranda told herself. You have to do something. "Catspaw, your father raised us both," she said breathlessly. "You're like a brother to me."

"Why, so I am," said the goblin King, stopping to smile at her.

"Do this one thing for me," she said. "Don't kill Nir. Please!"

The goblin King stared at her as he thought things over. "And will you do something for me, little sister? Say yes, and I might consider it."

"Yes!" cried Miranda. The King began absently shredding the bark off a tree with his claws.

"All right," he said slowly. "I promise not to go after the elf lord and not to authorize any other goblin to attack him. No goblin will harm any of the other elves, either. I'll follow the treaty."

Miranda scowled at him. "That's just what your father did," she retorted. "He said he wouldn't authorize anyone to follow Seylin, and instead he allowed Seylin to be followed without his express permission. You know anyone in Sable's family will try to kill Nir, starting with Tinsel and Tattoo."

"Clever girl," said Catspaw approvingly. "But I'll command that there be no attacks on the elf lord. No goblin violates a direct order. The only way your precious elf will be killed is if he attacks one of us goblins. I can't promise away our ability to defend ourselves."

Miranda turned over the promises in her mind. Surely Nir would know not to attack the goblins. There were thousands of them, after all, and the goblin King was so powerful.

"What do I have to do?" she asked suspiciously. "It will be horrible, won't it?"

"Miranda, these elves have corrupted you," said Marak Catspaw benignly. "You just have to come back home where you belong and live under my command. You're my subject, you shouldn't be out in these drippy woods. It's a wonder you're not sick or dead."

"But I won't see Nir again!" whispered Miranda.

"That's the idea," he replied. "Don't just glare at me. Tell me yes or no. I can't wait long, I have an elf to kill."

"Yes!" hissed Miranda. "You know I don't have a choice."

"Fine," said the goblin King. "I'll give you a few minutes to arrange your affairs."

He walked off to speak with his Guard, and Miranda turned to find Hunter standing behind her. "You know I have to leave," she told him, struggling against tears. "You heard what they were going to do."

"Yes," said the blond elf, his handsome face grim. "I'll gather some things we'll want to take."

"But you can't go," protested Miranda. "The elf lord needs you."

Hunter gave her a tight smile. "Sika, Nir left you in my charge," he pointed out. "If he comes home and learns that I let a goblin have you, the first thing he's going to do is kill me. I've been Nir's friend for years, and I couldn't do that to him. Killing me would hurt his feelings something awful."

He returned with a pack and erased the camp character. Then he took Miranda's hand and crossed the boundary.

The goblin King turned as they approached. "Who are you?" he asked, eyeing the elf curiously.

Hunter was pale, and he flinched as those ghastly eyes raked over him, but he held his head up and looked straight at the King.

"I'm Hunter, and Sika was left in my care," he said loudly. "I'm not going to hand her over to you. Either I come with her, or she doesn't go at all. You'll have to kill me to get rid of me."

"I won't kill you," said Marak Catspaw, quite unruffled. "An honor guard. That's showing Miranda proper respect. Come along then. You can be her elf guard. And, Tattoo," he called, beckoning the young goblin from the line, "you can be her goblin guard."

Miranda frowned when she heard the familiar name. So they still want me to marry him, she thought. Another member of the Guard led up a horse. Hunter stared at it, appalled.

"Hey! Get that thing out of here!" he exclaimed, jerking Miranda away from it.

"The horse is for Miranda," observed the goblin King. "I have one for you, too. We'll have to ride because it's too far to walk."

"We will not have to ride," declared the blond elf emphatically. "I wouldn't let Sika near that frightful beast. Too far to walk! Do you have any idea how far I've walked in my life?"

Catspaw frowned. "I thought you were concerned about Miranda's welfare," he said. "It's a two-hour walk at least."

"Oh," scoffed Hunter. "I thought you said it was too far."

The goblin King, rather short on sleep, eyed the elf balefully. "All right," he decided after a minute. "We'll do it your way."

Whispering softly, he took off his long black cloak and held it so that it just brushed the ground. It dangled in the air alone when he released it. Then he spread out the sides and the hood, pulling the garment taut. When he stepped back, a half-circle of black cloth hung flat in the air before them, the hood forming a shallow cave at the top. It looked like a giant black bat.

"There you are," said the King to Hunter. "Just step through."

"That's not my way!" insisted Hunter.

"It isn't a horse," explained the goblin King. "Tattoo, you go first. Walk through the middle, and don't forget to duck."

Tattoo stepped forward without hesitation and vanished into the cloak. Hunter walked around it cautiously and studied it, but Tattoo was nowhere to be seen.

"I'm not risking Sika's life on a goblin trick," he said huskily.

"Elves are such cowards," remarked Marak Catspaw with satisfaction. "They're afraid of everything but trees."

Hunter's jaw tightened at that, and he strode into the cloth, pulling Miranda with him. A second of blackness, and a cliff face loomed before them, glimmering in the dusk. They stood on thin, scrubby grass about thirty feet from the forest's edge, and a line of broken cliffs barred their way. Tattoo stood to one side, casually surveying the area.

Hunter jumped in alarm. The goblin King's cloak hung in the air right behind him. He jumped again. Now the goblin King stood right behind him. Marak Catspaw studied the nervous elf as he retrieved his cloak. Miranda didn't even bother to look up.

"Here we are," announced the goblin King.

"Where are we?" snapped the elf. "And why?"

"This is Miranda's new home," replied Catspaw. "I can't bring her into my kingdom because of those stars, so we've renovated some old guest quarters. Right through there." He nodded at the cliff. "Go ahead."

Miranda looked up and remembered Marak bringing her through the front door only a few months ago. She had been so happy to be going home with him at last. Her happy future had crumbled several times since then. She wondered if it would continue to crumble every single time it appeared that it might possibly be happy.

Hunter glared desperately at the sheer, broken rock, his whole being rebelling against it. No worse destiny awaited an elf than being dragged into the goblin caves. He stalled for time.

"I'm not bashing my face into a rock wall," he told the King. "I don't want it to look like yours."

"Stop acting like a child," replied Marak Catspaw calmly. "Tattoo, you go first again."

The goblin promptly disappeared into the rock. Hunter couldn't let himself be outdone, so he closed his eyes and hurled himself at the cliff face, almost jerking Miranda off her feet. A second later, he collided with Tattoo. They were inside a large stone room.

"What happened?" demanded the surprised goblin. "Did he have to give you a push?" The distraught Hunter felt that rudeness could go no further. He couldn't even frame a reply.

The goblin King walked past them to a door in the far wall. "And through here," he said, pulling it open. Tattoo walked in and looked around with interest. Miranda stepped in looking at her feet.

Hunter staggered in and closed his eyes against the bright light. Marak Catspaw examined the elf. Beads of sweat stood out on his forehead, and his breathing was shallow.

"Miranda, you'd better help your guard sit down before he faints," Catspaw concluded.

Miranda helped Hunter over to a thick mat on the floor while Tattoo brought a handkerchief dipped in water. Hunter leaned back against the cave wall and slowly began to revive.

"I'm fine, really, Sika," he muttered, opening his eyes to glare at the goblins. "It's just that this place is so dreadful."

"What a shame you don't like it," remarked the goblin King, not sounding particularly sorry at all. "These quarters were designed especially for elves."

They were in a cave about twenty-five feet wide and so long that Miranda couldn't see the end of it. It curved away steadily in a shallow bend. Unlike the goblin palace, this cave had been left close to its natural state, or perhaps, decided Miranda, it was just supposed to look natural. The bumpy, irregular walls curved upward to become the sloping ceiling about twenty feet above them, and the cave floor was uneven, too.

The cavern, full of shadows to her human eyes, was just light enough that she could distinguish colors. The walls and floor shone milky white, as if they were covered with ice, and hanging globe lamps cast a dim, pearly glow. Columns stretched from ceiling to floor here and there, like stalactites or tree trunks. They were the color of fine jade, and they matched the wide, thick green mats scattered on the floor near the walls.

A few feet in front of Miranda, a fountain bubbled up in a wide basin, bobbing in five uneven jets of water that sparkled and sang. The water spilled over the sides of the basin into a shallow channel three feet wide that ran down the center of the cave room; composed of large chunks of light blue stone, it was designed to look like a brook's natural bed. It broke the flow of the water into small rapids as it twisted out of sight around the long bend of the cavern room.

"The elf lord Girzal was our last guest," said the goblin King. "He stayed here for several months as his ransom was being arranged. He and Marak Blackwing became somewhat cordial, and he pronounced the place quite livable. Hunter, I realize it's bright for you, but farther down the cave, you'll find a small cavern off to the side that isn't lit. It has hooks in the floor for your tent."

Hunter looked slightly relieved. "Ransom?" he muttered, looking around with a little more interest. "What ransom could elves pay?"

"The elf lord's youngest daughter Lim paid it for him," answered Marak Catspaw. "She lived with the goblins for three months as a guest before she accepted the terms of the ransom. Then she became the goblin King's Wife, and her father went free." Hunter grimaced in disgust.

"Miranda," continued Catspaw, "the dwarves have added new rooms suited to a human, and you can reach them through the staircase over there. This door will be locked, these quarters will be guarded, and the guards in the outer room will bring you your meals. Hunter, you may stay here as long or as short a time as you like. You're a guest, not a prisoner, but if you leave, you won't be allowed to come back. Tattoo, you'll remain here as long as Miranda does, and I'll have the guards bring you whatever you need. You can sleep in a tent, too, if you like," he suggested. "Remember, you did when you were little."

Under the scrutiny of his monarch, Tattoo tried not to look dismayed. Miranda felt no such constraint.

"So I have to stay locked in here for the rest of my life," she declared.

"Of course not," replied Catspaw. "Just for the rest of the elf lord's life. Then you can come back into the kingdom."

Miranda gave him a suspicious look. "You promised me," she warned, but he only smiled at her.

"Don't worry," he answered. "I'll keep my promise." And the goblin King left.

Elf, human, and goblin sat and gazed dejectedly at the fountain for several minutes, each depressed for a different reason.

"Tattoo," began Miranda, "is your mother really—I know what Catspaw said—but Sable can't be dead, really?"

"We're making her stay alive," growled Tattoo, "but it doesn't work very well, and I don't know what good it does when she won't stay alive on her own."

"You don't mean that elf woman is your *mother*?" exclaimed Hunter. "Stars above!" Then he turned red when they both looked at him. "Sika, don't you believe that goblin claptrap," he insisted. "Nir would never attack a woman, much less an elf woman. He didn't even let us hurt the revolting humans we found near camp—no offense," he added hastily. "They didn't look like you."

"It's not a lie," declared Tattoo. "I was on duty when my mother came in. She looked horrible, dead white and covered with dirt. First, she told Marak"—he hesitated—"well, she said what he told you, anyway. And then she fell right down, not four feet from him. We thought she'd fainted, but she wasn't breathing. Seylin said he knew some spells that could do it, but not delayed and at a distance like that."

Miranda covered her face with her hands, overcome at the thought of Sable dying because of her.

Hunter furrowed his brow in thought. He pulled his set of knucklebones out of his tunic and began absently tossing them and catching them. "Nir didn't put a spell on that elf woman to kill her," he said slowly. "And he didn't attack that other elf woman, either, the mother of the goblin King." He glanced bemusedly at Tattoo's silver face with its faint black lines. "It's a shame you both didn't take after your mothers a little more. But Nir just affects elves, that's all. I can't explain how he does it. He can be too much," he continued, waving his hands. "Too much, and not even know it."

Tattoo raised his eyebrows. "So you're saying that the elf lord affected my mother to death?"

"I just mean," said Hunter, "that if he told her to drop dead, she'd do it."

"*My* mother? You don't know my mother!" scoffed Tattoo. "She's not about to drop dead to please an elf man, and don't think they didn't try to make her do it, either. No, I know what happened. The elf lord told her to take herself off, and she gave him a piece of her mind. He just wasn't used to being talked to like that, him with all his affected elves."

"No, no, no!" declared Hunter. "That isn't what happened."

"Well, it happens that my mother's dead," pointed out Tattoo. "And your elf lord is, well . . ." He trailed off, glancing at Miranda again. Another silence fell.

"Let's have some food," suggested Hunter, opening his pack.

Miranda raised her face from her hands and gazed at him reproachfully. "How could you think of eating at a time like this?" she demanded.

"At a time like this?" he wondered. "Well past the time for the evening meal, which we haven't eaten yet. I know, we'll take a walk first and see the rest of this dismal hole. That'll work up an interest in food."

It took the three of them almost an hour to reach the end of the curving cavern. The milky walls and randomly spaced pale green columns continued, as did the occasional mats. The small artificial brook hurried along the middle of the cave floor, bridged periodi-cally by narrow slabs of stone. It reminded the wanderers that they were walking downhill.

After some time, the curve of the cavern became more pronounced. Hunter stopped and looked around suspiciously. "It's as if we're in a giant snail shell," he said.

"We're walking in a spiral, yes," agreed Tattoo. "It makes sense if you think of this as an elf prison. You elves are active, and a spiraling tunnel gives you plenty of room to take walks without using up too much space. These mats are for elves, too, to use instead of chairs. Marak is right, this place was designed just to suit you."

Hunter looked unimpressed, but in another minute he gave a cry of delight, unintentionally confirming Tattoo's remarks. They had come around a sharp bend and arrived at the center of the spiral, a large circular room. The channel of water ended in a deep pool as large as the room was wide. Stone steps in front of them descended into the clear water, and ripples cast their waving lines on the walls and floor. Hunter couldn't have been more thrilled.

"A place to bathe!" he cried. "Even underground."

Tattoo dipped a finger into the water. "It's frigid," he announced sarcastically. "It's everything an elf could wish."

Miranda was hungry by the time they made their way back uphill to the fountain. A low table waited by the door. On it were plates of meat and cheese, rolls, buns, meat pies, sweets, and a bowl of fruit. Miranda and Tattoo realized that someone had thoughtfully raided the pantries for them, but Hunter was very wary.

"Don't touch that stuff, Sika," he ordered. "It's probably poisoned. I thought of this, so I brought food with us."

"Oh, good," said Miranda loyally. She sat down and surveyed the dinner Hunter handed her. A strip of dried deer meat and a stale round of bread. Then she watched Tattoo devour a meat pie. The goblin caught her wistful look and grinned.

"I'd especially avoid these jam tarts," he suggested, biting one in half. "The cooks always poison them first."

"You're probably right," said Hunter, relenting. "We shouldn't be rude. I suppose we could bring ourselves to eat a little goblin fare. Here, Sika." He handed her an apple.

Miranda was happy to discover that the Daylight Spell worked underground. She wished it could keep her asleep night and day. The months since she had left home had been a series of painful sorrows and shocks, and this last setback had put her beyond feeling altogether. She wasn't even unhappy. She just felt worn out and listless. After all, she reasoned, she wouldn't be able to see Nir anyway. He was still on his trip. She couldn't face even imagining how she might feel when she knew the elf lord was back home.

Hunter took Miranda on walks with him and fed her his elf food until it ran out, but his attitude completely baffled her. He hated the subterranean prison intensely, and he had lost all of his old companions, but he was much more cheerful than she was. She didn't realize that elves were naturally optimistic and didn't ordinarily worry, as Nir had pointed out. Hunter wasn't really happy, but he didn't see any reason why that should interfere with his fun.

In Miranda's room was a shelf of books, and a couple of nights after their arrival she came downstairs deep in the tale of Robinson Crusoe. Hunter was examining a buttered croissant suspiciously. Tattoo dozed on a mat nearby. Lonely and homesick for goblins, Tattoo spent as much time with the two of them as he could.

"That's not elvish," commented Hunter, looking over her shoulder at the book as he ate. "Is it goblin?"

"It's English," she said absently. "A story."

"Oh, chronicles," said the elf.

"I can read it to you if you like," offered Miranda. "It's about a man who suffers shipwreck at sea." Then she thought that Hunter might not understand this. "His ship, his boat, sinks in the middle of the sea—that's like a huge lake. And the man has to live all alone on an island and find everything he needs."

"I didn't know your family knew how to do that kind of thing, Sika," admitted Hunter, considerably impressed. "Nir says we elves used to go fishing in boats made of hides, but no one in my family knew anything about it. My father fell through lake ice, though, and drowned."

Miranda was puzzled by these remarks, but Tattoo was a veteran of Kate's English classes and spotted the confusion at once. "That man on the island isn't Miranda's relative," he said from his comfortable position on the mat. "He isn't anybody's relative; he's just made up. Imaginary, like a dream."

Hunter was astounded. "You're learning the history of a man who didn't exist?" he demanded. "Why would you bother to do that?"

"Because it's interesting," said Miranda. "When I think about his troubles, I forget mine for a while."

"You want imaginary troubles to forget real troubles?" asked Hunter. "I don't have to read a big long chronicle for that. I'll just imagine I have a stomachache."

He rolled around on the floor, moaning and holding his middle. Miranda was disgusted. She headed back to her room to enjoy her book in peace. Hunter sat up laughing as she passed.

"Wait! My stomachache's gone!" he exclaimed. "I feel wonderful." But she marched up the stairs without looking at him. "She's mad at me," he sighed. "Now we'll never find out what happened to the man who didn't exist. And what will we do for fun now that we can't tease Sika? I know," he suggested, giving the goblin an appraising glance. "Do you know how to play knucklebones?"

Miranda was glad to have normal food again, and she thought that Hunter would like it as well, but the poor elf simply hated it. He couldn't reconcile himself to his new diet at all.

"I can't get over how horrible it is," he insisted to Tattoo one evening before Miranda came down. "Like this brown stuff. What do you call it?"

"Chocolate cake," answered Tattoo, glancing at the wedge Hunter was waving about in the air.

"This chocolate cake," continued Hunter. "I can't even begin to guess what it's trying to taste like."

"Like chocolate?" suggested Tattoo, helping himself to a slice of his own. Hunter gave him a pitying glance.

"I don't know how you ever got to be so big and hulking on food like this," he remarked. He rummaged in his pack for a minute. "Here," he said, handing Tattoo a piece of dried meat and taking a piece for himself. "The last of my stock. Just wrap your silver lips around that."

Tattoo tore off a shred and ate it. "Haven't you people ever heard of salt?" he demanded.

"Now, that's food to savor!" exclaimed the elf, brandishing his piece. "My own kill, too, the night before we got locked in here."

Tattoo looked more interested, and gnawed at the meat again. "My father used to hunt with the old goblin King," he said, "but I've never hunted, myself."

"You've never hunted?" cried the elf. "At your age! Where does your meat come from, then?"

"Mostly from sheep," replied the goblin. "Sheep walk right up to you if they know you."

"Oh, you've missed so much!" exclaimed Hunter. "There's noth-ing like it, your own food running wild, beautiful, and carefree through the forest. And you find it and follow it, bring it down and bring it back home, and you feed your whole camp with your efforts."

Tattoo watched the animated Hunter, mildly impressed. The goblins didn't respect the pretty elves, but this was an achievement he couldn't boast of.

"Why, you take that deer you're eating now," said the elf. "I didn't even have my hunting partner that night. I had to stalk her and bring her back alone."

Tattoo choked and swallowed with an effort.

"Her!" he shouted. "And now I'm *eating* her! Oh, you people are just barbarians!" He flung the rest of the meat onto the ground and stomped off down the cavern. Hunter watched him go, more bewildered than offended.

"What's wrong with him?" he wondered as Miranda came down the stairs. She had heard the last of the conversation.

"Goblins never eat female animals," she said. "They think mothers are sacred."

"Now, that's funny, Sika," remarked Hunter. "He just called me a barbarian. Doesn't he know that goblins are the barbarians?"

A few nights later, Miranda sat staring at the fountain, despondently wondering where Nir was.

"Miranda," whispered a soft voice. She looked around in surprise. A large, fluffy black cat crouched on the stairs that led up to her room.

"Seylin!" she cried. The black cat flattened his ears and switched his tail.

"Do you mind keeping your voice down!" he hissed. "I don't want Tattoo to know I'm here."

"It's all right," she said. "Hunter talked Tattoo into going swimming with him. He didn't want to, but Hunter teased him and made fun of him until it was just easier, I think. Why don't you want him to know you're here?"

"I didn't just come to cheer you up," replied Seylin. "I need information. Within the last two months, something completely unexpected has happened: a healthy band of almost seventy elves has returned to their ancestral homeland. But almost immediately, things have started to go wrong. They've lost arguably their most magical female to a goblin marriage, and they're about to lose their most magical male as well. The band doesn't have very many descendants of the noble families. I'm afraid they won't survive it."

"Catspaw promised me that he wouldn't kill Nir!" exclaimed Miranda. "Why are the elves going to lose him?"

"The goblin King means to keep his promise, but that won't save the elf lord for very long," opined the cat. "The lord has already caused enough harm to get himself killed several times over, and I very much doubt that he means to stop."

They went upstairs. With a shimmer, Seylin changed back into his regular form and pulled from his pocket a pen, a bottle of ink, and a small scroll. He unrolled it, and Miranda saw that it was blank.

"Recent events have shown me just how little we understand the elves," he said. "I have to find out why the elf lord keeps doing these irrational things, and you're the only one I can talk to."

"I'll tell you anything that will help," she promised. "But why would Tattoo care that you're here?"

"He won't, but he'll tell the guards, and they'll tell Marak Catspaw," answered Seylin. "The King's mind is already made up about this, and he's happy with his conclusions. He's already forbidden me to discuss this with Arianna. If he knew that I had been here, he might tell me not to come see you again, and I would have to obey him. That would limit my choices in a very critical matter."

Miranda had not been able to talk to anyone about Nir since the day she had met him. She talked about life in the elf camp for hours. Seylin was a good listener, and he surprised her by taking frequent notes, unrolling the small scroll farther and farther as the night progressed. By the time he ran out of questions, the scroll was several feet long.

Miranda lay on the bed with her hands over her eyes. The talk had stirred up her battered feelings, and her heart was aching. Seylin tapped his pen against his knee, looking back over his copious notes.

"I still don't understand it," he remarked. "The more I know, the less I understand." He rolled up his notes into the same tiny scroll as before. "And here you are, at the center of a fight between the two greatest lords of our day. I suppose you could consider that an honor."

"I wouldn't say that they're fighting over me," protested Miranda gloomily, staring at the stone ceiling above her. "Catspaw certainly tossed me aside without a fight. Now Nir will come home in a week and find out that he has to give me up, too. He'll just pick one of the elf girls to marry. It won't be hard, they're all beautiful." She sighed. "And now I know that I haven't even saved his life."

"That's not true," observed the handsome goblin. "The elf lord would definitely be dead tonight if you hadn't struck your bargain with Marak Catspaw. You bought him time—and more important, you bought me time as well. Maybe I can find the key to this puzzle before it's too late."

"I'll go downstairs and get rid of Tattoo for you," she said. "Come back and visit me again, Seylin. I'll be glad to talk to you."

She found her guards playing knucklebones by the fountain. "Let's take a walk," she suggested, and the three of them started off.

As soon as they were out of sight, a large black cat crept out of the shadow of the stairway. He froze in concentration for a second. Then he leapt into the fountain's wide basin. No splash sounded, and no ripples rose as he hit the water. The black cat simply disappeared.

⌒

Miranda spent the next several days in her comfortable room, read-ing and rereading her books. Meanwhile, the two guards killed time below. Hunter was growing restless, trapped inside day and night. He was missing howling winds, autumn storms, and the leaves cascading from the trees. It began to wear on his temper.

One night, he pulled out his pipe and tossed it back and forth for a minute. "This is no life for an elf," he declared.

Tattoo was reading *Robinson Crusoe*. "It's not much of a life for a goblin," he noted.

Hunter glared at him. "I thought you goblins just adored caves," he said.

"We prefer the ones with goblins in them," replied Tattoo. He grimaced as Hunter began playing his pipe. "Look, do you mind?" he protested. "That thing hurts my ears."

"Your face hurts my eyes," snapped Hunter, "but you don't catch me complaining."

He put away the pipe, but Tattoo had picked up his bad mood. The goblin put down his book and began wandering around the fountain with a scowl. For some time he maintained silence, determined to keep up appearances in front of the enemy, but finally his frustration got the better of him.

"At least you know why you're here," he burst out. "Your lord left you responsible for Miranda, so you have to be. But me—I'm here day and night for no reason at all! My mother's dying, and I can't even be there."

"I know why you're here," announced Hunter casually.

The tall goblin stopped and stared at him.

"You don't! You can't!"

Hunter shrugged, picked up his pipe, and started playing softly. "It's goblin revenge," Tatoo suggested. "And what a revenge!" The blond elf shook his head. "All right then, why am I here?"

"Because that lying beast you work for is going to kill Nir as soon as he gets home," responded Hunter, "and then he wants you to marry Sika."

Tattoo stood still for a long minute. "Marak isn't a lying beast," he said automatically. He sat down to give the matter further thought. "How do you know he wants me to marry Miranda?"

"The elf goblin told her so when he came into camp to fetch her," replied Hunter.

Tattoo stared despondently into the distance. "I call that meanness," he sighed. "Seylin knows perfectly well I've wanted to marry his daughter Celia ever since we were little pages. So they're going to make me marry a foreigner. They did the same thing to my father."

"I'd say your father was lucky to force some poor elf girl to marry him," observed Hunter.

Tattoo pulled his knife from his boot and began to play with it. "Technically, Mother forced Dad to marry her," he said moodily. "I don't know how anyone could force Mother to do anything. And now I'm stuck here in this boring place, facing marriage with a human. What did Miranda say about it when Seylin told her?"

Hunter opened his mouth to convey Miranda's passionate refusal, but he looked at Tattoo's miserable expression and stopped. He hated goblins, he reminded himself, and he would be happy to face Tattoo in battle, but there were some things that a man simply shouldn't do.

"It never mattered," he answered with a shrug. "Nir wouldn't let her leave."

"Oh," said Tattoo. He turned his knife blade and studied it. "It's a great honor, being chosen to marry a nongoblin bride," he muttered. "I know my family would be thrilled. But you take it from me," he said earnestly to Hunter, "elves and humans are nothing but trouble!"

After Hunter's revelation, Tattoo avoided his potential bride's company, leaving Miranda puzzled and hurt at his quick departures. She came downstairs less and less often. This left the goblin and elf with nothing but each other for entertainment, and neither one was pleased about it.

"No!" declared Tattoo one evening when Hunter began tossing his knucklebones invitingly in the air. "I refuse to play that stupid game one more time!"

"I don't blame you," replied the elf. "You always lose. What do you goblins do for fun, then? Make faces at each other?"

"I don't *always* lose," grumbled Tattoo. He thought for a minute. "Adding corners is a game we play in the guardroom." He retrieved a piece of meat from the table and laid it on the ground between them. "Adding corners is really just illusion magic, a variation on the solid shape manipulation drills you did as a child." Hunter's stare went blank. "Oh, good heavens!" Tattoo groused. "Didn't you learn anything at all?"

"I surely did," responded the elf promptly. "I learned how to be hungry. My mother and father were dead by the time I was nine, and I was hunting to feed myself and my little sister."

Tattoo was taken aback. Maybe these pretty elf men were tougher than they appeared. "I'll show you how," he continued more respect-fully. "You take anything at all"—he gestured at the meat—"and you change its appearance into a simple solid shape, like this."

The meat became a shiny silver triangular pyramid, a tetrahedron. Bemused, Hunter picked it up. It felt heavy and cold, like metal. Each face of the tetrahedron was a perfect equilateral triangle.

"That's a game?" he wanted to know, putting it back down.

"That's just the start," said Tattoo. "The next person has to add a corner to it." As he looked at the tetrahedron, it changed shape. Now it looked like a silver ax head. "Go on, it's your turn."

Hunter studied the figure. It dissolved and became the piece of meat once more.

"You lose," said Tattoo. "That happens when an opponent can't visualize the shape and add to it."

"What a stupid game," remarked the elf.

"No, no," insisted the goblin. "It's fun once you learn how." The meat became a tetrahedron. "Your turn." The tetrahedron became meat again.

"A really stupid game," commented Hunter.

"Oh, come on!" said Tattoo impatiently. "Even our children can work this magic." The meat became a tetrahedron. After a long moment, a spike appeared from one face.

They played for several hours, and Hunter always lost, but he improved steadily. They finally reached the point where the goblin had to do more than glance at the figure to change it. He looked over the spiky object before him and added another spike.

"Your turn."

Hunter stared at it for several seconds. It turned bright pink.

"Hey!" exclaimed Tattoo. "What happened?"

"I don't know," sighed the elf. "I got a little bored. Our games don't make you think so much."

Tattoo studied the figure. Then he shrugged. He turned it purple with green dots.

When Miranda came downstairs, her two guards were staring at a brilliantly colored object that was covered in spikes, nodules, and twists. A blue eyeball on the end of one spike appeared to be watch-ing her. She let out a shriek. Tattoo flinched, and the creature dis-solved into an ordinary piece of meat.

"You lose!" exclaimed Hunter with satisfaction. "Hello, Sika," he said, smiling up at her. "I just won a goblin game."

In a quiet room in the palace, Tinsel sat by his wife Sable's bedside, his silver face haggard. Sable's breath hissed in the room, loud and shallow, as her daughter Fay chanted the spell that forced the elf woman to stay alive. They no longer let Tinsel work the lifesaving magic. He was too tired and distraught.

The magic that sustained the black-haired elf wasn't working terribly well. The unconscious figure on the bed had grown gaunt. Her skin was dry and dull now, and her lips were cracked. Little by little, she was becoming a corpse before their eyes.

The goblin King and his two lieutenants came into the room, but when Tinsel looked up with a hopeful expression, Marak Cats-paw shook his head. The Scholars had done a full review of every spell in the kingdom's books, and they had found nothing that would help.

The silver goblin dropped his head and began to sob. His daugh-ter put an arm around him as she continued her work. "Don't keep her like this," he begged brokenly. "If you can't bring her back, just let her go."

"We will," promised his sovereign grimly. "But not just yet. That murdering elf will die before she does. He's back in three days. We'll surround the camp with the entire Guard and terrorize it until he decides to attack us. Then we'll annihilate him bone by bone. After that, we'll stop the magic. Sable will die avenged."

Tinsel wiped his streaming eyes. "I want to help," he whispered.

"You'll have to get more rest," warned Catspaw. "Then we'll see." He left the room with his lieutenants.

As the door closed, Seylin turned. "Goblin King, I would rec-ommend that you reconsider this plan," he said. "Revenge is one thing, but you must consider the cost. Your father—"

Marak Catspaw exploded.

"My father!" he exclaimed. "Oh, yes, I know all about it. Father never hurt an elf. But he'd have hurt this one, and long ago, unless I'm very mistaken. Father wouldn't have stood by and watched his ward turned into a slave, and he wouldn't have gotten Sable killed, either. It's time, gentlemen, that you faced a sad fact," he concluded angrily. "My father is not ruling this kingdom."

Seylin glanced away, embarrassed, and Richard studied the floor with a frown. Catspaw glared at them both, frustrated and discouraged, but neither one looked him in the eye. The King was just opening his mouth to say something far more bitter when a voice behind him spoke.

"And why is that a sad fact, dear?"

Kate stood behind him in the hallway, surveying the three of them. Delicate and beautiful she might be, and they were undoubtedly the rulers of the realm, but she had watched them grow from boys into men, and her steady gaze told them so.

"Marak was a great King," she said quietly, "but he would be the first to remind you that his brilliant plans only worked half the time. His revenge on my guardian brought disaster, and he promised a human girl that she would be your wife when he had no right to do so. Don't turn him into something that he wouldn't want to be. He would laugh at you for making him into a legend."

Richard gave a wry grin at this, and Seylin looked thoughtful, but the goblin King crossed his arms, unmoved. "You've always known it," he pointed out with cynical fatalism. "You said yourself that I wouldn't be a King like my father."

"Of course you won't," replied Kate with a smile. "Because you're more like your mother. Did you think that would disappoint me? Excuse me now; it's my turn to watch with Sable." And she disappeared through the door.

Marak Catspaw stared after her for a moment with a very odd expression on his face. When he turned around, he found that Seylin was smiling, as if he were calling to mind an old and well-loved joke.

"Catspaw," he pointed out, "one of your parents saved this kingdom. Sometimes I make the mistake of forgetting which one."

The goblin King nodded thoughtfully, frowning a little, but his unmatched eyes were alight with satisfaction. "Very well, adviser," he said calmly. "Give me your advice. I'm ready to listen to reason."

"I only wanted to point out," replied Seylin, "that if you take your whole Guard to the elf camp and carry out a brutal revenge on their lord right in front of them, you're likely to cause such despair that the elves won't submit to your rule. They'll refuse your commands and die provoking additional attacks."

Marak Catspaw considered this. "That's quite true," he agreed.

"Instead, I suggest that you call for a meeting and have all the elf warriors come to the truce circle. They won't be able to launch an attack in there, and they can consider your proposals more calmly. Send your Guard in as well, to protect goblin lives."

"He's right that the elf lord is likely to take some goblins down with him," opined Richard.

"And what do you suggest we do with the elf lord?" demanded the King, growing angry again. "I suppose you want me to send him into the circle, too."

"No," said Seylin resignedly. "I know you better than that. I've been doing quite a bit of study on this issue, and I see no way to avoid a fight. The best plan I can suggest, to minimize loss of life, is this: Meet the elf lord outside the circle. Propose a duel. And then kill him yourself."

Chapter Fourteen

Miranda awoke to a feeling of dread. This was her elvish eighteenth birthday, the night she was supposed to be married. This was the night when Nir would find out that he would never see her again. For two weeks she had remained numb and disinterested in life. Now her grief surprised her. The last thing she wanted was to be alone. She hurried downstairs to find the others.

Hunter and Tattoo had cleared the low table. They knelt across from each other, staring at an ordinary bun. As Miranda watched, the bun wavered back and forth on the table between the opponents. Then it flew into the air and socked Hunter in the stomach.

"Ha! I win," declared Tattoo.

"We were playing three buns out of five," protested Hunter.

"That *was* three buns out of five," said the goblin. "Hand it over."

Scowling furiously, the elf pulled his deer-bone pipe from his belt and gave it to Tattoo. "At last!" exclaimed the goblin happily. "A peaceful evening!"

"Not exactly," remarked a voice behind them. Seylin stood in the doorway. "Tonight will be remembered for many things," he said, "but it won't be remembered for peace. The elf lord returned last night to find Miranda missing. He sent a message to the goblin King, declaring the treaty null. He intends to meet the goblins in battle and fight to the death—to his own death, and the death of every warrior he has."

The three stared at Seylin in shock for a moment. Tattoo was the first to speak. "Twenty-two warriors against the King's Guard. That won't last long. Sorry," he added to Hunter.

"It means the end of the elves!" breathed Miranda in dismay. "Catspaw won't let that happen."

"Marak Catspaw sent a messenger asking the elf lord to come to the truce circle," replied Seylin. "He doesn't intend to kill the warriors, just the lord himself. The goblin King thinks he can reason with the elves once their leader is dead."

"Well, he's wrong," snapped Hunter.

"The situation is desperate," agreed Seylin. "It calls for careful handling. Even with the best intentions, it may well end in disaster, and the end of the elves will mean the end of the goblins. I can think of only one way to avoid this catastrophe. I need Miranda's help."

The guards looked puzzled and stared at her blankly. She stared just as blankly at Seylin. "I'm nothing but an ordinary human," she protested. "I can't even work magic."

"Elves and goblins need their magic to survive in a human world," said Seylin. "I'm not asking you to work magic. Just come with me to the truce circle and swear to stay there until I give you permission to leave. Whether you like it or not, or even understand it, you're at the heart of this entire conflict. As long as you're inside the circle, that's where the conflict will be, and the truce circle magic will keep it from being bloody."

"I'll come with you," promised Miranda.

"Not without my permission," declared Hunter. "She's my responsibility."

"And I can't let her go anywhere," announced Tattoo. "I have my orders."

"Which were what?" prompted the elvish goblin.

Tattoo paused to think. "I have to stay here as long as Miranda does, as her goblin guard."

"Fine," answered Seylin. "She's leaving in just a minute, and that leaves you free to go, too. I'll bring both of you men with us if you'll swear to remain with Miranda inside the circle. Otherwise, I think I should explain something. I learned magic from the old goblin King, I taught magic to the new goblin King, and I don't intend to let either one of you jeopardize your own race's future."

Both guards looked at each other and then at their feet. They didn't know what to do.

"Don't you want to be at your old friend's side tonight?" Seylin asked Hunter. The elf brightened at the thought. "And, Tattoo, I had a suspicion that you wanted to marry my daughter Celia," he remarked. The goblin gave him a deeply reproachful look.

They followed Seylin out of the cavern and into the guardroom. Tattoo gaped at the bulky forms lying on the floor.

"You sent Lash and Jacoby to sleep?" he demanded frantically.

"Yes, well," demurred Seylin. "Their orders were different from yours."

Tattoo gazed in disbelief at his snoring comrades. "He's going to kill me, isn't he?" he sighed.

"The goblin King?" asked Seylin. "Oh, I wouldn't think so. Probably just me," he suggested with an encouraging smile.

Outside, they found bright twilight and a crisp breeze blowing. Seylin collected them at the cliff. "I need your permission to conceal you," he said, "for your protection and mine."

"You'll make us invisible?" asked Hunter.

"No," lectured Seylin. "Real invisibility is impossible. The spells either make you look like something else, or they make you be somewhere else. This spell makes us look like shadows, so stay in the shadows or you'll be spotted at once. Hunter, hold Miranda's hand, and you and Tattoo, hold my hands." The four large black shadows hurried self-consciously across the grass and vanished beneath the trees.

In half an hour, they arrived at the truce circle, and Seylin rendered them visible, or at least conspicuous, again.

"The elves won't arrive for at least another hour," he told them. "Miranda, swear by the magic of the truce circle not to leave until I give you permission." He guided her through the oath. "And you two, swear by the magic of the truce circle to remain in it with Miranda." They did so. "Now, Miranda, see if you can leave."

Miranda walked to the outer line of trees and stopped, unable to go farther. She glanced down at the stars at her wrists, but they were dark. "I thought force was forbidden in the circle," she said, rejoining her companions.

"It is," answered Seylin, "except what you force upon yourself. What you swear here you have to honor here. Now I'll conceal you again. Please trust me and stay concealed until the two lords enter the circle. After that, you're free to be as conspicuous as you like."

He changed them back into shadows again, and they sat down under the trees. Twilight deepened into night, and the stars came out. They heard a crowd approaching and Richard issuing orders. Seventy-five of the King's Guard filed through the trees and formed ranks. The rising full moon began to light the interior of the circle.

"The elves are coming," whispered the shadowed Hunter to Tattoo.

"I don't hear anything," murmured the goblin.

"I know," replied Hunter proudly.

"Elf lord!" came Catspaw's shout from outside the circle. "You may have broken the treaty, but I stand by my promise. I mean to do what is best for the elves."

"You stole Sika from my camp through lies and threats," called the elf lord's clear voice. "In doing that, you have already destroyed the future of the elves."

The shadow that was Miranda leaned toward Seylin. "Is that true?" she whispered, dumbfounded.

"I'm almost positive it is," answered Seylin. "Except for the lies, of course."

"I encouraged my subject to flee a murderer and return to safety," responded the goblin King. "I and my goblins remain the friends of the elves. We refuse to attack your warriors, and we will disarm them if they attack. If you wish to fight, send your people into the circle and face me alone."

"Very well," replied the elf lord, and the warriors began to file into the circle.

"But Seylin, he can't do that!" whispered Miranda to the shadow next to her. "Nir has absolutely no chance of winning!"

"True," answered Seylin, moving away. "But I wouldn't worry about that. I don't think the elf lord expects to win."

She followed the sound of his voice to the outer circle of trees and looked out between the great oaks. Lit by the full moon, goblin and elf stood face-to-face not ten feet apart. Catspaw was a little taller and heavier. He held his great paw outstretched, his lion claws bared. Nir held his own right hand up, his cloak thrown back from his shoulders.

"Seylin, you're going to do something, aren't you?" she whispered to the shadow beside her.

"Of course," he answered. "In a minute."

"In a minute?" she echoed frantically. "Seylin, you have to do something *now*!"

As the last elf man reached the circle, the two leaders sprang at each other. A blast of wind tore the branches around them, and they disappeared behind a sheet of white flame.

The howling wind drowned out all other sounds, and the sheet of flame became a fiery ball. Crackling and arcing, it rolled across the ground, its brilliant glare now purple, now golden. Trees split and splintered as it rolled by, and the wind whipped leaves and twigs into a whirling column. Dimly, within the glowing heart of the flame, moved the black forms of the magical warriors.

Inside the truce circle, the assembled men broke ranks and

scattered, crowding to the gaps between the trees. Elves and goblins jostled together, unheeding, intent on watching the combat. But no one set foot outside the great trunks, no matter how advantageous a view this might offer. Torn tree limbs, caught on the spiraling wind, crashed into one another, and flames ran along the ground and licked the very edge of the enchanted ring. No one inside it dared to leave its safety.

The flaming sphere, spinning and flashing, rose high into the air. The wind whirled into a scream. With a crash like a thunderclap, the heaven-bound globe split open in a shower of sparks. Stark against the bright light, two dark figures plunged to earth. They landed with twin thuds a few feet apart on the ground outside the truce circle.

Seylin walked out and stood between the prone leaders, his hands behind his back.

"And did you enjoy your refreshing combat, my lords?" he asked. "I trust that you're both well."

The men looking up at him appeared not to know whether they were alive or dead. He smiled reassuringly at their stunned expressions.

"In fact, I'm sure you're both well," he concluded. "And since each of you firebrands has failed to annihilate the other, perhaps you'll come into the circle now and look for a less drastic approach."

They climbed shakily to their feet, gazing around in amazement. The scorched earth smoked, and shattered tree limbs littered the ground. They studied their own hands, their clothes. They watched each other out of the corners of their eyes. Not a scratch, not a bruise, not a rip in a cloak. Their clothes weren't even dirty. Avoiding each other's gaze, they followed Seylin into the circle.

A shadow flung itself at the elf lord. "Nir!" cried Miranda, the spell falling from her as she reached him. Nir put his arms around her and stood still, holding her tightly, his head bowed over her bright hair. He had fully expected to be dead this minute. He had never expected to see her again.

Catspaw turned at Miranda's cry. Then he examined his adviser's careful expression. "Seylin," growled the King, flexing his claws, and it was fortunate for the handsome goblin that they both stood inside the truce circle.

"A good subject anticipates his monarch's wishes," remarked Seylin smoothly.

"And what does that have to do with *you*?" roared the King.

"Thank you, friend goblin," said the elf lord with dignity, "for doing what you knew was right."

"Well, he didn't do what I know is right!" snapped the infuriated Catspaw. "I hope you don't think I'm letting Miranda leave here with you. She's not tagging after some itinerant, half-mad, flute-playing elf and living the rest of her life on deer meat and rainwater!"

"And the life you have planned for Sika is better, is it?" replied Nir hotly. "Living in some airless hole among malformed people who can't even touch her, with no possibility of the marriage she wanted or the children she's been worrying about."

"Children? Don't be ridiculous," declared the goblin King. "She's not having children with you."

"That's a lie!" asserted Nir.

Marak Catspaw stared in surprise. "It is not, you crazy elf! Goblins don't lie."

"Tell him how you know it's a lie," Seylin prompted the elf lord.

"How he knows?" cried the goblin King. "Seylin, you taught me that law yourself!"

"Not exactly," observed his adviser. "Go ahead, elf lord, tell him how you know."

To Miranda's surprise, Nir stiffened and carefully pushed her away. Then he stood, head high, glaring at the goblins as if he were back in combat again.

"Just as I thought," mused Seylin. "He won't tell you because it's a secret. A dark, shameful, terrible secret that he hasn't told a single elf. You see, goblin King, the elf lord knows that Miranda can have his son. He knows it because his own mother was a human, and she had his father's son."

A murmur arose at this from the assembled men, amazement from the goblins, dismay and disappointment from the elves. The elf lord stood perfectly still, ignoring them all, and stared at the rising moon.

"An elf-human cross?" growled the puzzled goblin King. "With that kind of magic? Seylin, it's not possible!"

"He'd tell you if I lied," observed Seylin. "But I didn't. And that isn't the only secret this elf has been keeping. Miranda thought that he would give up on his lost human sweetheart and marry some elf girl, but I knew he would fight to recover her with every warrior he has. Because Miranda isn't his sweetheart. She's his wife. And she's been his wife from the very first night they met."

The murmuring grew louder. Miranda stared at the elf in confusion. Married from the first night they met?

Nir looked at her, at the shock and bewilderment in her eyes. "I'm not a monster like you are," he said angrily to Marak Catspaw, "to drag home a young girl and announce that she has no choice in such a personal matter."

"Oh, no," retorted Catspaw sarcastically. "You're so much more noble than I am. You dragged her home, gave her no choice, and then didn't bother to tell her."

"I don't think a single elf knew what he'd done," Seylin remarked to the King. "There was none of the customary dancing or the presents of flowers for the new bride. I suspect that when he swore to give Miranda all that his world had to offer, he did it very quietly."

Catspaw frowned. "Seylin, you're talking about the Seven Stars Spell," he observed. "In its original form, it is a marriage vow, yes, but you can't pretend that it applies to him."

"Doesn't it?" asked Seylin in excitement. "Look at this elf, not as an opponent you personally despise, but as an academic puzzle instead. He marries a human using the Seven Stars, and she's so well protected that she can't even run her finger along the edge of a knife. He heals without spells, which not even a strong healer can do, or Sable would have managed to save her friend Laurel. He knows by magic the location of every elf and collects them by twos and threes, and they obey him so completely that Arianna couldn't even drag her feet when he sent her off to become your wife. He faces you in single combat and emerges without a scratch. But all you really need to know is that he is the son of a full elf man and a full human woman. Answer the riddle, goblin King. Do you know who he is?"

Marak Catspaw walked around the elf lord, studying him. He was beginning to enjoy the situation hugely. Nir ignored him, staring at the full moon. He obviously was not.

"The real question is," mused Catspaw, "does he know, himself?"

"No," answered Seylin. "He knows everything he needs to know, and not one thing more. But we should have known sooner, and would have, if we'd listened to Miranda."

"By the Sword!" exclaimed Catspaw. "Seylin, you're right! Tell us, Miranda, what did Father raise you to be?"

The girl looked at him and then at the silent Nir. She was angry that they were laughing over him and puzzled that he wouldn't defend himself.

"Marak raised me to be a King's Wife," she snapped.

"Well, you're a wife now," observed Catspaw, "so that means your husband must be a king. You're married to the prettiest elf there is, Miranda. You're the wife of the elf King."

Chapter Fifteen

Dead silence reigned in the truce circle. No one moved. Then Nir dropped his contemptuous gaze to Marak Catspaw's face.

"Don't mock me," he said coldly.

"Mock you, brother?" said the goblin. "There's nothing I'd love better. Unfortunately, I'm not mocking you."

"The elf King is dead," declared Nir. "He died hundreds of years ago, and he left no Heir."

"We know that's not true, or you wouldn't be here," observed Catspaw. "I don't know how you happen to be his Heir, but I do have a chief adviser who generally knows this sort of thing. Adviser!"

"Goblin King?" responded Seylin.

"Can you tell us how this upstart elf-human cross came to be a King?"

"I can do better than that. I can read it to you," answered Seylin. "Dentwood, did you bring the books?"

"Yes, Father."

A young man came forward through the assembled goblin Guard. He looked like an ordinary human, with thick brown hair and brown eyes, but when he turned to hand Seylin two books, Nir saw that he had pointed elf ears. "Thanks, son," said Seylin absently, and the human-elf-goblin walked back into the ranks.

"This is the last of the elvish Kings' Chronicles," announced Seylin, holding up one of the books so that they could see the markings on the spine. "I'll read you part of the story of the last elf King's father, Aganir Melim-bar, the elf King named Saturn's Ascent. But in English, because I think it's only fair that Miranda be able to understand it.

"'The King's Wife of Saturn's Ascent,'" he began, "'was much praised by the advisers because she was a strong and gifted woman. She studied her new people, mastered their language, and won their hearts. But her vain and weak husband did not love his human wife because she was not beautiful. Having enslaved her heart through the amnesia drink that destroyed her memory of her world, the elf King treated her devotion to him with disdain, and when at last she was pregnant with the Heir, he put her aside altogether. His wife confronted him about his cruelty, and words passed between them which neither would forgive. He gave her the choice of living in any other camp she wished, but he would keep her in the King's Camp no longer.

"'The King's Wife toured the camps, and the elves mourned her disgrace. At last, she settled in the Camp of the Bright Shoulder Star because the lord of this camp had died and his lady also waited to bear a son. The two bereaved women, one human, one elf, took each other to their hearts, and they comforted each other through the long months of their pregnancy. And so strong and brave was the King's Wife that she delivered the Heir alone and then rose from her bed to help her friend through her difficult labor. At the end of the night, the two women lay side by side in the midwife's tent, and their two new sons lay with them.

"'But here is a strange thing, for as noble and as good as this King's Wife was, she hated her own son. She sent him next evening to his father's camp without shedding a single tear. But she begged the right to name the son of the lady of the camp, and because of their love, the lady gave her consent.

" 'When the full moon came, the King's Wife held her friend's son, and she kissed him and cried over him. She said that here would be no cruel elf King who would bring torment to a human girl, and she named the baby Ash, which means "unique," or "alone."

" 'The King's Wife ceased to eat from the night of her delivery. The people lamented, and the advisers were angry because the King would not save his wife. But the elf King himself was pleased because he had never cared for the sight of her. She died two nights after the naming of Lord Ash, and only the elf King did not mourn her passing.' "

"She switched the babies!" exclaimed Marak Catspaw in amazement. "She sent the lady's son to the King. She kept the Heir in camp and named him Lord Ash!"

"And there, goblin King, stands the heir of Lord Ash," said his adviser. "Ash is his proper name, the name he received from his father and his father's father."

Nir stared at the book in Seylin's hands, pondering the story. "They were wrong," he said quietly. "The King's Wife did love her son."

"But she hated her husband enough to destroy his entire people," countered Seylin. "The recognized Aganir U-Sakar, the elf King named New Moon, was an unwitting impostor, the son of a camp lord. His advisers were astounded at the weakness of his magic. They couldn't persuade him to marry for years because the elf King is the only elf man capable of feeling an interest in a human woman. The impostor found the thought of marrying a human revolting. When he finally did marry, he had enough magic to place the Seven Stars, but the stars were always dark. His human wife didn't bear a child because their marriage was sterile, and when she killed herself, the stars couldn't stop her.

"By this time, the impostor King must have been assailed by terrible doubts. He took to dangerous amusements, in which the

King's defense magic should have kept him safe, but New Moon had no defense magic. Changed into the form of a white fox, he jumped into a trap, and the trap broke his neck. The master of Hallow Hill displayed the beautiful fox pelt on his wall until the elves stole it back, and the despairing elves set fire to the Hall as a revenge. Fire isn't a normal elf weapon, but it was the worst thing they knew, and that's why Hallow Hill has one wing that has been completely rebuilt."

"Why didn't the true elf King step forward to lead his people once the impostor was dead?" demanded Catspaw. "He would have had the magic to know he should do it."

"He couldn't because Lord Ash, the true King, was dead long before the impostor," said Seylin. "He died before New Moon even married. Clear signs of his real identity were present in his life. He married three different elf women, and the first two died childless. That's because the elf King, like the goblin King, can't have a child until his magic matures, some time past the age of forty. Lord Ash's magic doubtless got rid of the first two wives, just as this elf King's first wife, Kara, knew that his magic was getting rid of her, and as Arianna was instinctively afraid that his magic would do to her, too.

"Then Lord Ash's niece was stolen by the goblins, and he was determined to rescue her. Because he was really the elf King, no member of the Guard could withstand him, and he fought all the way to the iron door, destroying every goblin in his path. Then the iron door called on the goblin King to save it. If the Kings had fought together as you two did, the goblin King would have recognized his opponent, but he brought down the ceiling on Lord Ash instead, and that killed the last true elf King. His young elf wife bore her dead husband a son, but the child was a great disappointment. He had almost no magic at all.

"What happens next is lost in the confusion of the elf harrowing, but it's easy enough to guess. One Lord Ash followed another: plain, unremarkable elves. The powerful magic of the elf Kings stayed dormant because they were the sons of elf women. At last one final Lord Ash came along: lonely, the last of his band. He fell in love with a human girl, and he lured her away from home. She longed for her own world, but her husband loved her ardently, and so, two hundred and fifty years after the death of the last true King, another elf King was born."

Nir looked at Miranda. "My mother was from a large family," he said softly. "She loved my father, but she was so unhappy. She tried to smile for him, but when he was out hunting, she would cry and cry. My father always thought that if she could just have a daughter, she wouldn't miss her sisters anymore. But she never had a daughter. Only me.

"When my father died, I released my mother from the spells so that she could return to her people. She tried to convince me to come with her because she said I was half human, but she and I both knew that wasn't true. My people were the elves even though I didn't have any people. I watched my mother walk away into the dawn, and the next evening I started searching for elves."

"Which I did, too," remarked Seylin. "But I didn't have your knack for it. Just imagine, goblin King," he continued enthusiastically, lapsing into his old tutor's role, "we always tell the Kings that they embody the magic of their race, and then we teach them so carefully that they never have to rely on it. But here was a young King, completely untaught and completely alone. He had nothing of his heritage but his language and his name. And within twenty years, he had found every scattered survivor of his race and restored their ancient way of life. It's all completely intuitive. He even keeps moving to the sites of the King's Camps, although I'm sure he doesn't know it."

He proffered the other of the two books to Nir. "This, Aganir Ash," he said, "is the next spell book we should loan you."

Nir took the slim volume and studied its title. *"The Spells of the Elf King,"* he read.

"It has only scholarly interest for us," said Marak Catspaw. "No one but the elf King can work them."

Nir paged through the book for a minute. Then he looked up at them with a smile. "It doesn't have much interest for me, either," he said. "I already know most of these spells. Here's the Border Spell. That's what I've been working since the new moon."

"So I guessed," replied Seylin. "Miranda described it to me because you tested it on her, the spell that kept getting her lost. The Border Spell used to protect the elf King's forest, and every new King had to walk the border and renew it. It was the decay of the Border Spell that made the elf harrowing possible. Once it was gone, the goblins could sweep through and attack the elf camps as they pleased."

"You can't do that now," said Nir, his dark eyes shining. "I passed the north side of the truce circle and left you the strip of forest between the lake and the human mansions. I don't think you'll be sending your spies to watch my camp anymore."

"Spies!" sighed Seylin. "That was our huge mistake. The elf King should never come face-to-face with the goblins' captive elves, but none of us knew you were the elf King."

"Now I know what you did to Mother!" exclaimed Marak Catspaw. "When you tested her, you put the Call of the King on her, but Mother can't leave us to follow you."

"And we've wondered what would happen if a goblin disobeyed his King," Seylin remarked. "Since goblins—elves, too—are brought to the King and Called right after birth, they're incapable of disobedience. Your mother isn't the only one to find the Call profoundly unsettling. Marak said that Richard here cried like a baby when he was Called. Sable must have had an instinctive fear of it: she had never touched or even looked at the elf King. He caught her work-ing against him, and then he put the Call on her. The only reason she didn't fall dead at his feet was that he gave her an errand to do."

"Dead?" echoed Nir, considerably startled.

"Dead," confirmed the goblin King. "She delivered your mes-sage to me, and she fell dead at my feet instead. We've kept her body working by magic, but nothing I've tried has restarted her heart."

"I thought that was just a lie you told to trick Sika into leaving," Nir admitted, deeply troubled. "I never meant to harm that elf, only to banish her. If I see her, maybe I can bring her back."

"Then come with me," suggested the goblin King. "Not inside. I'll bring her out." And turning to Richard, he ordered the Guard to return to the kingdom.

"It only remains to confirm the treaty," declared Seylin as the goblins trooped past. "Do both of you agree to honor the old covenant between the Kings?"

"Yes," answered Nir, "provided that the goblins will respect my marriage."

"Oh, by all means," replied Catspaw. "I can't fight a prophecy, especially one my own father made. I hope you're happy with your King, little sister. If you ever find yourself in trouble that he can't help you out of, just send a message along to me. And don't believe every-thing the elves tell you about us. They have some shocking ideas."

"Thank you," said Miranda. She said it a little stiffly. But then she remembered Marak and all his love and pride in her. "Catspaw," she said hurriedly, and then stopped, a lump in her throat. "Cats-paw, I'm still glad that I was raised by a goblin King."

"Well, of course you are," he said with a smile.

"Miranda, you may go," said Seylin. "And thank you for your help."

Nir walked her to the edge of the circle. "Sika, go back to camp with Hunter now," he said. "I'll be there soon."

"Can't I stay with you?" she asked in a low voice. "I don't want to leave. What if this is another of Catspaw's tricks?"

Nir's dark eyes danced. "Then he can try to kill me again."

Half an hour later, Marak Catspaw walked out of the cliff face that was the entrance to the goblin caves, carrying a bundle in his arms. He knelt on the grass and laid it down, propping it across his knee. As he unwrapped the blanket, Nir's heart sank. There lay the elf who wasn't an elf, pitifully emaciated and shrunken. Her long black hair, coarse now, straggled across her hollow cheeks.

He knelt down beside her and took her hand in his. "Come back," he commanded softly.

The elf woman stirred and opened her eyes. There was fear in them, all the fear of a bullied slave whose bare survival had been bought with tremendous pain. Nir looked into those eyes and read her past, a past as dark as any he could imagine. Her past, and the past borne by thousands of elf women like her. Terrible suffering, count-less deaths, which had brought his people down to a handful. It could all be laid at the door of his own family—vain, foolish Kings who had cared nothing for others and everything for their own petty pride.

"What do you want of me?" whispered Sable in terror. The elf King bowed his head.

"Get well," he answered gently. "Be happy with your goblins. You don't owe me your allegiance. I wasn't there to save you when you faced certain death. You had to face it alone. I wasn't there to free you when you lived in a slavery so profound that the goblins' captivity seemed like a blessing. The goblins were there, and I'm glad they were there, and I understand that you love them. But, Sable, don't hate your own people."

Tears stood in those sunken eyes, and Sable wrung her thin hands. "When has an elf ever been kind to me?" she asked bitterly.

"Never," sighed Nir. "Kindness died in your elf band when the mothers died. But it isn't the fault of the dead mothers that they failed to teach their children love, and it isn't the fault of the orphaned children that they failed to learn it."

"You could have taught me," muttered the gaunt woman. "You showed me no kindness."

"I should have," admitted Nir. "And I never meant to harm you. But you caused suffering, too. You told lies that damaged my wife's trust in me and undid all the kindness I had shown her."

"Miranda, your wife?" wondered Sable. She stirred uneasily against Catspaw's knee. "Oh, I understand now," she whispered. "I know who you are. Your wife. Miranda wanted that. I was furious because you broke her heart." And her dry lips twisted into a little smile.

"I'll try not to," promised Nir, smiling back at her. "Don't give up on your people yet. Go to sleep now, and wake up when you're rested." He watched her face grow peaceful. Then he looked up at the goblin King. "Thank you for keeping her alive for me," he said.

"I certainly didn't keep her alive for you," retorted Catspaw with a frown.

"She's had her children," the elf pointed out. "She won't do anything more for your bloodlines and pedigrees."

"For pity's sake!" snapped the goblin. "She's my faithful subject and my mother's closest friend! I don't know what you think we goblins are—a race of heartless cretins, obviously. You wouldn't even have that forest you've just walked if my father and my great-grandfather hadn't walked it first. They placed the Ax Spell on the border trees to keep them safe from logging."

"Why would goblins do such a thing?" asked the puzzled Nir.

"They did it out of respect," growled Catspaw, "and that's a word you could stand to learn. My father respected the memory of his brother Kings and the elvish race."

Nir pondered this as he watched Marak Catspaw tuck the blanket around the sleeping Sable. He was surprised at the gentleness of the action.

"How is Arianna?" he asked cautiously.

"Oh, she's fine," answered the goblin King proudly. "She's terribly brave. Just last week she gave me a smile because I brought her some branches of holly. What she likes best is to sit on our balcony with Mother, Irina, and Sable, and they work on one of Irina's projects together, and they sing. They can sing for hours sometimes, and it cheers her up tremendously. It hurts my ears," admitted Catspaw with a grin.

Nir smiled to think of this tiny group continuing their elf ways in the goblin kingdom. "That's what Arianna's magic is for," he said. "Her magic that you admired so much relates to music. Galnar has her harp now, but I'll send it along to her. I didn't think that you would let her play it."

Marak Catspaw scowled at this last remark, but then he relented. "I'd have given a great deal to see Miranda married to someone else," he confessed.

"You'd have given my life, for example," observed the elf bitterly.

"Absolutely," agreed the goblin. Nir was amazed that he could be so direct. "I'd have given much more important things than that. Miranda's welfare matters to me."

"Miranda—what a name for her!" Nir grimaced. "A lie of a name. I used to hate it because it means 'in the coils of the snake,' but now I hate it because it means 'seeing.'"

"Seeing?" asked Catspaw in surprise.

"Yes, in some language that humans speak," sighed the elf King. "I can't think of a worse name for someone who's blind at night."

The goblin King studied his rival for a long minute. "There's a spell for that," he pointed out.

Nir looked up, his dark eyes gleaming with excitement. "I have to have that spell," he declared emphatically. "That is—please share it with me," he added.

"Certainly," promised Catspaw. "I'll send it over tomorrow night. Do you know, I'm glad there's an elf King again. Life has been terribly dull: nothing to plan for, nothing to defend against, the King's Guard out picking flowers. It's a shame we signed that treaty, isn't it, brother? But our sons will have a thrilling time. And they'll tell stories about us, too. They'll begin, 'In the reign of Marak Catspaw and Aganir Ash, the elf King named Alone.'"

◦━

It was early morning by the time Nir walked back to his camp, and he paused on a rise to study it. The elves were delirious with joy. Every single one of them was dancing. Mothers were dancing with their babies in their arms, and Galnar was dancing as he played. Even the elves assigned to prepare the morning meal were dancing along with the rest. That meant no bread, and the stew was doubt-less stuck to the pot. Other races held feasts in celebration, mused Nir, but elves always burned their meals when they were happy.

But the elf King didn't join his delighted elves. He spotted a light roving the boundary line back in the shadow of the trees. He walked out of the darkness into the circle of that light, and there stood the worried Miranda, keeping watch. The anxious look in her eyes changed to relief as she caught sight of him, and he took her into his arms and kissed her.

"You've done more crying than laughing in the goblin caves," he observed, "and it's your marriage moon, and you're not dancing by its light." He sat down with her right inside the boundary line. "We'll have to dance tomorrow night instead."

The elf King studied his young wife. Now that he understood the riddle of his own existence, he understood her role as well. He realized why the plans of the First Fathers had placed this stranger among his deferential people. She was a captive, but she was freer of him than any elf ever could be. The patterns of her mind were beyond his understanding, and her secrets were hers to keep. Her human heart would be the only one he would have to earn.

The elf King realized that his weak forefathers had rejected this challenge. They had found their one truly free companion to be a burden not worth the bearing. They had emptied their wives' minds and forced their devotion because they didn't want to earn their hearts. But those pitiful, subjugated women were still free to hate their worthless husbands, still free to reject a race that could inflict such cruelty. And an unmagical human, bound mind and body into slavery, had studied this strong, magical race and accomplished its devastation. She had deliberately destroyed thousands of beautiful, powerful elves so that some other human girl, her sister in mind and heart, would remain free and not endure the ghastly slavery that she had known.

Miranda looked up at him, her brown eyes very grave. "What did your magic tell you about me when you met me in the truce circle?" she asked. "The secret that made you feel so sorry for me? The one that would bring me no comfort in my life, except that I had a special destiny?"

"It told me that you had to marry me," he said. "It told me you were the mother of my son."

Miranda smiled at him and shook her head in disbelief. "And

you felt sorry because of that?" she exclaimed. "I can't imagine that there's a woman alive who wouldn't want to marry you. You must never have seen your face in a mirror!"

He could have argued the point. He could have explained that his father's good looks hadn't made his mother any less lonely and wretched, or their meals any less meager, or their nights any less hard. But he held his wife close instead.

"As long as you want to marry me," he said, "I don't care about mirrors. Your face is the one I'd rather see."

Chapter Sixteen

The next night, the goblin King sent over the spell that he had promised, and with it a blank volume. The following message fell out of the
book: "It took me all afternoon to enter last night's events into the
Kings' Chronicles, brother, and I send this so that you can start
a Kings' Chronicles of your own. Your lazy ancestors fell out of the
habit, but Kings should record their own reigns. Just remember not to
write down all those nasty grudges you have against me. This is an
important record for the Scholars. Particularly for the goblin Scholars,
once your kingdom crumbles and we take away all your books again."

The next night the elf King sent over Arianna's harp, and with
it this message: "Thank you for the book, brother. I have put it to
prompt use. I am sure I was as flattering to you as you were to me.
You'll have to be patient for those books since you can't barge around
my land anymore. If you feel like hunting in your little scrap of forest, let me know so that we can chase a few deer your way. It's the
least I can do to show my respect for my brother King."

A few nights later, Hunter and Tattoo met beside the truce circle.

"Oh, hello," said Hunter. "It's good to see you again. I'm on
border patrol tonight, walking the edge between our lands and keeping an eye out for goblins."

"I'm assigned to border patrol, too," said the goblin, "keeping an
eye out for elves."

"Great!" declared Hunter. "We can walk together. We won't take
our eyes off each other even if we bump into a tree."

"Actually, I was hoping to run into you," said Tattoo as they started off. "I still have to give you back your pipe."

"No, keep it," answered Hunter. "I'll make another one." He thought for a minute, and his expression softened. "I'll tell you what, give it to the goblin King's Wife for me, and tell her Hunter misses her."

The process of changing Miranda's eyes took months. The darkness slowly rolled back, and colors emerged for which she had no name. The stars steadily increased in brilliance and magnificence until she realized that they were something more than pretty, and one moonless night she stood with the elf King on a high hill and saw everything that he saw.

When that night came, Nir removed the Daylight Spell, but Miranda didn't go to the meadow to watch her first sunrise in over a year. Instead, she lay in the tent with Nir's cloak pulled over her eyes to protect them from the blinding glare of the day.

"Are you sorry to lose the sun?" he asked her as she squinted against the dazzling whiteness.

"No," she said. "The moon is more beautiful." And the elf King was happy.

Marak Catspaw and Seylin agreed that an untaught ruler was more dangerous and unpredictable than a properly educated one, so Seylin embarked on the astonishing career of tutoring a second King. He spent weeks at a time in the elf camp teaching Nir history, strategy, and magic, as well as the scintillatingly beautiful elvish mathematics that had struck Marak as so absurd.

Both Kings marveled at the friendship that continued between Miranda's old guards. Hunter taught Tattoo to stalk deer, and Tat too taught Hunter to ride a horse. Their friends became cordial with one another, organizing gatherings and competitions, and the military commanders even encouraged mixed patrols.

Hunter came into camp one night with a letter for the elf King's Wife. "Tattoo and Celia had their baby," he told her. "Do you know what? They named him after me!"

"Sumur told me," answered Miranda. "He heard it from Mongrel when they were on duty together. Have you seen the baby yet? Sumur said it has a rhinoceros horn."

"Hunter is a remarkably handsome child," stated the elf firmly, and his blue eyes dared her to comment. She managed to keep a straight face, but she took her letter from Kate and hurried off.

"I was interested in your idea about comparing King's Wife tales," Kate had written, "so I started to write the story of my early life with Marak. I let Arianna read it, but I was rather shocked. She laughed so much that her sides hurt. I assured her that it was a frightening and tragic story, but she kept right on laughing anyway. She said that she had no idea a goblin could love jokes and pranks as much as the elves. Honestly, Miranda! I know Marak liked to tease, but I never thought he was that funny."

Miranda smiled over the letter and tucked it away in her cloak. She looked up to find herself surrounded by children. "You promised!" they clamored, and she had, so she let those little hands drag her away.

The elf King was debating the future of the two races and disagreeing forcefully with his opponent. This was perhaps not surprising since his opponent was a goblin.

"A lasting peace is impossible, despite the friendships that are building now," stated Nir. "Eventually, the goblins will want elf brides, and we will never give them up without bloodshed. That happened only one time, and it will not happen again. The elves will not buy peace with the misery of our children."

"Misery!" exclaimed Seylin. "Elf brides don't have to be miserable."

"Elf brides lose their whole way of life," declared Nir. "Many may recover from it, but not all do, and none of them should have to."

Seylin looked at his royal pupil's determined face. "You can't possibly be objective," he said. "You aren't just the ruler of the elf way of life, you embody it magically. Marak Catspaw is the same. He embodies the goblin way of life. You can study each other, but you will never understand each other, and you will never really like each other, either. You are the living argument between the two Greatest of the First Fathers, and that argument will last as long as the races exist."

"The First Fathers quarreled over whether their race should be beautiful or strong," said the elf King. "The goblins seek for strength in the elves, and the elves look for beauty in the goblins. With such different viewpoints and such different ways of life, how could they possibly sustain peace?"

"Within the hearts of both races lies the same code of conduct," answered Seylin. "With minor differences, the same laws apply to each. These laws come down from a source higher than the First Fathers, and they unite the two sides of the argument. Kindness and cruelty, honesty and treachery—these have the same meaning to a goblin or an elf. After all," he remarked, glancing away significantly, "you can't condemn the goblins for behavior that the elves also practice."

The elf King followed Seylin's gaze. There sat Miranda, surrounded by the children, playing an old elf singing game. Opponents took turns singing the first verse of a song until someone ran out of choices or forgot the words. Miranda was playing against all the children and holding her own very well. Just now she was singing in German, her clear, sweet voice competing with Galnar's playing in the meadow. She couldn't have looked happier, but the elf King remembered a night when he had dragged home a terrified, furious girl and enchanted her to force her into a way of life she dreaded. And that frightened girl had told him that he was even worse than a goblin.

Miranda was deep in a vigorous rendition of Beethoven's "Ode to Joy" when her husband jerked her to her feet and kissed her passionately. When he let her go, she couldn't remember what she had been singing. Several seconds of silence passed, but the words had gone right out of her head.

"What was that about?" she demanded as the children cheered their victory.

"It's your goblin friend," complained the elf King. "He's making me think too much."

"Who, Seylin?" laughed Miranda, looking past him at the handsome goblin. "He always does that to everyone."

"Well, not to me," declared Nir firmly. "He can't make an elf work hard. Come on, Sika, let's go dancing." And they did.